GROUND
MANNERS

GROUND MANNERS

A Novel

Cynthia D'Errico

To order additional copies of this book, contact:
Xlibris Corporation
1-888-795-4274
www.Xlibris.com
Orders@Xlibris.com
88732

Dedication

Without the unflagging enthusiasm of Dave Miller, this work would never have seen the light of day. Dave re-ignited a dying torch lit decades ago by my mother who supported my love of writing long before anyone else even knew I wanted to write. My gratitude to them is endless.

This is in memory of my beloved Fred whose gentleness, civility and love dwell within me every day, and for Fuddy, a purebred *Canadien* who inspired a woman to open a horse sanctuary well over 20 years ago.

This book is also dedicated to my father who, in making me stronger and more fearless than my own nature could bear, drove me to investigate both the light and the dark of life and made me go where even angels fear to tread.

You don't throw a whole life away
just cuz it's banged up a little.

Tom Smith, trainer of *Seabiscuit*

Cast of Characters

Ausencia: an Argentinian polo horse. Lived for a brief time at Holdout Bay and then Huis Clos Stables.

Belle Spahro: Skye Spahro's daughter.

Cam: an older pony in Zia's herd.

Chano Trottier: a doctoral candidate assigned to carry out field research at Holdout Bay.

Contessa: a registered Canadien mare retired along with the stallion Marquis to Holdout Bay by Lucien Deschambault.

Darquise (DeeDee) Brucy: a doctoral candidate in Québec history. Solange Deschambault's cousin.

Delphine deBeauvilliers: turn-of-the-century diarist. Deceased.

Guyanne Deschambault Rutherford: Solange's daughter. Heir to the Deschambault and Rutherford legacies.

John Rash: CEO of Metropole Enterprises.

Justin: a blind pinto, part of Zia's herd. Living at Holdout Bay.

Letty: a student at Université Jean-Talon who has a crush on Chano Trottier.

Lucien Deschambault: former manager of a provincial stud farm in Deschambault, Québec. Guyanne's grandfather. Deceased.

Luka: a young pony rescued by Skye Spahro, now living at Holdout Bay.

Matteo Volpone: John Rash's employee; a former product renderer.

Olibade Ouellet: Lucien's stockman, now living at Huis Clos Stables.

Skye Spahro: an animal communicator; director of The Institute of Nature Communications.

Solange Deschambault: well-known investigative reporter. Lucien Deschambault's daughter and Belle Spahro's long-time friend. Owner of Huis Clos Stables.

St. Lawrence River: dominant waterway in Québec made up of the freshwater reach, estuary and gulf.

Toby: a bluejay; friend to Skye Spahro.

Ulric the Red: a Belgian draught horse retired from his work harvesting Irish moss in PEI, now living at Huis Clos Stables.

Zia: a Canadien mare with special DNA. Herd leader.

Contents

Part Three

Part Four

Index of Illustrations

*   based on illustration by Janek Syzmanowski in *The Complete Guide.*
**   photo by kind permission of Jim C. Taylor. *www.jimctaylor.com*

PART ONE

A Mare without a Herd

'I T WAS QUIETER here, the residents much calmer and friendly, according to their natures. Some grunted as they went by; others came to a dead stop and peered, weighing me and finding me wanting. Still others scampered by soundlessly, thinking something more dire and leaving it unuttered. I knew I was out of shape so I tried to ignore the stares. I could smell water nearby but I couldn't see it, and all I could really hear was the occasional snorting of some of the horses. I could see the little herd if I inclined my head a little to see beyond the big tree in the front pasture. Their curiosity to know me, what I was doing here and where I was from was strong, so I stayed in their line of sight as much as possible to satisfy them. An old champagne mare was so startled when she spotted me that I thought she was going to make a run at my enclosure. I could tell she was important, free and loose on her own, so I let her eyeball me all she wanted. They all knew I was a foreigner although I ate the same food as they did.

The country I come from is beyond the equator, a tropical place with foliage so rich and variegated that tourists visited all the time. They were never disappointed by what they saw: the ancient, unruly slopes, the waterfalls in the most surprising places—and even, what were to them, really odd-looking trees—were extraordinary, well worth the Travelocity special. Not like the trees here. Here they were all of a piece, as if some obsessive artist got stuck on the same theme: firs, cedars, spruce—just a stream of bristly green. Some outstanding for their height or breadth, but most just aligned endlessly in a deadening repetition of form and principle. The same. Everywhere. *Repetitio principii.* One of my former owners, a retiree, had been a scientist. He said we couldn't solve problems by using the same way of thinking that had created them in the first place. He said that science was like a mule dressed up in fancy horse harness. I didn't know what science was and I didn't always understand everything he talked about, but he was my first owner and I've always remembered him for his kind ways and little sayings.

I hoped I could stay here—wherever here was. A bluejay had visited me briefly to say that I was at a special place, a place especially for horses, and that the owner was trying to find room for me. I figured that soon I would meet the other horses and the usual greeting scenarios would take place. Through their body language—pawing, snorting, vocalising—they'll let me know who the lead mare is and who the favourites are. There are always favourites, even in a herd as small as this one. The thrill of being a favourite is something I had, on occasion, experienced. It had never lasted long because I was often on the move, but I always remember that heady feeling. Unlike so many other favourites, though, I never abused my status because you never knew when a newcomer might come along and take you down a peg. I'd seen it happen and the humiliation of it could put some in a blue funk for days. I felt for the timid ones especially who became wrapped up in thoughts about running off forever; running, running, and then running away finally from the will of man who uses up your speed and your strength, rationing your essence out like a miser, whim by measly whim, until you are grounded, hobbled—forever at the mercy of a puny master species. If you lost rank in the herd, those kinds of thoughts could overwhelm your spirit, and that would affect your relationship with master. Herd trouble often led to problems on the outside, altering a biddable mount into an edgy, intractable one. I'd seen it happen many times.

As I was saying, I hoped I could stay here. The owner here seemed to be a brown-eyed lady with sunny hair. She was very busy, but visited several times a day to see if there was anything I needed. She worried over something different every day: was there enough shade? Did I have enough water? Would I like something for the pain in my leg? I could hardly tell her that all I really wanted was to join the others and more importantly, I wanted to know what work there was for me. This was most essential—life-saving, really. I'd seen what happens when you couldn't work anymore or were deemed unfit for work of any kind. Up to now, I'd been lucky. I'd always been given work to do; strenuous and demanding, the kind that makes you sweat and pant. You had to be steady and swift to be a polo mount. I was all of that, and more. My cv spoke for itself, and although my leg right now was less than it should be, I could still manage to run and play if I had to. It wouldn't be because of shirking work that I would risk losing this peaceful, roomy place. Despite a landscape indented with those seemingly endless trees, this was, in many ways, far from a sticky wicket.

Almost as soon as I thought it, I could hear a horse trailer pulling up.'

Herd Leader

ZIA WAS FUMING, silently at first, her ears up and forward as if she were a Doberman. 'Why wasn't I told? Skye knows she should check with me first.' She danced and trotted then wheeled, back and forth, back and forth, never taking her eyes off the stranger mare. When finally she whinnied, it was a deep and loud bruiting of her displeasure. A minute later, she began to paw the ground, each strike of her hoof calibrated to convey meaning to the herd as well as to the honey-coloured stranger. 'After all, I'm herd leader. This is my herd, my family, mine.' With each crescent of disturbed dust, her grievances grew. 'My herd, mine, mine . . . .'

It wasn't that Zia gave newcomers a hard time—well maybe she did a little—but there was a protocol to observe, to respect—something Skye Spahro knew better than most; a fact which only made Zia feel even more aggrieved. In the normal order of things, Skye would first consult with her, as herd leader, and then the newcomer would be introduced via Zia. Additions to an established herd, even smallish ones or ones made up of rescues and discards like this one, had to be carried out with some sensitivity to the pecking order already in place—otherwise, chaos ensued. Injuries, bullying or ostracism, as in any community, were destabilising and inimical to the comfort of the herd overall; and, as Zia saw it, keeping a herd of prey animals calm was nine-tenths of her job. All of this was certainly true for *domestic* herds, anyway. Zia was aware that some Mustang herds took in elk and deer—equids yes but a whole other species—and provided them full herd protection: a practice she didn't necessarily deplore if exigent predatory threats called for it. For Zia, formerly of La Petite Vallée Slaughterhouse, safety and security were all.

On top of everything, she already had a newcomer to deal with: Luka, the pony with the wound in his neck, not yet here a full week, and so skittish and scared, she could barely approach him. Without missing a beat, she looked around to see where Luka was. Cam, an older pony, was with him. 'Well that's all right then,' thought Zia, 'I'll see to him in a while.' Right now, she had three quick questions for Skye: Who is this mare? Where is she from? Is she staying?—and one urgent one: why wasn't I consulted beforehand? With a dismissive toss of her head—she would set Skye straight anon—she turned and walked over to join Cam and Luka.

A Flight Risk

"**I** REALLY DON'T know what to think," said Luka nervously as Cam groomed his young friend's neck, low along its crest. "After all you've been through, that's no surprise," replied Cam quietly, careful to stay clear of Luka's neck wound. "I was abandoned," Cam continued, "left to starve for months; a fairly common backstory for many of us who come to Skye's place." Luka began to relax and lean comfortably against him. "Zia could tell you more about Skye and where you are now, the Institute, but for now, all you need to know is that nothing of what went on before will happen here."

"Zia scares me," Luka replied. Cam nodded slowly. All his movements were calculated to calm, not to alarm, Luka.

"I know. Zia can be a bit . . . intimidating, but Zia's been everywhere, knows everyone, and she knows what's what. She's seen things, brutal, horrible things, she says. She doesn't go into detail or anything . . . all she'll say is 'not knowing is the worst thing.' She says order and routine are the best defense against—against, well, chaos, I guess. But she looks out for us and, well—take Justin over there: feet the size of dinnerplates and as blind as a bat."

"Why, if it weren't for Zia," continued Cam, "our Mr. Magoo would've run right into that tree over there and cracked his skull in two by now."

They both looked over at Justin, the big pinto, and then at the fir tree, a solid monolith of nature if ever there was one. Luka couldn't help himself. His laugh was muffled, more like the snuffle of a pig, but it was laughter nonetheless, and Cam was pleased. Justin did look funny, standing, as he often did, with his whole neck and head down low angled to the right, looking a bit like an ostrich with one ear to the ground. Suddenly Luka felt, rather than saw, Zia approaching. He stiffened immediately and his eyes grew wide.

"Don't panic!" whispered Cam, "She'll just give you the once-over, a nip 'n' twist here and there, and you'll be fine." But Luka had already gone somewhere in his head beyond the sound of Cam's calming voice. Terror was Luka's fall-back position and he took off like a bullet. "How rude!" Cam barely heard Zia's aggrieved tone as she barrelled off in pursuit. Sighing, Cam followed at a comfortable trot. 'Aw, she'll destroy all the progress we've made. Hang it all,' he thought. 'If she were just a little more . . . and a little less—'

Luka, meanwhile, didn't have a hope in hell of outrunning Zia. She was bigger and faster, and like a cowpoke, seemed to anticipate his every move. If he zigzagged, she zagzigged. If he flew into the woods, she met him exiting, in the clearing. Cam watched it all, partly annoyed and partly admiring both Luka's deftness and Zia's doggedness. But he knew the outcome of this little drama, enacted every day in every herd, everywhere. Shaking his head, he turned to go back and, just then, saw Justin making his way towards Zia with powerful strides. Zia had posted herself, still as a sentinel, for yet a third time at the clearing, the only way out of the dense woods, and was waiting for Luka to show himself.

'Oh no!' thought Cam, 'Justin's going to plow right into Zee!' Cam turned away. 'I can't look!' But he did look, and he saw Zia, with a lightning swerve of her whole backside avoid Justin by a hairsbreadth. Cam gawked, his bottom lip trembling. "That must be what they call a jackknife!" As far as Cam knew, only two horse breeds in the world could jackknife on a dime. Justin, oblivious, stopped dead, feeling a swoosh of air close by. "Is that you, Zee?" Cam heard Justin say. Zia, annoyed beyond words, replied by butting Justin hard in the shoulder and began to lead him away from the woods. 'Ohh, if it were anyone else, she'd tear a strip off him,' thought Cam. By now, he had two competing needs: food—it was close to suppertime—and finding Luka, who, thanks to Justin, was nowhere to be seen.

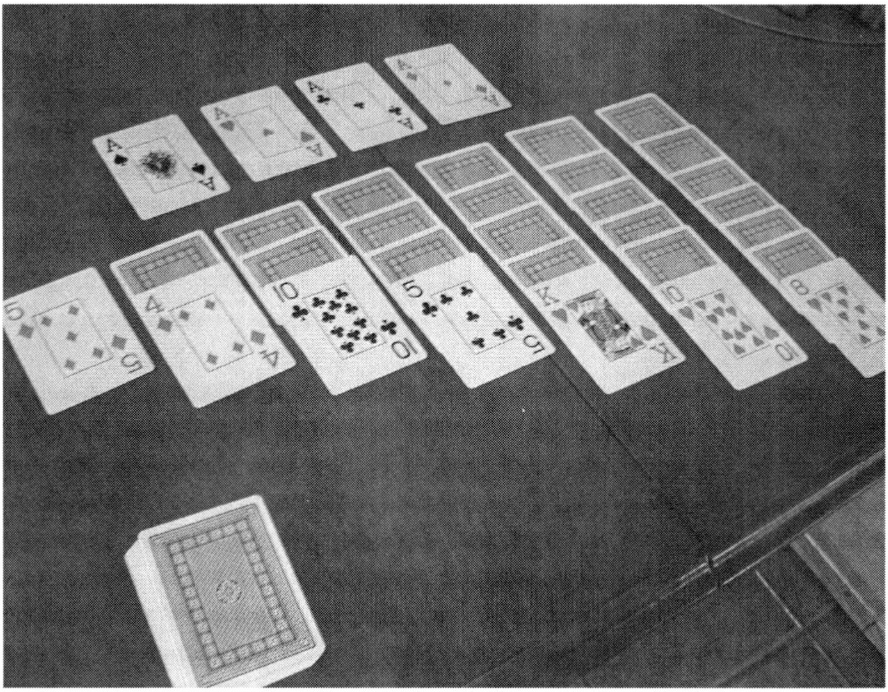

Solitaire

THROUGH THE BIG bay window, Belle Spahro watched her mother Skye talking with Zia. Apparently Zee had a lot to say because Skye seemed to be mostly listening, nodding at intervals like a bobble head.

". . . so you see, Skye, when you bring in a new resident, it's essential that I know beforehand . . . . And now, I don't even know where she's got to. Where is the new mare?"

Belle scanned the area to see who was watching besides herself. Ah yes, there was Toby, hunkered down on the branch of a nearby fir. 'Such a busybody, that blue jay,' thought Belle with a faint smile, and he, of course, could hear what was beyond Belle's hearing.

"I agree with you, Zee," said Skye, "but sometimes, things happen so fast that I don't have a chance to let you know. In Ausencia's case, we found a good foster for her for the time being, so I had her moved the other day. But we're expecting the polo mare back soon and—"

"So her name is Ausencia. Why wasn't she put in my pasture right off?" Belle saw her mother pull Zee's head closer and lay her cheek against the mare's. Belle didn't need to hear what was being said to know that Skye was intent on calming the anxious mare.

"Zee . . . Zia," Skye cradled Zia's face, "you are so good, such a treasure. I could never do without you. But you must trust that things that happen elsewhere will never happen here—not ever—and I will always take care of you all. All the decisions I make . . . and all the changes I make . . . are all for good reasons and always to keep you all safe. Safe, Zia . . . safe for always." The mare seemed to relax, as if just for the moment setting aside a burden she carried with her always. Zee nuzzled Skye's arm and nestled in closer.

"But I have seen things . . . unspeakable things and I—"

"I know, Zee. I have seen them too. And I have felt them. Sometimes I can hardly breathe at the horror of it. But all of you are safe here at the Institute, as all of my friends before were, and all of those to come, will be. Forever. I promise."

Belle watched as the once-stunning champagne mare snuffled Skye's hair and face as if just the scent of her could dispel all those nightmarish memories. Toby, who had left his perch and was fluttering around noisily, was bursting to let them know what he thought of their exchange. Always eager to express himself, was Toby. Now enjoying Zia's careful grooming, Skye managed to look up at the blue jay, and began laughing. Belle didn't often hear her mother laugh like that—just hearing it made her laugh out loud herself. The nature of their work didn't offer much occasion for laughter—an occupational hazard—but somehow, Toby could always make Skye laugh. Still smiling, Belle walked back to the desk to finish her paperwork.

One of Belle's first memories was of walking down a street with her mother and seeing an unleashed dog rush up to Skye, sit directly in front of her and quietly stare at her for several minutes. Belle, her little hand in Skye's, looked at both of them looking at each other, the whole time knowing something was going on, something was being said; she just didn't know what exactly. It was a soundless exchange; not once did her mother's lips move. As soon as they got home, Skye was on the phone, giving the address of a puppy mill to the Sûreté of Québec and then to the SPCA. Belle, who was busy leafing through the new Wonder book Skye had bought her, only partly listened to what her mother said during those phone calls. But somehow she knew that some puppies had that dog and her mother to thank for the rescue that took place that same afternoon. She just knew. When she was old enough to put the question into words, that's exactly how Skye had explained it to her:

"I just know," Skye had replied at the time. "Like when I wake up in the morning, and you say, 'you're happy today, Mom, aren't you?'—how do you know, my bell-elle? You just do, don't you? Even though I'm not smiling or laughing, you know I'm feeling happy at that moment. You sense something so clearly, with details so vivid that you know it's a fact. Or when you yell: 'Mom, phone!' even before the phone has rung . . . and you know you do that very often, my bell-elle, usually when I'm in the shower. Well that's what it's like with me and the animals. I know and *they know* I know." Then, laughing, she had scooped Belle up in her arms. "So it's lucky for you that I can't read *your* mind, eh my little bell-elle . . . 'cuz you're just a little critter too, aren't you, my sweet girl?" Then Skye tickled Belle and Belle tickled Skye, until they tumbled together onto the sofa, giggling and laughing so much that their eyes teared and their bellies ached. That was all the explanation Belle ever needed.

The way Belle saw it, being the daughter of a woman like Skye was a gift in itself: a fortunate case of arrested development, as if the fontanel of infancy had never closed up, shutting out all that didn't fit, was a bad fit, was unfit; refusing to move towards an adulthood which would inevitably breed cynicism, scepticism and other isms even more pernicious. This openness made Belle's world-view very rich and full indeed. Still-life didn't exist in her consciousness because life was teeming all about and around her, here, there and everywhere; all beings present and accounted for, all acknowledged, none gone unnoticed. In a nutshell, what Belle took from her mother was the knowledge that all separateness is false and that the syntax of life is discoverable everywhere, in everything and in everyone. Belle's energy, as a result, seemed to spill out beyond the rim of her self, as if embodiment had not quite fit the bill, leaving a luminous excess around and about her. Her person fetched others to her in the same way and by the same mechanism that brought animals to Skye's doorstep. And even though Belle could not experience the larger, communicative reality that Skye could—giving Skye a much wider interlocutory field to operate in—Belle was otherwise, in every important respect, very much her mother's daughter. Since there was no way to describe this charisma that both mother and daughter exuded, the most that could be said—and that which was most commonly said—was 'there is just something about her' and that indefinable 'something' was a draw for both people and animals: in the case of people, always without rhyme or reason, reason being the quality least likely to provide an answer to this imponderable of their natures.

When questioned by the curious or the cynical about her mother's special gift, Belle would say that it was just as much a part of her as her blonde hair or her green eyes or the way she walked or the way she laughed. For Belle, as for Skye, no explanation possible was the same as no explanation necessary. If pressed, she'd just shrug and say: "Some things just are . . . c'est comme ça," for Belle was no philosopher by nature. In fact, when Skye first opened the Institute of Nature Communications, it was Belle—at the time, just a young teenager—who insisted that Skye meet with the Board of Certification for Animal Intuitives. And when Skye tested way over the scales, her energy causing one small circuit board to fry, Belle simply smiled and said: "C'est comme ça."

Later that day, when Skye came in, still dishevelled from Zia's loving nuzzles, she pushed aside the pile of phone messages and reached for her cards. When Belle saw that, she quietly put the kettle on; Skye would be at it a while. Playing Solitaire—or Patience as Skye sometimes called it when she needed some—was not so much about strategy, like, say, chess. It was more about winning without sacrifice; winning by restoring each card to its rightful place. Each card had to be reclaimed from the somewhere, the anywhere, the deal lands it in the isosceles frame of life's lottery and returned home, to the primum mobile, the home ace. Aces promise restoration of the displaced. For Skye Spahro, who had a deathless desire for justice, this very old and simple game was all about rescue and restoration.

Like most card games, Solitaire pits randomness against the rules of order, but first engages the player in a foreplay meant to divert from the real agenda, which is the privilege of the aces. Laying down the cards in alternating colours is nothing but a diversionary tactic, far from the true aim. This is always where the player's short-sightedness and greed for an immediate return foil him. The initial set-up abets this lie because each row of cards beggars the one that precedes it—first card of the row open, yes—but more cards per row and one more face down, one more unknown variable, than in the previous row. Perhaps by force of symmetry or a diabolic nod to linearity, the law of diminishing returns is already in play. The player places a black on red—black queen on red king for example—and thinks he's making progress, doing well. Yet this is nothing but coaxing the deck to reveal itself, card by card, so that you can predict how quickly you can transfer to the ace—of whatever suit—but to an *ace*—to the win. If you run into trouble, you can borrow from whatever you'd already placed on an ace and replace it in the triangle. You lose points for such a move, but it is, perforce, only a temporary gambit. Or you can take a numbered set from one row, say a black five of spades through three, and move it over to another row needing a black five, just so you can pick up that red diamond six from the first row, and place it on the red diamond ace pile, whose highest number would now be six. Now the red diamond ace pile is only seven cards away from being a complete suit: restored to wholeness. For Skye, each card represented a human obstacle to securing the rescue of a horse: some cards were obstacles and others were opportunities to advance faster and rescue sooner. In her mind, the opponent wasn't feckless chance:

it was man himself, post-lapsarian, post-industrial, now become the beast without a head.

The game on this particular late afternoon revisited her encounter with a certain Mr Contrecoeur, a Montreal calèche driver, unwilling to give up his 28-year-old draught horse to the Institute even though she was lame and burned out after 25 years of pulling tourists through filthy city smog and mind-numbing noise. She hadn't seen grass since she was a foal. He planned to sell her to a friend of his in the north who wanted a big draught to show off when he rented out to trail riders. Their immense size and gentleness always impressed people. The friend would pay half as much as the slaughterhouse—about twenty cents per pound—so where's the harm? She wouldn't go to slaughter (his friend assured him); he'd make some money off her—after all, now that she was lame, she was no good to him—and she could still be useful to somebody if only as a marketing tool. Here was an immediate return that looked like progress, like success—but it was far from the win. Skye nodded agreeably as Contrecoeur pointed out the many advantages of his plan to her, and learned, by the by, that it was only a three-hour drive to the friend's place, and lovely country up there, too. Skye borrowed a card from the ace of spades pile and placed it back in the triangle—an interim gambit but a useful one. In fact, they'd had quite a lovely talk about horses, she and Mr. Contrecoeur. When she left, he felt good. Horses were his life, he'd told her; he'd gone through dozens. She was a real horse-lover like him; he could tell. 'We're a dying breed but there are still a few of us around,' he thought, as he downed another beer.

Skye drove up north as soon as the mare was sold—Mr. Contrecoeur had promised to let her know when the deal went down, and he did, being a man of his word—and collared the new owner the day before the unhappy mare was scheduled for slaughter. There was no trail riding outfit; there wasn't even a stable, and slaughter always held an immediate return. He could get double per pound what he'd paid his friend. Skye reminisced as she transferred the borrowed card to another row; the next card dealt would give her an edge or stalemate the game. Of course he hadn't lied to his friend, she'd said, not really. Things happen. It's perfectly understandable. Yes, sometimes we plan to do things—like, say, start a riding school—and it just doesn't pan out. But no point waiting for the kill-buyer; he'd probably say that that lame bag o' bones wouldn't survive transport—and DOA's sometimes bring trouble from those animal people—you know they're everywhere now. The buyer probably won't risk it. Skye made sure to wave amiably as she and a volunteer loaded the old mare onto the trailer. She relaxed only after they'd driven an hour's distance: sometimes they think twice and come after her, but this one didn't. She eased up but didn't smile. She had nothing to smile about though she'd won this game; a win without sacrifice. She'd already organized the mare's retirement: at a trusted stable named 'The Four Aces.' With nary a scruple she re-named her long-suffering friend 'Patience.'

That game won, Skye sipped her tea and thought back to the mare's gaunt face, her ears, her eyes, when the trailer stopped in the middle of reams and reams of grass: limitless pasture. For twenty minutes or more, Patience rolled and rolled in the soft green, and then rolled again, trying this patch out, then another, as if greeting a long-lost friend. Her bliss destroyed all onlookers, their soppy tears engaged fully in the mare's trouvaille; all of them feeling, in that long delicious moment, how deep her hopelessness of ever seeing grass again had been. 'Patience' was finally home, reclaimed, restored to her rightful place in the natural world. And, to Skye, it was a place of righteousness.

"Was that Patience or Solitaire tonight, Mother?" Belle asked playfully. "It was definitely Patience," replied Skye, eyes smiling, ". . . and she won."

Belle watched as Skye gathered up the cards and placed them perfectly straight on the mantel. There was always another game right around the corner and she had to be ready to play. To win. Then mother and daughter went outside to the pastures to check on their friends and secure the Institute for the night.

Orphans

B Y NOW, CAM had covered all of Luka's favourite haunts. After suppertime, that is. Cam had decided that food would sustain him while searching and anyway, it was a long time till tomorrow's feeding. He stood in the middle of the field, undecided as to what to do next or where to look. He thought of asking Zia for help, but nixed that idea. It wasn't that she wouldn't know what to do; it was the way she'd go about doing it. He looked over at the almost sightless Justin who was standing by the culvert, apparently transfixed by some oversized dragonflies hovering among the bulrushes. Thanks to a negligent owner, Justin's eyesight was so poor, he sometimes mistook a Shetland quietly grazing for a tree stump. He felt Justin would be more of a hindrance than a help. In the end, he decided to go find Penny. The copper-coloured pony was usually good at this sort of thing and wouldn't spook Luka the way Zia would.

As he went in search of Penny, Cam looked back once more at Justin who now seemed to be talking with the flies. Justin was taller than average and his coat had just enough dollops of white in it to make him an overo pinto. He dwarfed the tall bulrushes, and even in the dusk, his white splashes stood out against their brown crowns as if part of a paysan tableau. Cam was out of sight now so Justin took two measured steps down into the culvert. Cam was half-right. Justin was indeed talking—to Luka who had hidden himself in the middle of the culvert, still shaking from his encounter with Zia.

"So what did you do?" asked Justin, hearing Luka's story for the first time. "What *could* I do?" replied Luka, still unsure of Justin's motives. "He'd tied me to the ground by three feet of chain—by my neck. I couldn't even get to my feet, much less stand up." Justin moved in a little closer, hoping Luka would relax and at least stop shaking.

> *From the Sûreté Report, Offence #14001-42 Animal Health Protection Act P-42 (RSQ) R.R.10, St-Francis.*
>
> *Two ponies found abandoned and starving at above address. No water or food. One animal tethered to ground in lean-to smelling of decomposition and befoulment. Attempts to reach property owner since yesterday unavailing.*
>
> *Determination: Emergency rescue and medical intervention needed to prevent property loss (chattel).*
>
> *Phone request at 5pm to animal care consultant for farm and large animals, Mme Spahro (Institute of Nature Communications), to come onsite.*

> *Skye could hear the officer's fatigue over the phone. "Écoute madame . . . il faut que tu vienne. Ca me dépasse . . . . Icitte j'ai 2 poneys dont un est quasiment garrotté. Emmène le vet parce que c'est sur qu'on ne pourra pas les sauver ces pauvres bêtes-là."*

"Before Skye arrived," Luka continued, almost in a whisper, "there were men there in blue jackets with flashlights that hurt my eyes. They scared me and I couldn't see Mother anymore. I thought they'd taken her away—and she was all I had, all I had to hold on for. I strained as I'd always had against the chain, trying to break it, trying to free myself. One man came over and spoke to me softly. But all I could think was, where was Mother and what had they done with her . . . what now were these vicious animals going to do to us?"

As he listened, Justin's head hung down low, almost to the ground. Luka's anguish made him shiver deep inside. Justin barely remembered his own mother. "Then Skye came. There was a light around her that wasn't from the lights in the men's hands. I stopped struggling and tried to speak but I was so weak. She knelt beside me, and I could feel her hand touching gently where the chain had embedded itself into my neck."

> *After getting directions from the Sûreté officer, Skye grabbed a jacket, two halters, and the keys to the pick-up. On her way out, she yelled: "near St-Francis, 2 ponies, maybe 3. I'll call Dr. Scott on the way." Belle yelled back, still keyboarding: "What's the case number?*

Don't forget the camera!" But Skye's 4x4 was already backing up the long driveway to the gate. Belle could just make out Toby above the cab, keeping clear of the wake of dust skirting the fast-moving truck.

Institute consultant arrived at 6pm. She first approached the older pony running loose and agitated; calmed it sufficiently for securing. Madame declined a flashlight and sanitary mask (see release forms), and entered shed (no stables on property).

Veterinarian (contacted by Mme Spahro en route) arrived fifteen to twenty minutes later, and began emergency surgery to remove chain impaled in animal's flesh (behind ears).

From Skye's dictation to Belle. To: Sûreté du Québec; cc: SPCA

After I spoke to the mother—Sheba was her name—I entered the shed to see to her son. The stench was overpowering. But the mother said her boy was strong and still alive. I found him bound to the ground by a strong chain looped tightly over his poll, restricting head rise to three feet, unable to sit or stand. Filth and excrement were stuck onto his flesh and all around him. His constant struggling had driven the steel links right into his flesh, at least two inches deep. It stank of decay. I touched carefully around the wound to see its extent; it was a mass of viscous scabs and congealed blood. Parts of his flesh were already in a state of decomposition. Then Dr. Scott arrived and he went to work. Once stabilized, both Sheba and yearling were transported to the equine hospital in St-Hy. Institute Contract #340-621. Prosecution pending.

Then Skye said to me: "I've made your mother a promise, Luka. You will feel much better very soon." I tried to ask if she knew where Mother was, but I couldn't. I wanted my mother so bad . . . so bad." Now Justin moved closer and nuzzled his little friend's withers.

"How awful for you, Luka. I can't begin to imagine . . . and where is your mother now?" Justin's faith in Skye drove his innocent question. "She's dead they tell me. She never made it back here, to Skye's. One night, she got sick and never recovered."

"I am so sorry, Luka. But you know she loved you so much and must have been so happy that you were rescued. And I know Skye and she must have—"

"—oh I know. Cam told me that Skye spent days and nights at mother's side, trying to bring her back to health. But I think Mother had had enough of the world of men and only stayed long enough to make sure of me, to make sure that I was okay. I think Mother liked Skye. I think she trusted her."

"And do you trust her?"

"I, I think I do. She's so different from that terrible man who tied me up and left us to starve."

"Oh, she is, Luka, she is. The special thing about Skye is, she can talk to us and understand us. She is the only human I've ever known who can . . . and . . . ." Justin hesitated. He'd seen Zia standing quietly by the water trough; she'd been watching for some time now. "And Zia is her right-hand man, you know. Skye and Zia are like one and the same—one with less of a coat than the other, but the same nonetheless." The mention of Zia made Luka tense up but, Justin noticed, not as much as before. "Zia is old, you know, Luka, and she has been around the block a few times. She knows things and has seen things. She is very protective for just that very reason. You know, I can't see very well . . ." Justin took a step back, always shy to talk about his handicap. "And it's been Zee, Zia all along, who's kept me away from very dangerous things—barbed wire and electric fencing, upended nails in old planks of wood—all sorts of things. She's taught me to rely on my other senses so that I can get around without hurting myself—or hurting others because as you can see, I'm a big boy. She's taught me—well, she's taught me not to be afraid, Luka. And I'm sure she can teach you too."

By now, Luka had caught Zee's scent. But he'd listened hard to Justin whose earnestness had won his trust. Luka hesitated only a moment. He looked up to where Zia was, patiently waiting and watching, and emerged from the culvert into the open where she could see him clearly. She made no move towards him. He knew he had to go to her. She wouldn't come to him; not after what had happened earlier. Cam had said that all she'd do is nip 'n' twist here and there, a horse-talk thing; a posturing of respect. But Luka didn't know horse talk. He'd lost his mother before she could teach him such essential things. And he couldn't bear being touched since the chain scar had become a permanent reminder of cruelty beyond measure. But as he took in Zia's calm and even maternal mien, he thought it had been a while since he'd felt a mother's nuzzle, a mother's touch—and he was so lonesome for Mother. He looked back at Justin who was standing just a few feet away.

"Go on," Justin whispered. "She's waiting. Don't be scared, Luka." On Justin's urging, Luka walked towards Zia and presented his muzzle. Toby, who'd been watching everything from a comfortable perch, sang out. He flew off, still singing, to find Cam and then Skye. He loved having good news to share. Mostly, he loved being the first one to tell it.

How Belle Found Holdout Bay

WHEN BELLE FIRST happened upon Isle-Saint-Jean-Baptiste, she felt she had discovered one of those little-known paradises hidden all over the vast province of Québec, and, as it turned out, this perfect little island—no more than 30 square kilometres around—was right on Montréal's doorstep. Convinced that a permanent home for the Institute was an idea whose time had come, she had spent months researching areas north, south, and east of the greater metropolitan region. At first, she had looked around the gentrified country areas. There was Bromont: a mecca for the skiing set surrounded by picturesque lakes, but with a *Lafleurs* Hot Dog and a *St. Hubert BBQ* fronting the main drag there, Belle knew hungry developers pretty much owned the whole area. To the north, near Sorel, biker gangs ruled, and around Rawdon, off the main roads, puppy mills abounded, cloaked by thick, impenetrable cedars. Anyway, the land around the waterways in that region was unstable, and she wanted a solid location on robust ground. When Belle found herself driving through Isle-Saint-Jean-Baptiste, she was delighted by the acres of immense trees lining only two boulevards that arched gently into second-gear slopes, each ending at the St. Lawrence on the far side or Lac Saint-Louis on the other.

Looking back now, Belle wondered why the island's name hadn't struck her as a bad omen. After all, the little island was named after a saint whose severance of parts was devoutly to be avoided. But she'd had other things on her mind at the time. This was the year after the Québec Ice Storm of 1998, and there had been an uptick in cases of abuse and abandonment of service and farm animals. This wasn't unexpected in the province of Québec whose animal protection laws were enforced by no more than a wagging finger and a fine equal to the cost of a carton of cigarettes. But the devastating storm had created a low-lying panic that surfaced on the radar in the guise of more domestic violence, more violent child abuse, and of course, animal abuse—incubator of serious personality disorders and deeper psycho-pathologies. Fortunately, there were almost as many companion animal shelters in Québec as there were abusers—some very prominent and others more low-key—but all seemed completely unable to work in concert, not unlike bureaucrats who never looked beyond their own cubicles. That left only the Institute to deal with all animals bigger than an Irish wolfhound, largely because a certain expertise was needed to care for an animal who couldn't survive on kibble or cream, no matter what your Aunt Adèle said. As a result, the Institute's annual rescue numbers had streaked up the graph by almost forty per cent. This didn't include organizing the rescue, finding interim foster homes (riding stables were out—they rarely kept their word), and more important, finding permanent homes willing to retire a 1,000-pound mammal until he died of natural causes. This was in addition to Skye's 24/7 on-call status with the Sûreté du Québec, the main enforcers of the province's animal protection laws.

Skye denied help to no one because, for her, every chance to save the life of a horse was a gift. 'An embarrassment of riches' she would say to her daughter when the number of weekly cases would ramp up and Belle started to drown, not just in the extra paperwork, but in what she called this 'endless sea of abuse.' Skye, on the other hand, had taken on the task decades ago, knowing full well how big it was, had been and was going to be; and throughout, remained unfazed by it all—or, if not unfazed, then undeterred. Skye's f-word was fatigue; she never seemed to feel any or if she did, she never complained. Like a hummingbird never completely resting its always shuddering wings, she had taken on this herculean task working out of a post office box the size of a birdfeeder, settling here and there only for a brief time—always on the move. But Belle was getting tired—tired especially of dealing with draconian laws, overwhelmed inspectors, and infighting amongst the shelters. Belle felt strongly that the Institute—known across the country with an unimpeachable reputation—could now risk being grounded somewhere, somewhere permanent. It took some months of discussion before Belle was able to persuade her mother of the value of a fixed location. After a long while, Skye finally agreed that if Belle should find a place—a suitable one with lots of pasture and sufficiently private—she would at least consider the idea. Satisfied that Isle-Saint-Jean-Baptiste fit all Skye's criteria, Belle tested the waters with her mother before contacting a real estate agent.

"So what do you think? Could you work there? It's ridiculously close to the city—you're on and off the bridge before you know it, and—"

"I know the island well, Belle, extremely well, in fact. I spent a few years there as a girl, one of the happiest times of my life."

What surprised Belle wasn't that Skye knew the island: it was that she'd spent 'a few years' there. That was a long time for her nomadic mother.

"Well then. You know the island. Then you know there's lots of space, land, water. It's like a huge tree farm, wooded areas everywhere—the trees alone provide privacy—not to mention you're never further than five minutes from the shoreline. And the people are—"

"—I remember the people well—in fact, that's what I remember best. They call themselves 'jeanistes,'" Skye answered quietly. Then, without looking up from the map in her hand, she said, "Find us a property, my bell-elle, and then . . . we'll see."

Relieved and excited, Belle reached for the phone and called Hugh Rutherford, a top realtor in the area. When she returned to the living room, Skye was deep in conversation with Toby who was perched on the alcove ledge, and as had happened so many years before with the stray dog on a sidewalk and a thousand times since, Belle was not privy to the exchange.

Standing Beside Time

T HE REAL ESTATE agent felt sure he had a bird in hand here. He'd shown Belle just about every part of the island that he thought met her specs—except of course the freehold near the cemetery. Few people were comfortable living near a graveyard, and this one was a state tourist attraction. An eon ago, when the glaciers receded, the Gulf waters had scalloped deep into the cliffside, and, whether by a random or a guided hand, had carved into the rock and foliage, a perfect stairway, snaking its way right down to the St. Lawrence River. 'The only one of its kind in North America,' the tourist brochure boasted. And along those serpentine ledges, now expertly landscaped with the best Kentucky bluegrass, were graves and headstones dating back to the 1800s—the ones that could be dated, that is. The locals—les jeanistes—claimed that dozens, if not hundreds, of sailors' bodies had washed ashore as early as the 1600s when Champlain sailed down what he thought was the way to China. In fact, none of the real estate agents ever bothered showing the land near the cemetery to potential buyers, even though the view across the water to Beauharnois was as relaxing as any in the more popular Eastern Townships. So when Belle phoned and said she'd found the perfect place, waterfront, near a big cemetery, and could he meet her there around two o'clock, the realtor was beyond surprised.

"It's called Cimetière de la Sirène, if I'm reading this properly," she said to him on the phone as she stood in front of a lectern set up for tourists. "Do you know it? There's about six or eight acres alongside it . . . no, not on the church side . . . just beyond the little quay that's there—'Holdout Bay' it's called—where the water is all marshy and reedy."

Hugh knew it all right. Could he be there before two? Definitely. Hugh Rutherford, fully chartered real estate agent, was the top in his field, and with good reason. But sometimes, even he—after 28 years in the business—could be surprised. Like right now. Not skipping a professional beat, he finished his showing in St. Lazare, stopped at a *Lafleurs* for some dogs and fries—two stimés moutarde, chou—and made over six phone calls while driving to his two o'clock with Belle Spahro. A bird in hand, indeed.

It was through Hugh that Belle met up with her dear friend, Solange, again. They'd attended the same college in the late 70s; Solange just a year ahead of Belle. Both spent all their free time in the second wave groups that were going to change the world—again: Solange to keep abreast of current events and Belle because there wasn't a righteous cause she could ignore. They'd been friends the way one is a school friend—intense, devoted, caught up in the whorl of each other's daily dramas—their friendship framed by the social and cultural unrest of the times. After graduation, realizing that a longish time had passed between phone calls, an awkwardly long time, when careers were being launched and new bonds were being forged, that their great friendship had been an intimacy of circumstance—full and unforgettable but short-lived—they lost touch. Still, Belle had followed Solange's career as a reporter: for a short spell, a TV journalist, and then, best of all, an investigative journalist. It pleased Belle to see her friend do so well; even her mother Skye who rarely watched TV would point her out, saying, "Belle, there's your friend, the one you went to school with, remember?" And Belle would leave her desk and look at Solange's face and hear her voice, always poised and clear as a bell, and she would. Remember, that is. It was like standing beside time, hearing that voice and looking back to then from now—in her prime, at school, fighting the good fight shoulder-to-shoulder with Solange.

When Dee overheard the pretty blonde woman talking on her cell phone, apparently to a real estate agent, she walked casually in her direction, all the while recording in her laptop dates and names from the gravestones. 'Épouse de feu.' DeeDee typed the phrase engraved on the headstone into her laptop as quickly as she read it. 'Wife of the late monsieur. And did it mean the same in 1872 as it does now?' She typed underneath: 'check Larousse or Island archives.' Dee could type almost as fast as she could think. Dee looked up for a minute and squinted at the sun. It was a fine summer day to be among the dead. 'Nothing focuses the mind so much as death,' thought Dee, 'probably the reason most people found cemeteries to be such relaxing places. Meditative . . . restful.' The names were all familiar to Dee. Generations of their descendants still lived on the island; in fact, most were relatives of hers, or in-laws of relatives, or friends of relatives. There was something biblical about the way the first arrivals from France—les habitants as the history books referred to them—stuck together, learning from the Indians while they diligently avoided the English and the Spanish. Cimetière de la Sirène had been re-named in the fifties when the diocese had the ancient stone church rebuilt. The crude flagstones were painstakingly taken down and then re-assembled in an authentic—and much neater looking—facsimile. The parishioners made the case that naming a Christian burial ground after the mythological sirens who seduced sailors into foundering their ships was blasphemous, and after all, the cemetery belonged to the county of Our Lady of Vigils. The cemetery was therefore re-christened 'la Cimetière de la Garde.'

As Dee approached, the woman, still holding her cell phone, said in a pleasant voice, "Mon dieu ça l'air pesant ce computer-là!"

"Oh you get used to the weight after a while," Dee replied, shifting the laptop straps to one shoulder.

"Is this your first visit to the Cimetière de la Garde?" Dee asked.

"Oh is that the name? I thought I read Cimetière de la Sirène on one of the tourist cards."

"Yes it was called that originally—and the locals still call it by that name—but you know, naming a French Catholic cemetery after a Greek myth, and one so negative towards women—well . . . ." They both laughed.

"Ah non, ça ne se fait pas." The two turned and began slowly climbing the ledges together, up towards the church.

"My name is Belle."

"I'm Darquise. Call me DeeDee. So this is your first visit to our famous cemetery. Do you know the island at all? Isle-Saint-Jean-Baptiste is a well-kept secret, I always say. Oh, people come for the day to see the cemetery but they never think of moving here . . . which is good in many ways. We only have about 7,000 residents—most of them islanders, but not all—which is also good."

"It's charming—and so tiny. I had no idea it was here, actually; I sort of stumbled on it. And it's so great that everywhere you go, you're surrounded by water, though . . ." Belle said, looking across the river, "very placid water."

CYNTHIA D'ERRICO

"No there are no tides here to speak of. The water is present everywhere but unobtrusive, like a ribbon or seam sort of; no drama or raging seas—just here, there and everywhere sharing the air and light with us."

"Oh look, quelqu'un s'en vient. On a de la visite." Belle turned and saw Hugh hurrying towards them with quick, long strides.

"You're late, Rutherford!" Belle yelled to him with a smile.

"Hey Hughie . . . long time no see!" said DeeDee. Belle, still smiling, looked enquiringly at Dee.

"Do you know Hugh?"

"Bien sûr. Who doesn't know the real estate king of Isle-Saint-Jean-Baptiste?" As Hugh joined them, DeeDee said, "Actually he's my cousin's ex. Perhaps you know her—Solange Deschambault? She has the stable down by Pointe-de-la-Méduse—les écuries Huis Clos."

"Solange . . . Solange the journalist? Why of course I know her! We went to school together. Is she really here, here on the island?" Belle's delighted tone made both Hugh and Dee pause a moment.

"Actually Hugh could tell you more than I can. I don't get to see Solange that much . . . different lifestyles and all that. Hugh, isn't Guyanne staying with Solange now?"

Hugh, always well-mannered, addressed himself first to his new client: "Belle, how great that you know Solange. She's a special woman, as DeeDee can tell you. Come to think of it, I do remember Solange mentioning you, though it was some time ago." Then he deftly turned to Dee: "Yep, Guyanne is with her mother—for how long, who knows?" He looked heavenward and Dee rolled her eyes. "That girl has got to get a life. I've had hamsters that were livelier than her—and they sleep half the day! En tous cas, ça fait du bien te voir, Hugh . . . ." As the two caught up on family news, Belle's mind was busy processing the return of her dear friend to her neighbourhood—her neighbourhood-to-be, that is—and what was this about a stable? She knew Solange's Dad had run one of the provincial stud farms around Three Rivers somewhere—or was it Cap Rouge?—but Solange loved reporting and travelling so much, she hadn't spent much of her time there after she'd graduated. And now she kept a stable? Dee saw Belle turn to Hugh with a question in her eyes.

"Well I'll be sure to tell Solange I know you, Belle. In fact, if you like, I'll give you her number. You know, her dad, Lucien, died recently. He'd been ill for a while and Solange went on leave from the network so she could help take care of him. He was a great guy, Lucien."

"Yes, he was," agreed DeeDee. She'd been a favourite of *mon oncle* and he certainly one of her favourites. He was always full of stories from his past—a colourful past full of local intrigues and questionable political doings. A natural raconteur, he made everything sound like a French farce. And he had the most contagious laugh, finding his own jokes the funniest of all, which made everybody else laugh.

"I'm so sorry to hear that. Solange had great respect for her father, and he did a great deal for the Canadian horse, le Canadien. They would've become extinct, that breed, if not for him and—"

"Oh that's right. Your mother runs an Institute devoted to . . . to . . ."

Hugh tried to remember what it was they did there. It doesn't do to forget a client's occupation.

"Nature communications," said Belle, not really wanting to get into it just now. Hugh recovered quickly: "And how is Ms Spahro keeping these days?" DeeDee repeated the name to herself. 'Sparrow . . . like the bird? Sparrow . . . sounds foreign, not even English foreign . . . .' she thought. 'Well, Belle was a natural blonde after all—maybe Slavic, Norwegian?—not a bottle blonde anyway.'

"Oh she's fine, thanks. Just a little wobbly sometimes. There's always someone with her, though, if I'm not around." Belle meant Toby the bluejay, mainly.

"Could we go have a look at the Holdout Bay property now?" Belle asked politely. "I need to be home by four." Hugh had been late and Belle wanted to have a really close look at the land nearby so she could describe it in detail to Skye. DeeDee took the hint and shook hands with Belle, saying she hoped the Bay was what she was looking for. She often visited the Cimetière, collecting data for her dissertation on local Québec history, and perhaps one day, they could lunch together. Belle said she'd be happy to and she meant it.

When Belle finally got home, Skye was asleep on the sofa, the phones shut off. So Belle took all the phone messages, saw to the animals, and wrapped Skye's supper in case she was hungry when she awoke. Then she took the card out of her purse with Solange's number on it and picked up the phone. They talked till three in the morning . . . just as when they were young and yesterday was only hours, not years, ago.

Counting Her Blessings

AFTER EVERYTHING HAD been loaded and secured, Ausencia settled in to the comforting motion of the horse trailer. She didn't know where she was headed any more than she knew where she'd just departed from. More to the point, she didn't really understand why, after twenty years in the same place, doing the same job, living with the same man, her life had, almost overnight, taken such a turn. Not that she had ever believed in destiny or any grand design per se. As a service animal, all she could claim to believe in was constancy of purpose, an ethic reinforced every time a steel bit was put in her mouth. Her experience up to now had taught her that life was characterized by change occurring in small doses, micro-changes, hardly perceptible, until one day, you found yourself living in a new way, with new things around you. And through all of that, her purpose remained steady and solid, like the constant ground beneath her. So this unexpected turnabout caused her to question what she knew about life. For example, she knew that big changes like this one were not like travelling. Ausencia liked travelling. When you travelled, you left one home-like place temporarily and returned to it at the end. She liked meeting new competitors at polo events, was always amazed at how each country's flora and fauna were unique, with each country touting an indigenous species of its own, not to be found anywhere else in the world. What an odd boast it must appear to the species in question, she'd often thought, each having marked out their breeding, living and dying grounds long before man came along, as if flags and national flowers gave man any more claim to the land than the law gave to squatters.

In Ausencia's opinion, men, in general, were not unlike German Shepherds. A Shepherd had been her stablemate for a brief time. He was very good company albeit possessive in the extreme, always wanting to know where she was going and why. One day, he came home with a few pups that reeked of coyote and she knew then, that, like most of us, he wasn't at all what he seemed to be and that what appeared to be his obsession with control was really a cover for a crushing fear deep down inside him—a craven fear, not what you'd expect in a predator, even a domesticated one. She remembered being surprised at the time that he'd mated with a coyote and not a wolf. Weren't Alsatians descended from wolves, after all? After a time, after she'd watched him nurse the three coyote pups by regurgitating food for them to eat, he one day coaxed her into accompanying him into the woods. There Ausencia saw the half-eaten carcass of a young female coyote who'd clearly lost the fight to a bigger, stronger creature—perhaps a bear—but certainly something that had failed to recognise, in her ferocious posturing, a desperate attempt to defend her young. So the Shepherd wasn't the father at all. He was their rescuer.

The ache in Ausencia's leg worsened. She shifted her weight, trying for an equal distribution, knowing full well that the other legs would give out soon just from the double workload. She hoped this wouldn't be a long ride. The van was hot and steamy though both windows were open. She saw little out the window nearest her head; at first a procession of the by-now familiar green trees which she found calming, then car and city noise which she found distracting. The air had changed too as they trucked through the small town, with foul smells and a heaviness that hurt her lungs and made her wheeze a little. We're all imposters of a sort, thought Ausencia, as the van hit a particularly bad stretch of road. At least they had left the city behind and her wheezing had stopped. All poseurs, just like her friend, the fierce-looking but warm-hearted Alsatian. She shrugged a fly off her belly. All traces of her own nature, wild and free and what-have-you, had been eradicated years before, when she was very young. She barely remembered; something about running away and being used up came to mind occasionally but, like fragments of a dream, she couldn't finish the thought anymore. Domestication had hammered it out of her. As a result, she felt no fear of any kind, craven or otherwise. Nor trust either. As now, there was no guarantee that she wasn't headed for the abattoir.

As the van slowed and pulled into the driveway of her new home, the fourth pup came to mind. The Shepherd had brought him to the stall with his three siblings. Once he'd gently lowered the mewling tangle of legs and noses to the ground, he realized that this pup, much punier than the others, was also deformed. It had no head. None at all; it was just an unsightly stump like a smurf with more legs. The Shepherd didn't waste

CYNTHIA D'ERRICO

time checking it further. He promptly picked it up and ate it. The van came to a full stop and the sudden quiet told Ausencia all she needed to know: there were no horses here.

"Are you keeping this one?" asked the daughter as she squinted at Ausencia through the van's matchbox window.

"I said I'd keep her for as long as Belle needed. It's not like we don't have the room," replied her mother, Solange, a bit distracted. She found it odd that Ollie, the driver, had gone directly into the stable without saying a word. Solange unhitched the back doors. She didn't expect her daughter Guyanne to help, a heavy-set girl with bad skin and a defeated nature.

"She's supposed to have been a real gem in the polo world . . . won all sorts of awards and big money for her owner," said Solange as she released the ramp.

As new air flooded in through the rear, Ausencia pulled up her shoulders and head as far as the rope-tie would allow like a hopeful contestant in a beauty pageant. Always best to look fit and able for work.

"Past her prime with a gammy leg, they told Skye. She was going to slaughter so they only fed her enough to keep her meaty enough for the butcher. Belle and Skye intervened just in time, by the looks of her."

Solange looked Ausencia over, trying to remember what her father had taught her about conformation, the set of the head over the shoulders, fetlock-to-pastern ratios.

"Incredibly underweight, but apart from that, she looks pretty solid to me."

Solange stepped inside with her and ran her hand over her body, very gently around her sore leg. The van was dark, dappled in shadow. Ausencia thought the mother must have excellent eyesight. She checked Ausencia's teeth. In the meantime, Ausencia eyed the daughter, hoping it wasn't her ponderous weight she was meant to carry onto a polo field.

"She's mature, at least twenty-five, I'd say. I'll go see if Ollie prepped her stall while you unload her."

As soon as Solange disappeared into the stable, out of earshot, the daughter kicked a few pebbles onto the ramp and walked away from the van.

Ausencia had to pee and her leg throbbed. The two-hour van ride was nothing compared to intercontinental travel. She'd done that all her life. Most often, she'd been fully sedated. She didn't enjoy the drugs, but even a drug-induced sleep gave her a break from that relentless throb. As it was, she could do nothing tied in the dark fly-infested van but endure the steamy heat, and await the pleasure of this graceless creature who was already half-way down the driveway, unhurried and unconcerned. Grateful that at least they hadn't left her tied out in the searing heat of the sun, Ausencia decided to count her blessings.

CYNTHIA D'ERRICO

A Stalled Car

SOLANGE PAUSED JUST inside the stable door and heard Ausencia pawing the floor of the van. But it was what she didn't hear that annoyed her. She knew her daughter would delay de-trailering the damn horse. Guyanne had lived in the city with her father, Hugh, for most of her life and had only come to live with Solange in the past month. And that, thought Solange wryly, was probably because Solange had recently inherited her own father Lucien's large estate, a hobby farm complete with stables, three pastures and a barn, painted 'barn red' no less. None of his zest for life had passed on to Guyanne who, at twenty, seemed to have the personality of a houseplant. She held opinions on nothing, had no interest in anything in particular, and shrugged off everything with a cursory "ça m'est égal." Hearing it always set Solange's teeth on edge. Forestalling the hated phrase now, Solange walked towards her daughter saying, "If it's all the same to you, I'd like the mare de-trailered *now*, not tomorrow. And she'll need to be walked before the vet comes—that's in one hour, Guyanne—and put in the east pasture. And we—*you*—will set out her feed after the vet check-up."

Guyanne didn't turn to face her mother until Solange was alongside her at the very edge of the driveway, a threshold that faced a cul-de-sac.

"Mind this one has a bad leg; the left hind, so walk her easy. And her name is—it's Absentia, I think—something like that. It's Portuguese." Not that her daughter had bothered to ask the mare's name. They both stood there, looking out towards the same dead end until Guyanne jammed her hands into her jean pockets and walked back towards the van at a pace so slow, it made Solange bite her bottom lip hard.

Since Guyanne had come, Solange's usual high spirits had been sorely tested by the girl's joyless, often lethargic, nature. She couldn't very well ask her own daughter to leave, go back to her ex's, grow a backbone, get a life, some friends maybe, a character—hell, even having a vice would have made her more interesting, more human. She couldn't ask because it had been Guyanne herself who'd asked to come live with her. The only other time had been eight years ago when Yanne was twelve and her father had just re-married. At the time, Solange had gently explained to her daughter that her work as a journalist kept her travelling, sometimes for weeks at a time. It just wasn't feasible. Hugh, her ex, had agreed, saying that Solange's career made it impractical. But both Hugh and Solange knew that Solange had no nesting instinct at all; it would be better all around for Guyanne to stay with him—especially for the girl herself. Solange continued to see her daughter on holidays and whenever she could pencil in a quick visit during breaks from her extensive travelling. She felt now that, though her own flesh and blood, Guyanne was really a stranger to her.

And she to Guyanne apparently. The girl was always bewildered by her mother's lively interest in everything, in everyone—her passion for even the most everyday things, like sunsets or foliage or even the smell of fresh hay. When Solange would greet the day, saying, "What a beautiful, clear morning!" Guyanne never answered because she didn't have an answer. Like a cardboard cut-out pasted onto a pre-fab background, she just couldn't see it. There was nothing to say about the sky, the air, the smells or the sounds around her—they were only props—they had nothing to do with her. Ça ne me regarde pas. She had no point-of-view on such things because she lived only inside herself. Anything outside herself had no connection to her. Even the ground beneath her feet was suspect; had no solidity to it, no continuity. She often walked as if her very next step would plunge her into a void.

Over the years, when their busy schedules allowed, Hugh and Solange had fretted over this lack of spirit they saw in their girl; this lack of engagement with the world, with people. Early on, they'd had her tested for autism, hoping to give a name to whatever it was that ailed her and thereby find a remedy. All the doctors could come up with was 'flat affect,' as if her heart had flat-lined even though it still counted out plodding beats like a metronome. So they'd registered her in every sport, art, club, hobby available to young people, until from sheer exhaustion trying to keep up with their good intentions, she developed mono. By nature and by profession, they were both problem-solvers, oblivious to the fact that, try as you might, you could never fix people. You could either accommodate them or ignore them. They could do neither with their only child, finding, as time passed, that she was withdrawing deeper and deeper into herself, like a telescope slowly collapsing shut. Their desperation had made them stupid. They blamed the divorce, never thinking that it was a hard thing to be the child of such accomplished parents, each in their own field, Hugh in real estate, and Solange in journalism. Worse than that, family achievement went back generations—on both sides. Lucien Deschambault, Guyanne's grandfather, was well-known in political circles—a subset of the rarified rich—for having helped preserve a Québec heritage horse breed—le Canadien—known as 'the little iron horse,' a few decades before Guyanne had been born. On her father's side, her great-great-grandfather had been Canada's first Veterinary Director-General, Dr. Rutherford. Like Etienne Couture and Joseph Deland, her families were referenced in history books, so she had not only the present to live up to, but glories of the past as well, too insecure to know that high praise of one generation harboured no slight to the next. She couldn't even pity herself, the morose girl she had become, goaded on by her well-meaning parents, darting like a pacman from one thing to another; after a while, not able to recall what it was that she needed to connect to in order to feel whole, or even why she needed to connect anyway. And the odd time she could feel her power, the power to be herself, it was instantly extinguished by the thought that all had already been done, her forebears had seen to it all. There was nothing left to make her mark on, nothing they had left untouched; no torch she could light with a passion uniquely her own. They had stolen her thunder before she'd even taken her first step. Guyanne Rutherford was a person waiting to happen. Like a car out of gas, the young woman had stalled.

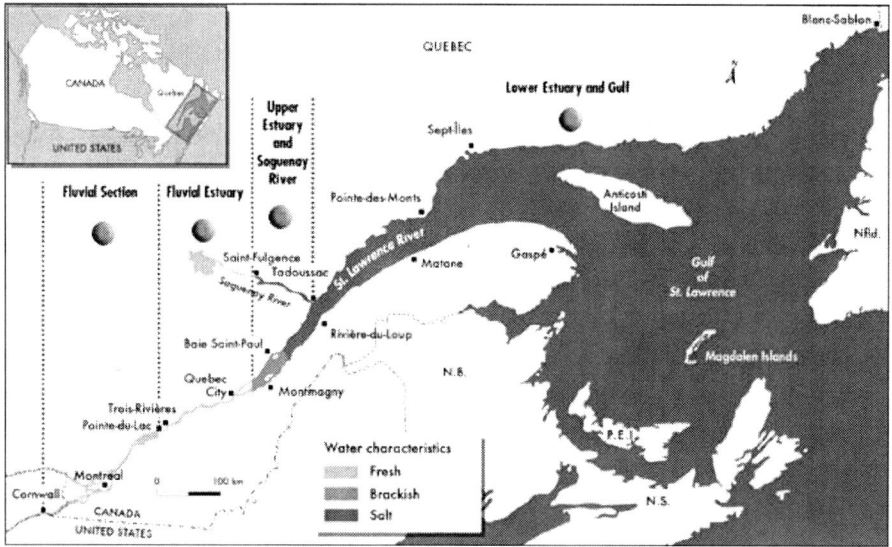

Blanc-Sablon

QUEBEC

Lower Estuary and Gulf

Upper
Estuary
and
Saguenay
River

Sept-Îles

Anticosti
Island

Nfld.

Fluvial Section   Fluvial Estuary

Pointe-des-Monts

Gulf
of
St. Lawrence

Saint-Fulgence
Tadoussac

St. Lawrence River

Matane

Gaspé

Saguenay River

Baie Saint-Paul

Rivière-du-Loup

Magdalen Islands

Quebec
City

Montmagny

N.B.

Trois-Rivières
Pointe-du-Lac

P.E.I.

Montreal

0   100 km

Water characteristics

Cornwall

Fresh

N.S.

CANADA

Brackish

UNITED STATES

Salt

CANADA

Quebec

UNITED STATES

An Oak in a Flowerpot

C HANO COULDN'T RECALL how to spell the Director's name but it reminded him of the bird. He scanned his letter once more. It read:

> *Institute of Nature Communications,*
> *Director, Skye Sparrow,*
> *Holdout Bay,*
> *Isle-Saint-Jean-Baptiste, QC*
> *J7V 5B4*

> *Dear Ms Sparrow:*

> *I am a doctoral candidate in the Department of Geosciences at Université Jean-Talon here on the island. My team is researching shoreline erosion along the St. Lawrence (fluvial freshwater reach), with particular attention to urban and industrial pressures exerted on shorelines as well as suspected deflocculation of marine clays, bank deforestation and concomitant loss of riparian habitat.*

He crossed out "deflocculation of marine clays". He didn't want to bore her with jargon.

> *We have just terminated our study in the Beauharnois/Maple Grove area, located immediately across from your Institute at Holdout Bay. Since your property sits close to where Lake Saint Louis, the Ottawa River and the St. Lawrence freshwater reach commingle, we request permission to carry out field research on and*

around your property. We estimate field work may take up to four months to complete. I will be conducting the research myself; in the event that my working superior or doctoral advisor need be onsite, I will request your permission in advance. We understand that there are large animals at the Institute. We assure you that our work and instruments will not disrupt your daily schedule, and that we will be very respectful of any residents of all species.

If required, the university and Environment Canada will provide release forms for insurance purposes. The enclosed brief provides more detail for your information.

I look forward to a positive reply.

Sincerely,
Chano Trottier,
Université Jean-Talon,
Graduate Suites, Dormitory Three,
5th floor,
Isle-Saint-Jean-Baptiste, QC
J7V 6D5

Enclosure

The St. Lawrence River is the dominant feature of the Quebec landscape. It flows a total distance of 1500 km, and over 70% of Quebec's population lives along its 4200 km of shoreline. The St. Lawrence is not a homogeneous unit. It is divided into three sections, (1) the freshwater reach, (2) the estuary, and (3) the gulf, on the basis of its natural characteristics: tides, salinity, vegetation, and sources of water. Natural Resources Canada. Climate Change Impacts and Adaptation.

Our study of the shoreline* near and at the Beauharnois generating station revealed high levels of industrial contaminants, such as PAHs and mercury, in local sediments. While other contaminants, especially PCBs and metals, make their way from Cornwall-Massena upstream, chemical contaminants such as mercury are the discharge of local industries. Our findings encourage further studies regarding how these pressures may be affecting the opposite shoreline, specifically that of Isle-Saint-Jean-Baptiste.

The surface area of Lake Saint Louis is 148sq.km (excluding Isle Saint Jean Baptiste's 28 sq.km) and its shoreline has been urbanized and recreationalized by human activity. Urbanization has altered the lake's wildlife habitats and significantly disturbed riparian wetlands. Increased boating and shipping activity both before and after the high-water flooding in 1972 and 1976 (issuing from the Ottawa River, one of the Lake's feeds) have also pressured shorelines by creating waves which break on, and may be weakening, island shorelines.

It is the effect on the shoreline soils, granular material (sand), marine clay and riparian wetlands (marshes) of the island we will assess, particularly since Lake Saint Louis provides habitat for 78 species of fish, and the island marshes are believed to provide resting and staging areas for large populations of waterfowl, some of whom may have been displaced by current industrial practices affecting nearby nature reserves.

*We have restricted our study to Holdout Bay whose shoreline perimeter is 8km. Since coastline data covers general line of coast without reference to inlets or bays, our base data will differ from published coastline indices.

Chano tucked it all under his arm and set off for Dee's room. She'd correct any spelling errors, and she was acquainted with the women who ran the Institute so she would know how to spell the director's name. DeeDee was nothing if not meticulous. A doctoral candidate in History, she was older than most and a bit of a mystery. It was suspected, though no one knew for certain, that Darquise Brucy was a sovereignist. She'd minored in Translation, she claimed, just so she could read the old texts in their original seventeenth-century French. And she was not only an islander—a jeaniste born and bred—she was also 'pure laine,' descended from one of the first landholders in Nouvelle France: the Lord of Brucy. You couldn't get more pure-blooded Québécois than that. Like Chano himself, she was impersonal and cool to those close to her, but fiery and passionate about the larger issues. Chano liked her and trusted her.

As he knocked on DeeDee's door, he looked down at the address on the letter and thought nothing, but nothing, could be further away from the hard and dry data he worked with than 'nature communications.' He could hear the banter now; he'd be onsite at a place where people talked to animals—telepathically, they would joke—and do all animals speak one language? Do mammals speak the same language as non-mammals? Or is it a specific mind-meld kind of thing—a very sci-fi, trekkie kind of thing? Do you have to meditate beforehand or perform some kind of ritual like throw salt over your shoulder?

He sighed. In truth, it was the amazing adaptability of other species that fascinated him above all else and kept him playing around in the dirt, collecting, sampling, classifying; studying soil levels, chemical makeup, types—all of it. He'd often wished he could ask a few marine animals or land insects how they managed to survive—or mutate and even thrive when the ecosystem threw them a curve. That would be quite the interview. In a way, the work that Chano did everyday was nature communications except that it was all one-way, like dictating into a recorder hoping all the while that it's really a two-way radio and one day, like Marconi, you'd get an answer. But educated guesses were the best he and his ilk could do, building upon centuries of scientific discoveries which weren't really discoveries at all, more like uncovering what was already there and giving it a name, like gravity or DNA.

Natural scientists like him were especially at the mercy of what they called the 'non-linear responses of biological systems:' the incredible ability of living things to adapt genetically to the environment as it changed around them or as we, clumsy interlopers, irrevocably altered it. You could never tell what they'd do. They were the unmeasurable variable in every equation; from crop pests to whales—size was irrelevant—and since you couldn't ask a pod of whales why they had beached themselves—and why there on that coast and not along this other coastline?—or ask that tree-eating beetle how it had become immune to pesticides that could bring down Godzilla—well, you were stuck with the old scientific method—pattern recognition—except that there was no recognisable pattern and therefore none to measure, record, categorise and predict from, leaving scientists scratching their heads and scrambling to revise and predict anew. After all, maybe it was a one-off, an anomaly; let's try a different baseline and take another shot at it. Let's return to 'first principles' and go from there. But the geosciences were not like other sciences: the encroachments of industrialized man had diverted what would have been predictable geodynamic and ecological evolution into an unprecedented decline—as if we had put the planet on speed or cocaine, and were surprised at the side effects. Trying to solve the problems we'd created was like trying to slay the many-headed Hydra: you cut off one head and two grow back. You can legislate the ban on phosphates in detergents that lead to toxic cyanobacteria in waterways but you can't—at least so far—ban speedboats, whose wakes create waves that break repeatedly against shorelines, weakening them and destroying the marshlands essential to local waterfowl; you can't ask people to stop sailing and boating and shipping—in short, living the way they have since a hedonistic consumerism became the lifestyle of choice. And there was no kind way to tell the well-meaning that those bank protection culverts which they'd assiduously put in place to protect the shorelines were so egregiously constructed that they were actually environmental bombs that would destroy flora, fauna, land and water in a decade or so. And you could barely begin to explain the effects of climate change without expecting the average citizen—exhausted from overwork and parenting—to suddenly learn terms as specialized as clay deflocculation and grasp their significance to hydrological disasters, like water shortages, water contamination and the end of developed civilisation as we know it. The undertaking that we now called the geosciences was like trying to empty the ocean with a teaspoon; and Chano, a realistic man, expected to spoon out about three teaspoons-worth by the end of his own petty lifespan if he was lucky, maybe a few more if he turned out to be lucky *and* gifted in his field.

Still and all, from a very young age, all Chano wanted to know was what God knew—all of what was knowable, nothing less. God, he was sure, was not a compartmentalist, dividing knowledge into convenient dualities, dichotomies—arts and science, nomine and antinomy, the rational and the irrational, human and animal, reason and intuition, action and reaction, the observer and the observed, thesis and antithesis. There was a palette of oneness hidden somewhere among all the two's: a numinousness occulted by the human mind whose consciousness only fired up in binary thought—a kneejerk operation at best; an epistemological solecism at worst. All he had to do was cross the line, traverse the boundaries and he would discover synthesis, so he had tasked himself with studying the nature of the breach itself, in all its natural manifestations; defining a forensics of the separate, the disparate, the discrete, the alienated. What causes such rifts, he wanted to know? These estrangements of nature from nature. What prompts these random cleavages of water from earth, earth from water, leaving scabby shores that had taken 400 million years to scarify into today's coastlines? And now, those same coastlines were in constant flux, sliding and slipping back, *sub marina,* as if they'd never seen the light of day or felt the heat of the sun. In PEI and elsewhere, ten metres of shoreline were disappearing every decade. Between Montréal and Lake

Saint Pierre, 270 kilometres of shoreline had been lost to erosion. The earth was tired, twitching and moaning, her seams rising and falling as if she were about to sneeze.

Chano was only vaguely aware that his obsession with shorelines and coastlines—lines and breaches of all sorts—harboured his own abiding alienation from a culture that disdained the very earth it trod on. He too held himself apart, aloof from his fellows' jaunty disregard for the terminal decay underfoot. What he called the global psychotic break was the key writ large to his own singular psyche. Comfortable only with the measuring and measure of boundaries, Chano had gotten stuck in the margins—the proverbial oak in a flowerpot.

As he knocked on DeeDee's door a third time, he saw Letty walking towards him. Some men grow into their looks. Letty thought Chano was probably born perfect: a real looker with that mass of thick shiny hair, so lean and trim—a tall cool drink of water. Everyone had a secret crush on Chano.

"Hiya Chano. How are you doing? Up for coffee?" she said, wiping the secret off her face.

"Sure . . . as soon as I get Dee to clean this up for me." Letty wished she'd worn mascara, as Chano showed her the letter and continued, "I've been doing some field work in the Beauharnois region for a paper I'm planning to publish with Environment Canada. When I saw the results, I realized that more work had to be done in the Lake Saint Louis area, near Holdout Bay."

"Oh . . . good for you. What do they do at this Institute anyway? 'Nature communications' . . . what does that mean?" Letty asked, feigning interest.

"I'm not sure exactly. It's some kind of animal communication centre or something. And they rescue abused horses too."

"They have horses there?"

"Not a lot, I think. I think they re-home most of the ones they rescue."

"What—so it's an animal shelter?" said Letty, her face expressionless as she studied the set of his chin.

"Sort of, I guess. Except this one takes big animals. The ones the dog shelters can't handle. And the owner, the director I should say, is supposed to be an animal intuitive—you know, one of those people who communicates with animals."

"Oh yeah? You mean like a Dr. Doolittle type?"

Letty smirked. "Oh this I've gotta see. Can I come with you when you go? I can carry stuff, if you have equipment or . . . ."

"Well, I don't know. You'd have to sign a release form and it'd be pretty boring for you, just watching me take samples and such."

Chano didn't like where this was going. Letty looked at the director's name again.

"Huh! 'Skye Sparrow'—what kind of silly, made-up name is that? I mean, that can't be her real name. It sounds like the title of a children's book, or a poem or something."

Chano didn't bite. He pointed out that it was misspelled. By now, he realized Dee wasn't home and he just wanted to go.

"Um, about that coffee. I think I'll take a raincheck . . . . If you run into DeeDee, tell her I'm looking for her, okay? I'll see you later."

He met up with DeeDee halfway down the corridor. Letty walked over to join them and said, "Shelters allow visitors all the time. I could come for a visit anyway. I'll bring carrots. Horses like carrots, don't they?" DeeDee liked Letty, though she found her a bit young for her age. Not really good at subtleties or jokes—and as far as that went—not the sharpest tool in the shed either. It was a mystery to Dee why Letty had picked Literature, of all things, as her major. She didn't know what had transpired before she—fortunately, it seemed—showed up, but Dee could see how uncomfortable Chano was, eyeing the exit door. It was only an arm's length away, maybe half a length more.

"Actually, it's more of a rescue centre than a shelter," said DeeDee. Letty looked at her as if to say, 'what do you know about it.' It wasn't a friendly look.

"Well, I know a little bit about animal rescue, you know. My cousin, Dorothy, volunteered for one for three years. In the city. She has six cats now. She said she stopped when she overheard one of the owners refer to her as 'a rescue bitch.'"

"That's disgusting! What does that mean?" said Chano, stunned out of his silence. DeeDee could see where this was headed.

Glad to have Chano's full attention, Letty explained: "A rescue bitch is a volunteer who'll do anything and everything that's asked of her—it's usually a woman—for no pay and never gets any credit for it at all. She's the grunt, you know, like a step-'n'-fetch-it person. Dorothy said that when she finally left, she told the owner that she'd treated Dorothy like one of the abused dogs she'd rescued—the owner used the threat that if Dorothy didn't help or didn't give money, an animal would die—and it would be all Dorothy's fault. She said they hold you hostage to your own compassion. She said some of those animal people were like terrorists. She'd had enough, poor Dorothy."

Dee was the first to recover but said nothing, fully aware that any chance Letty may have had with Chano had just hit a brick wall. By now, Chano had exactly measured the distance between himself and the exit and was gone without a word. On the other side of Dee's dorm room door, a cat was meowing loudly. "Poor Tawser, all alone all day, were you? Poor baby. Come in and have tea with me and Tawser," said DeeDee. "Come on . . . you'll be catching flies in a minute," she added, as she looked at her young friend staring open-mouthed at Chano's silent departure.

As far as people went, Letty was okay—more or less. But Chano didn't like cynics. They were the mirror image of fundamentalists but with better credentials. To him, meeting a woman who claimed to speak with animals was neither a hardship nor a joke. It was, in fact, one of those variables that he was willing to learn from if he could, and, in learning, there was no place for mean-spiritedness whether of sceptic or saint. He began to calm down as his stride of some length and speed put more and more distance between them; a strategic retreat he would soon learn to despise at Holdout Bay.

A New Spin on an Old Saying

DEEDEE HAD BEEN researching the history of the island for nearly a year now, and had never until now come across a piece of correspondence so personal in its tone and subject. This one involved the famous Intendant Jean Talon to boot—well, indirectly, she supposed, as it wasn't his wife that was 'different' but that of his friend, the doctor, Alcide deBeauvilliers. The doctor had played an important role in the settling of the island so this intriguing bit of information was relevant to—to what exactly, she wasn't yet sure—but something significant, something she'd discover as she ploughed on, excavating the origins of la patrie, the birth of the Québec nation.

She sat up and reviewed what she had pieced together from allusions found in official documents, but had mostly discovered in the epistolary collections of courtesans and servants.

Her summary read (including her margin notes):

> *The celebrated Dr. Alcide deBeauvilliers (1642-1702) was a man of substance and learning, who by profession and right of moderately high birth, had devoted himself to the small but fervent community which had settled along the shore of Isle-Saint-Jean-Baptiste. It could hardly be called a shoreline at all, he had written in a letter back home—'more like a rocky rim circumscribing a land mass no bigger on a map than the stump of a thumb.'* **[FtnoteAlcide-France correspondence, letter no. 313.]** *Nonetheless its importance to strengthening the prosperity of Nouvelle France was not lost on the then Steward of Lower Canada, the great Intendant Jean Talon. When he had ceded the Island to nephew-in-law, François-Marie*

Perrot in 1672, he knew that his niece's enterprising husband, a fur trader, would make a go of it, promoting the very industry which had become the prime selling point of the new world "for the glory of France, His Majesty Louis XIV, and in the name of God."

Dr. deBeauvilliers, or Dr. Alcide, as he became known, was a friend of the great Talon, corresponding with him as he curetted through the new land with an ingenuity and a vision that Dr. Alcide shared with enthusiasm from across the Atlantic. [**Confirm dates; footnote corroborative correspondence.**]

When it first became known that Dr. Alcide's wife, Eusèbe Rufiange, had been born with a veil over her face, there was some consternation among the titled, the godliest among them being the most mean-spirited. Others said it signified God's favour and still others whispered it gave the gift of second sight. But though this gossip cost Dr. Alcide some of his high-born patients, he was a man of science. He dismissed all and any superstition, as did his friend the great Intendant, ascribing such heathenish beliefs to a prior, ignorant age—truly the drawing-room fodder of wastrels and courtesans—as the new century loomed, enlivened by the discovery of new lands and newfound riches. 'Full on ahead and to the devil with the hindmost!' Talon had written to his friend Alcide when the court gossip had reached him in the new land. [***Ftnote letter no. 16, Talon-Alcide correspondence.***]

Dr. Alcide, a man rather more pious than his illustrious friend, Talon, further considered it immaterial to the sanctity of his or his wife's soul, as none of the papal edicts or encyclicals had anything to say on the matter of a veiled face at birth—not specifically, in any case. Therefore, nihil obstat. His wife, in comportment and obedience, was all that a wife should be, and her fondness for birds, of a wide variety, and with which she spent most of her time, was akin to the court's taste for falconry, so if anything, her avian pastime confirmed to him that she was, if not to the manor born, then was certainly a lady by nature. [**Check history of the sport of falconry in France.**]

Still and all, when Talon wrote of his endowment to nephew Perrot of an island convenient to the mainland, deBeauvilliers thought of the birth of his first-born, now just three months old. He had been disconcerted by his wife's insistence that the girl's name be Cassandra just when he had overcome his disappointment at the lack of a first-born male. "But this is a sorceress' name!" he cried, in shock at her stubbornness. "And a blasphemy to our Father who has bestowed naught but good on us always." **[Ftnote letter no. 16 from maidservant to brother.]**

In the end, Eusèbe relented and the child was baptized Jeanne-Marie. But Dr. Alcide deBeauvilliers was troubled by his wife's immodest demand, and as he re-read Talon's letter, he determined that his fortunes lay elsewhere than in the vicious mare's nest of His Majesty's court.

He wrote his proposal to Talon with care, offering his services as a doctor of some eminence to the Sulpician Order which had much influence in the new land. He felt sure his friend would know what was in his mind. **[Ftnote letter no. 3278 in Sulpicians' Archives.]** Once settled comfortably by the evening hearth, his letter duly posted, imagine his surprise when his wife joined him and said: "Preparations are underway, my dear Alcide. I have just to arrange for new homes for my dear downy friends, and you, I expect, will see to the disposition of the townhouse."

Not a man easily taken aback, Alcide kept his composure and asked quietly, "But my dear, how could you know of something I myself have only just decided a mere four hours ago?" In that incredibly soft, warm voice—the voice that had won Alcide's heart at their very first meeting, Eusèbe replied, "a little bird told me." **[cited in letter from Eusèbe to her sister, Armande: undated.]**

Dee read the last line again. She was fairly sure that that coy idiom of evasion was coined from the biblical reference that 'the birds will tell,' but it didn't seem to suit the character of Eusèbe, who, from what Dee had been able to gather, was an exceptionally sweet-natured and forthright woman. Neither wit nor coyness seemed consistent with such an earnest nature. It was completely out of character—a bit odd even—for a woman who had a special love and respect for birds—unless of course she really did talk to birds. 'Oh boy,' thought Dee, 'I'd really better call it a day. I must be more tired than I thought.'

It was getting dark anyway. DeeDee switched on the little lamp on her desk in the Archives room and sat back, twirling her pen in her hand. Up to now, she thought, all had been pretty straightforward, expected, predictable. The discovery and conquest of what became known as Nouvelle France had been a case of 'no birth without blood', her French forebears almost as bad as the Spanish and the English, shamelessly manipulating the natives and striving to dominate a land mass with temperatures so uncongenial and terrain so alien, that they may as well have landed on Mars. The more DeeDee had read, the more she felt how quixotic the whole enterprise must have seemed to the less far-sighted among them. And the greedy coneheads—the Catholic ecclesiasts—urged it all forward, having lost some ground with impertinent souls in the home country, and certain to recover their waning influence by converting the heathens in the new lands. It would be an enforceable persuasion of untold numbers, swelling the Catholic headcount by possibly millions. DeeDee's lips curled into a knowing smile. Religion always became currency: baptism and absolution in exchange for your fealty in war—our war, not your war, never yours. That's how it had always been done, after all.

Laptops weren't permitted in the Archives so DeeDee reached for her notebook and wrote:

> *More material needed on the Perrot and Rufiange families.*

Then, as she doodled in the margins, she remembered that the artifacts and collections' list for Dr. Alcide's family included a diary by one of his descendants, a Delphine deBeauvilliers, who'd lived as late as 1933. Whoever had noted the existence of the diary had given no clue as to its whereabouts but apparently, Delphine was a voluminous diarist with a keen interest in genealogy. If Dee could find it, it might shed more light on the correspondence between Alcide and Jean-Talon. She wrote:

> *Re-check collections for diary of Delphine deBeauvilliers (1880-1933) . . . diarist; may provide genealogical links.*

Though when it came to research Dee was like a dog at a bone, it would be a while before she found the diary and its present owner. When finally she did, she would be shocked at how irrevocably it would alter the life of someone dear to her: Belle Spahro.

She rang for the archivist and began packing up her notes, the deBeauvilliers letter topmost in her mind, giving a completely new spin to the third chapter of her dissertation.

The One That Got Away

SKYE SPAHRO WAS not a vain woman. Far from it. But she woke up that Tuesday morning and took a long look in the mirror, a look that asked an ancient question, one almost exclusively feminine: will what he sees please him? Am I still what I was? When she'd heard that Solange's friend, Ollie, would be picking up Ausencia, she knew immediately it was Olibade, her young man of old, the man she still met in her dreams, making her sweat and squirm, wet, alone in the dark. The nickname hadn't fooled her; the English always mangled French names to suit themselves, making René into "Rainy" and Angèle into "Angie." When she'd heard Belle making the arrangements over the phone, repeating Ollie's name as she wrote it down, a smooth, swift bleed of heat rushed through Skye's whole being, warm and enervating, not at all like the invasive hot flashes that used to ambush her unawares. No, she was one with this heat, flushing years, even decades, away until she was back then, back there, with Olibade, holding her like their lives depended on never letting go.

"Mother, are you okay?" asked Belle as she put the phone down. "You're all flushed. Come sit down for a minute and rest yourself." Belle was used to her mother losing her balance all of a sudden, but this didn't look like one of those episodes.

"No, I'm fine, Belle. But I think I will sit just for a minute." Skye looked up at her daughter and her green eyes were glassy, as if she'd been drinking.

"So Solange agreed to foster Ausencia for a while. That's very good of her." Skye tried to keep the tremor out of her voice. She was intoxicated in a way; 'pixilated' her father used to call it. When you're taken by the elves or the pixies, it might be by drink or it might be by memory. Both play tricks on the mind.

"Yes, Solange is being great. I'm so glad we've reconnected. And the man she's sending, Olibade Ouellet, he's a real horseman. He worked with her father Lucien at La Gorgendière."

Her mother didn't answer right away. Then she said: "Yes, it's a pity about Lucien; she must miss him. In all the years I've worked for horses, I never heard a bad word about Lucien, not from man, not from animal."

"Oh then you must have heard about Ollie, too. Solange said he's been with the family for ages, more like an uncle than a stockman."

"Yes," Skye replied, "actually I know Olibade; he's a jeaniste and—well—we knew each other for a time when I was young."

"Oh right. You did say that you'd spent some time here on the island when you were younger. Did you know him well, mum?" Belle asked, as she walked over to her desk, always preoccupied with the never-ending paperwork that consumed much of her day. Distracted, she didn't notice that Skye never answered.

So on the day the mirror stayed mute, Skye couldn't decide whether to go out and greet Ollie, or to stay in and pretend his being there meant nothing to her; that so much time had passed, that old loves were just that: old. But coyness was something foreign to her; she'd never learned how to fake that, or at least not well, not convincingly. The piercing green of her eyes always pre-empted any deception, telegraphing truths before she could even open her mouth. Finally, with a mild glare at the mirror, Skye tied her hair in a ponytail, and went outside as she heard a trailer pull up, bringing Olibade, her old love, right to her doorstep.

But it wasn't Olibade. A young man got out of an SUV. Skye froze for a minute. Running a rescue often meant trouble from previous horse owners who didn't respect the law or care about contracts. Once an animal came under the legal protection of the Institute, it was safe for life—especially from its abusive owner. Skye saw to that. Those horses were placed all over Canada and elsewhere; their location known only to Skye. That was the main reason the Institute had changed residence so often. If unscrupulous owners couldn't find her, they'd never find the horses either.

As he walked towards her, Skye noticed the crest of Université Jean-Talon on the van. She exhaled.

"What can I do for you?" she asked, blocking the verandah stairs.

"Hello, ma'am. I'm looking for Ms Skye Spahro . . . or, um, Belle Spahro," Chano said, holding a letter in his hand. Skye said nothing.

"My name is Chano Trottier. I requested permission to take some soil samples from your property here at Holdout Bay . . . for my graduate work . . . related to erosion levels."

"I'm Skye Spahro. May I see the letter?" Skye saw Belle's signature. She kept the letter and asked him to wait a few minutes.

"Belle . . . Belle! Where are you?" she called out as she entered the house.

"I'm right here, Mum. What's up?" replied Belle as she came downstairs.

"What is this, Belle?" Skye held out the letter. "Oh I thought it would be all right, Mother. He'll only be here a little while and I have release forms for him to sign, including that he agree to stay away from the horses."

"I'm not sure about this, Belle. People always mean well, but . . . . At some point, somebody always wants to give a horse a carrot and then—and then they start to think this is a petting zoo . . . and then they'll start bringing friends and—"

"—you know I won't let that happen, Mother. Let me go speak to him."

"Make sure he knows he is not a house guest and especially, Belle, especially, that he is not to speak of what goes on here," Skye said as Toby flew in the screen door Belle had just opened.

"It'll be all right, Skye. He looks pretty harmless to me," said Toby, as Belle walked onto the verandah to meet Chano.

"No one is harmless . . . as you well know, Toby. Even people with good intentions end up talking too much or talking to the wrong people, and then . . . ."

"Yes and then we had to move again. I know, Skye. But we've been okay so far since Belle set us up here. It's pretty remote, and the cemetery visitors can't even see beyond the woods. People probably don't even know we're here."

"Yes, so far, it's been good," replied Skye. But Toby knew she was thinking about Gemma, the one horse that all of Skye's precautions had failed to protect. Gemma and her foal. All those years ago. Her former owner, bent on revenge, had somehow found the retiree who'd adopted her—the kind old gentleman was so happy that she was in foal, too. But the old man could do nothing to stop what happened. When the Sûreté finally caught up with the sadistic bastard, they found the foal cut out of Gemma's belly and both of them, mother and baby, lying in their own blood with their throats slit. Skye stepped off the planet after that, nowhere to be found, even more determined that no one ever again—not nobody, not no-how—would get a chance to harm her friends again.

Skye suddenly felt a little wobbly. As she went upstairs to her room and closed the door, Toby watched a horse trailer pull up. Olibade had arrived to pick up Ausencia. Even before turning off the ignition, Ollie looked up at the house, but as had happened so long ago, his Skye had stepped away.

A Crystalline Space

A S CHANO TURNED and saw Belle step off the verandah to greet him, he felt as if he'd just stepped in from the cold into a very warm, welcoming place. Maybe she was a piece of the sky that had drifted to earth and was right here in front of him; now shaking his hand, now talking and smiling with the face of an earth angel. He tried to smile back and not stare stupidly at the curve of her cheek, her mouth, her eyes, but the smile he managed was so weak that he feared he hadn't smiled at all and appeared cold. Yet he felt the opposite of cold towards this dark-eyed blonde whose vibrato trilled all through his senses as if he were a tuning fork. Thoroughly warmed inside and out, he began to stammer and sweat. When she spoke, he responded; when she queried, he answered. It felt as if his own voice came from far away while hers seemed to have nested somewhere deep inside him, coiling and uncoiling with the in and out of his studied breathing.

Belle sensed that a personal disarray had come over the man and tried to put him at ease. She kept her voice light and casual, and as he pointed out items in the material he'd sent with the letter she still held in her hands, she leaned in close in a friendly, familiar way only to take a step back, surprised by a light-headedness that suddenly overcame her. Their eyes locked for long seconds and what Belle saw there, in that crystalline space, made her drop her eyes first.

She turned towards the sound of someone walking towards them. Chano, aware only of her, felt the warmth that was Belle turn away. Olibade, his eyes scanning the shuttered house, joined them, and Belle, relieved for reasons mysterious even to her, was very glad to see him.

PART TWO

Huis Clos Stables

AUSENCIA HAD BEEN settled at Solange's place, les écuries Huis Clos, for nearly a week now. And she'd been wrong: there were other horses here. A big Belgian, for one, named Ulric the Red. When she'd arrived, he was at the far end of the pasture with some dogs, and only appeared at feeding time when he walked straight into his stall. Ausencia noticed that there was no stall chain barring his way, in or out—and of the twenty-three stalls there, his was choice, built especially for draught horses like him.

It's hard to surprise a Belgian. Ulric paused only a moment on his way in when he saw Ausencia in the stall across from his. He took note of her presence and then turned to eat. Mindful of her manners at all times, Ausencia waited for him to speak first. As it was, he seemed to be digesting the very fact of her presence as he chewed his hay. He was a good eater, she noted. He didn't roughhouse his food like many did or attack it as if it were trying to escape. No, Ulric's eating was a collected, sober activity: a snoggling of hay punctuated by select pauses, as if interesting ideas came to him mid-chew. He'd raise his head from the bale, jaws poised, before rejecting each idea in turn—an idea, a snoggle, another idea, a more spirited snoggle and so on until he was satisfied with both his selection of ideas and his food. Ausencia liked him right off.

"Hello," said Ulric, done eating and now facing her from across the way. Ausencia, shy, nodded, aware that she had lost her figure. "I'm Ausencia." Ulric turned his head so as to get a better look at her. She was appallingly thin. 'Fine head though,' he thought.

"I'm glad you're not a Thoroughbred—they're so full of themselves, so touchy—too much inbreeding, you know, and not very good company."

Ausencia turned full around, her hind leg now on the mend and hardly dragging at all.

"My name is Ulric. You can call me Rick, everyone does. Did you come from Skye's place? I mean, are you staying or are you just visiting?"

"I don't know. I was at a place with lots of green trees—was that Skye's?—and then I was brought here. Where is here, anyway?"

"This is Solange's place—well it's her Dad's really. My owner was a friend of his and he wanted to retire me somewhere nice, so Lucien brought me here three years ago. I was in PEI working the Irish moss harvesting. Not bad work if you don't mind getting your belly wet. Hard though—and lonesome. Those of us left are few and far between." Ausencia had no idea what Irish moss was and had never heard of Prince Edward Island.

"Are there others here or, or is it—is there just you—just us, I mean?"

"Just me. Yup. For now. There's Contessa. She's away somewhere. They're always showing her off here and there . . . not sure why. She's a Canadien, pretty friendly. But Marquis the old stallion died a while back, just before Lucien passed away. Losing Marquis cut the heart right out of Contessa; she's real quiet now. When she's home, she keeps herself to herself. But now you're here. That's good. Skye may send others from time to time, but lately, well, there's just been me and I've—I've been hoping for some company."

Ulric took a few steps closer, into the passage, hoping his massive size would impress, not intimidate, the mare. Despite her wan looks, he knew she was a lady. Breeding always tells.

"I mean, the dogs are all right but they're so barky, always showing off, and Solange—she's great. But she's not like Skye. No one's like Skye . . . hey, didn't you talk to Skye? Didn't you even meet her?"

It had just occurred to Ulric that since Ausencia didn't even know who Skye was, she didn't realize how lucky she was to have been rescued by her. Ulric thought that, by now, everyone knew Skye or knew of her. Ausencia didn't know how to answer Rick's question. The landlady she'd met at the green place was very nice, very caring but she'd certainly not *talked* to Ausencia—at least, she thought, not in the way Rick seemed to mean.

"Oh," Rick understood now. "You must have met Belle, her daughter."

"She—Belle I guess—she was very, very good to me though. I wanted so badly to stay there. It seemed like a paradise, like nowhere I'd ever been before—but—" Ausencia pressed her chest against the chain, thrusting her head and neck as close as she could to Ulric's big face—"but I think I like it better here."

A trait of the breed not to wear their hearts on their sleeves, Ulric accepted her grooming stoically. Privately, he gloried in it. "Oh then I have a lot to tell you, Ausencia."

The next morning, when Solange came to help Olibade muck out the stalls, she found him leaning against a stall post, a big smile on his face. The chain to Ausencia's stall was on the ground, downed easily by one of Rick's massive hooves. The two horses were in Rick's big stall, standing nose to tail. Solange laughed at the sight of them, as cozy as cats in a cradle.

"Ah, it's good he's a lover, that Rick, and not a fighter, for sure," said Ollie, still smiling. Solange watched as he stooped to examine the bent chain, filled with the gratitude she'd felt the day he'd told her he would stay on at Huis Clos shortly after her father, Lucien, died. She didn't know how she would have gotten through the months that followed without Olibade. Solange had known Ollie Ouellet all her life. He'd started working for her father when Lucien was still in charge of the provincial stud farm in La Gorgendière—one of the last outposts for the hardy Canadian breed, the renowned Canadien. Ollie was his best and most trusted stockman, as horse-savvy as Lucien himself, hard-working and close-mouthed, always willing to go the extra mile when called for—just like the beautiful blacks, the Canadian breed they both loved. So in 1981, when the state dismantled the stud farm, selling off the remaining twenty or so Canadiens to members of the Canadian Horse Breeders Association, and Lucien, then 71 years of age, retired to Isle-Saint-Jean-Baptiste, Ollie went with him. Olibade knew the island well, a jeaniste born and bred, and wasn't unhappy to leave the breeding facility with its score of white, flat-topped buildings and sanitized stables. And it wasn't just Ollie who'd had enough of sterile working conditions: Marquis, #3455 in the Canadien registry, an old but prolific stallion and direct descendant of the famous mare, Belle Bayonne #1531, was retired and brought to the island, much to the annoyance of some private breeders. Now past his prime, Marquis had unfailingly sired top-of-the-line progeny, and many coveted having his famous name at the top of their stud lists. But Lucien always distrusted private breeders; he knew they wouldn't give Marquis his well-deserved retirement. They'd work him till he dropped and then send him to slaughter. And though he trusted the CHBA members—people who, like him, were devoted to preserving the purity of this special Québec breed, unique to Canada—he couldn't part with his magnificent old stallion.

When Lucien and Ollie moved lock, stock and barrel to Isle-Saint-Jean-Baptiste, Marquis and a pretty broodmare, Contessa #3456, went with them. Lucien bought an old, rundown hobby farm on a cul-de-sac, with lots of pasture and named his new, private little stable 'Huis Clos' because, as he told his daughter Solange, "we're all of us—me, Marquis and Contessa—at the end of the road, but at least, it will be our road and no-one else's."

The Things Papa Knew

GUYANNE LOOKED IN the mirror and saw nothing but pimples and pustules. She'd been a late bloomer, but she'd always hoped that by the age of twenty, the cruddy skin on her face would have miraculously disappeared. She applied the dermatologist's cream, carefully rubbing it in to blend with her skin tone, like the directions said. She rinsed her face lightly, then looked up at her reflection. Just more of the same. She looked away wishing all 5'6" of her would just disappear. She pulled on her boots with some effort and headed outside.

"Bon, allô, allô ma'mselle Guyanne," said Olibade, continuing to wrap the bandage around Ausencia's leg, a daily ritual.

"Hi Ollie. Is her leg any better?" Guyanne found Olibade much easier to talk to than her mother, Solange, partly because he was always working, head down, and rarely looked at her face. "What happened to her anyway?"

"Who knows? These polo ponies are worked hard, and then stabled away with just a couple of hours a day on pasture. That's never good. They like to be moving, horses, and they can't move much in a stall."

He stood up and stuck a finger between the leg and the wrap, gauging the tightness.

"Or they're worked too much, with no downtime at all. It's hard to know. This one, she could've had this problem for a long time and the owner didn't notice—or didn't care as long as she played well. Mature sport horses like her, they just keep on going until a bone breaks or a tendon goes."

Ollie continued explaining, pointing out the different parts of a horse's anatomy, something he knew like the back of his hand. Ulric the big Belgian, now never far from Ausencia, stood a short distance away, grazing.

When he came up behind Guyanne and nosed her in the back, Guyanne stepped back, startled but laughing.

"Ah so your mother, she's wrong, eh? You do know how to laugh."

"Why do horses do that, Ollie?" Guyanne's grey eyes actually gleamed a little as she stroked Ulric's massive neck.

"Well what do you do when you want to talk, when you want attention?" replied Ollie. Guyanne never wanted attention. Most times, she wished she could fade right into the woodwork.

"Comme nous, les chevaux veulent jaser de temps en temps. Horses are sociable—and curious. They like to know what's going on and what's what, just like we do. Mostly they're sociable with each other. But see, Ulric likes you and he wants you to notice him. Go ahead . . . talk to him."

"Oh he probably only likes me because I help you feed him every day."

"Non, pas vrai," Ollie replied. "Horses are very particular about who they like. He didn't bump me in the back just now, he bumped you." Ollie stood up for a minute to stretch his back.

"You know, I've noticed that you're good with the horses, but you never talk to them; you never spend time with them. There's more to taking care of an animal than just seeing he's fed and watered."

Guyanne flushed red. In fact, she'd been secretly pleased that someone, even a horse, preferred her to someone else. But it was a new feeling; it surprised her. She'd opened her mouth to speak but the fact of it left her mute, moreso than usual. Ollie crouched again to smooth out Ausencia's bandage. Guyanne kept stroking Ulric whose eyes by now were half-closed, his head hanging low and loose, leaning into Guyanne as if she were as solid as a tree.

"Your grandpa, Lucien, he always said that he knew everything about a man just by how the horses reacted to him . . . he always used to say that horses didn't know 'doubt' and 'doubt' didn't know horses . . . they just knew good from bad and bad from good." Guyanne could just make out Ollie's profile as he spoke. She liked feeling Ulric's weight against her, the big old boy now fully relaxed, enjoying her long, deep stroking along his chest and neck.

"Yeah he said he could tell if a man was a wife-beater, or if the man was a big talker—gros parleur, 'ti faiseur—or if he was just a big nounours—a foolish man. He said he could even tell if the man was happy, within himself like, or if he was unhappy or disappointed with his life or himself, you know," Ollie glanced at Guyanne and continued, " . . . and was looking for something, something he thought he could get back from being around horses . . . huh, as if the horses knew something he didn't. Yeah, he was something, your grandfather . . . the things he knew." Ollie shook his head slowly. "He used to say that he learned everything he knew about life and about people from horses . . . everything he needed to know and a lot of things he didn't really want to know. That's what he used to say, alright . . . all the time."

When the day was done—and Guyanne made a point of noticing the sunset though she wasn't yet sure why she should—she crawled into bed with the books she had bought just the week before on horses, how to care for them, what role they'd played in history, and how to train them, and began to make notes in her notebook. After a while, she fell asleep and dreamed. She dreamed of Papa, her grandfather Lucien.

Je me souviens

GUYANNE LOOKED DOWN. She was wearing an apron. It was her grandmother's, a woman who'd died before Guyanne had learned to talk. She was arguing with her husband, Lucien, Guyanne's grandfather.

"Mais qu'est qui te prend Lucien?" his wife had asked at the time, upset that her husband could even think of breeding horses for the provincial government—a dying breed at that—one no-one had any use for anymore, not even farmers whose equipment now came well-discounted from John Deere.

"The war has changed the world, Lucien. People don't need horses anymore. These new machines can do more work, never need to be fed or watered or vetted; they don't get old, they don't get sick . . . ."

"The feds throw money at the stud farms at St. Joachim and at Ste-Anne-de-la-Pocatière. We can do as well here with the province giving us the same money . . . and after all, my dear, this is a breed de chez nous—our breed. We should preserve it. We did not get this far except on the back of a horse."

This wasn't a story her grandfather had ever told her so Guyanne didn't know how she knew this. The intimacy of it mortified her a little. But somehow her dream self—who was reporting it all back to her—convinced her it was true; it had happened. Lucien continued eloquently, now most of what he was saying largely incoherent. Then the scene changed and a meeting was going on with two men in suits addressing Lucien with soapbox passion.

"Monsieur Deschambault, it is crucial to Québec, to the future of our nation, to ensure that le petit cheval de fer, the Canadien, does not get thrown away by les grands manitous in Ottawa. Without even a nod in our direction—not even a memo telling us what they were up to—the feds shut down all the stud farms except for Ste-Anne. It is unacceptable. Unbelievable. What we need to do—"

"—yes, what la patrie needs from you, M. Deschambault—may I call you Lucien?—Lucien, what we need to do is to preserve anything and everything that our ancestors fought for and died defending. This breed belongs to us and to us alone. We brought it here. It landed 400 years ago in Tadoussac just like we did, and then it was stolen right from under us—by the English, the Americans, everybody—just like everything else they took from us. Ça fait partie de notre patrimoine—"

"Gentlemen, gentlemen . . . let us be frank," Lucien interrupted. "You cannot construct a nation by glorifying farm animals. Why we've only just finished eating a supper that featured the best cut of un bovin canadien—a cow breed that will become rarer and rarer as we import the Jersey and the Holstein—ah! Ha!Ha! Do you see the joke, messieurs—'rarer and rarer'—the best cut of a Canadian cooked rare—ah hahaha—"

Lucien liked to play devil's advocate; he especially enjoyed a good joke like no one else. The two men from Agro-Québec watched Lucien double over with laughter and looked at each other. Guyanne giggled in her sleep, both at her grandfather's silly joke and at the humourlessness of the men in suits.

"Hah, I see that pleasantries such as these are not to your taste, messieurs."

Lucien sat up, began to re-load his pipe, and continued in a tone they had not heard until now. Guyanne didn't remember her grandfather ever smoking anything—much less a pipe. She wrinkled her nose in her sleep.

"What you want is to find reasons to support the separatist claim, to bring Québec to realize its independence—ah oui, le grand destin québécois. Do you ever wonder, messieurs, why our patron saint is Saint Jean le Baptiste—the one saint in all the canon whose head was cut off—he lost his head, messieurs—and to a king—yes it was served to a foreign king. On a platter. Il était dans son assiette. Pleinement. A lost head, ah yes, and we all know that a beast with no head has no—what shall we say?—has nothing to look forward to."

Guyanne shivered. Now suddenly, she was one of the high-collared martinets. She whispered to her confrère, "the Department has obviously made a mistake in selecting this man for our project." Her grandfather went on, unheeding.

"From whom and from what this independence is to be won is not my concern. I and my neighbours give not a fig whether the money for our farms comes from les anglais or from you. Money speaks only one language, messieurs—the language of survival . . . and I can say 'tank yew' just as easily as I can say 'merci.' Do you think I am just an ignorant farmer who knows nothing about nothing? I know our history as well—better—than you two. My ancestors—four generations ago—fought in the Patriote Rebellions in 1838—the last one, the one that crushed us—when the English burned and pillaged our villages. But what made those brave souls cry, what made them sob like children was when they took 800—*eight hundred*—of our horses, les Canadiens, purebred, perfect—the horse the Jesuits called 'magnificent in his devotion' . . . and left us without the one thing, the one loyal friend, that could help us rebuild our burnt out farms . . . le petit cheval de fer."

The two men opened their mouths to speak but stayed silent, their usual ripostes to such a man seeming foolish and even, a little absurd right now. They stood up and began to gather their papers. Lucien leaned back in his chair and smiled.

"But where are you off to, gentlemen? We have not yet had dessert . . . and my wife's dessert is to die for. She would be very insulted for you not to say so. I am happy to do what you need, and you will not find a better horseman in these parts than myself. Why, my grandfather was one of the founding members of the French Canadian Horse Breeders Association—yes, messieurs . . . alongside the great Monsieur Deland himself."

As the men hesitated, Lucien leaned forward and said: "Most of all, I have not yet told you the story of Belle Bayonne, or how the general—the great Montcalm—insisted his mount be a Canadien stallion. He would accept no other, no other, mes amis—and I'll tell you why . . . ." He had them now. Guyanne became her grandmother again, bringing in dessert and serving it to the men. Now she knew her grandfather would tell them his stories, stories she'd heard him tell over and over since childhood about the souche mares—not registered but of pure blood—and how it was because of the little mare, Belle Bayonne, that le Canadien became known as the Iron Horse. Belle Bayonne, #1531 in the old Registry of Purebred Canadiens, could travel 20 miles an hour carrying five people in a buggy, nonstop, at the age of 22. "Imagine the weight of five people, mes amis—and in the dead of winter, with snow as high as this table."

He told how Marquis' sire, Bazola #2485, won the ribbon at the Toronto Royal Winter Fair in 1946.

"They had two great stallions, see . . . and they thought both had a great chance at winning the ribbon. And they'd made a deal that whichever one did win, they'd exchange their ownership papers. But they could only afford for one of them to get in to the fair, see, so one of them hid under the hay in the hay wagon as they went through the entrance gate. And when the stallion Bazola won—and he took all the honours—the two men exchanged ownerships and that's how I got my Marquis, son of Bazola. Ah, 'une race, la nôtre' . . . that's what old Mr. L'Amoureux used to say. He was the mayor, you see, of Henryville, an exceptional breeder, and one day, he . . . ."

The men in the dream were sitting back now, nodding, relaxed, smiling. Guyanne smiled too in her sleep. Clearly, the dream was no respecter of times and dates. Many of those stories took place long after Agro-Québec had started funding the stud farm. No matter. Guyanne loved her grandfather's stories. The sound of his voice in the dream, telling story after story, lulled her into a very deep, very comfortable sleep after that.

As she opened her eyes the next morning, her mind was still coursing from one stream of thought to another, pell-mell, images and memory all atumble, in and out of real time. She tried to shake it off as she washed her face, but paused, her face still dripping, and smiled a great big smile that turned into a laugh. Then she looked at her silly laughing face in the mirror and that made her laugh even harder. Life was pouring back into her, stirring deep, banked fires inside her that made her flush red all up her neck straight through to her hairline. As she grabbed a nearby towel, she was hardly aware that she'd made a decision; one that was reshaping her interior landscape. She had found a way in; a connection to the world that till now had stymied her growth, constellated in a sentimental dream about horses—no, about Papa and his love of horses. A distinction she realized was important because it explained why Ulric's attention had touched her in such a deep place. She shook her head in wonder that a sensation so strong could be seeded by an old retired horse, but then Ollie had told her Papa said horses could fix whatever ailed you; that horses didn't know 'doubt' and 'doubt' didn't know horses. Maybe Papa could see from above what an unholy mess of a girl she was, stuck in a gooey, gelid bog of indifference, unable to free herself by herself, and had sent her the dream as a signpost. She was living in Papa's old home after all, where memories of him stood silhouetted everywhere; especially around the stable door, where the backlight of the fading sun often gave more substance than shadow to the image of her beloved Papa Lucien.

She finished dressing quickly, knocking the face cream onto the floor as she reached for Le Canadien, historique, and her notebook, and made a beeline for the stable, the place really, she thought with a start, she had felt most at home ever since she'd come to live at Huis Clos.

POINTS OF A HORSE

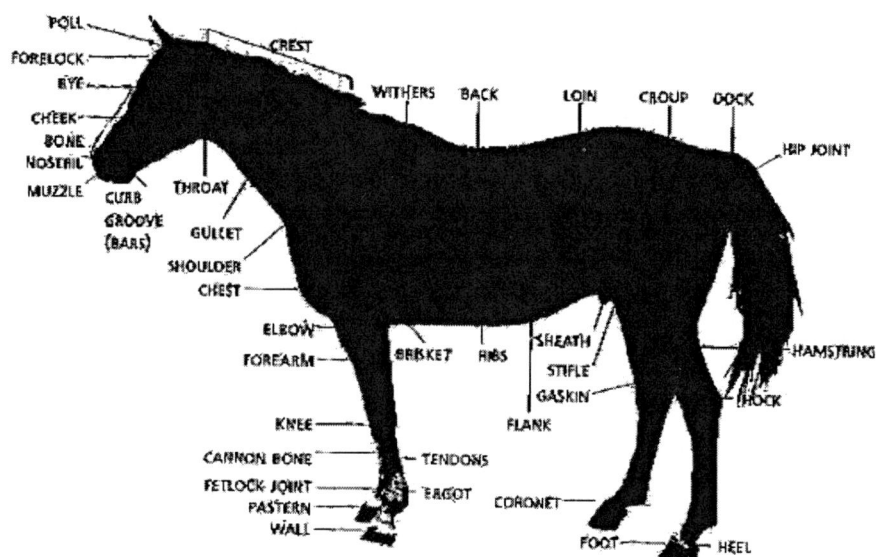

POLL

FORELOCK

EYE

CHEEK

BONE

NOSTRIL

MUZZLE

CURB
GROOVE
(BARS)

CREST

THROAT

GULLET

SHOULDER

CHEST

WITHERS   BACK   LOIN   CROUP   DOCK

HIP JOINT

ELBOW

FOREARM

BRISKET   RIBS   SHEATH

STIFLE

GASKIN

FLANK

HAMSTRING

HOCK

KNEE

CANNON BONE   TENDONS

FETLOCK JOINT   ERGOT

PASTERN

WALL

CORONET

FOOT   HEEL

The Beautiful Blacks

GUYANNE STUDIED THE enlarged sketch of equine anatomy and held it up parallel to Ulric as if it were an x-ray. Ulric turned to watch her, as she looked from him to the sketch and back again. After two minutes, his curiosity overcame him so he moved over to get a better look at the paper she was holding up, and began nosing and lipping it. Before Yanne knew it, his entire mass was more behind her than in front of her.

"Oh Ulric! Don't move. I need you to stand, just stand like normal so I can—I can get it all in my head." She tacked the sketch to the wall and sat her book on an upside-down bucket. She considered tethering Rick in crossties to keep him still, but decided against it. For one thing, Ollie never used them unless the farrier insisted on them, and for another, she felt Ulric would be supremely insulted. He was a horse who'd spent his whole life in human company following human orders, and knew almost before they did what they wanted done. In the end, she adjusted herself to wherever he decided to place himself—which as it turned out was better than where she'd placed him because the light was brighter there—and began a diligent study, touching and reading, reading and touching.

Horses' eyes are the largest of all the land mammals. Apart from two blind spots, horses have near-panoramic vision. Their eyes, placed laterally wide apart, give them a very full peripheral field which is crucial to a prey animal. However, they cannot see clearly anything about six feet directly in front of or beneath their nose nor can they see directly behind, around the tail area. A horse that backs up or turns its head sideways when approached is compensating for those

*two blind spots; such movements are often misinterpreted by novice
riders as shying or recalcitrance.*

Guyanne looked carefully at Rick's eyes and then went to stand
directly behind him. Ulric mulled this change over for a minute then
angled his body broadside by about forty degrees; he gave her a brief
look and then resumed his classic draught stance. As she observed his
reaction, Guyanne thought of the blinders on carriage and calèche horses.
She knew blinders prevented their seeing things that would alarm or
frighten them, but what a limited way for such an intelligent, curious
creature to live. It also explained why blinders were not standard gear on
police horses, like those of the Montréal police cavalry. The horses' much
more generous viewscape would give the riders eyes in the back of their
heads or close to, foiling ambushes and other furtive approaches—and
Guyanne knew for a fact that only 'the beautiful blacks' qualified as
Montréal mounts. Like Contessa, their calm natures and sure-footedness
make them best-suited for civil peacekeeping. Contessa brought Papa to
mind. Papa always said les Canadiens were royal horses, sent by Louis
XIV direct from the Gran Écurie to the new land for his military and
other important people. The Sun King had spared no expense, Papa
would say in an almost hallowed voice, in the breeding of these special
mounts. His Majesty imported Iberian stallions to breed with the native
Cotentin and Breton mares, combining the hardiness and intelligence
of the compact French dams with the elegance and courage of the exotic
imports. The tar-like blackness of these superb specimens, with their
thick and wild manes and long trailing tails, were natural assets in battle,
for the enemy—facing a noirceur en masse, eerily still and steady—would
be intimidated beyond reason.

Ulric watched as his young friend sat down cross-legged on some
straw, flipping through her book. Papa knew so much, she thought, and
he'd shared what he knew with his granddaughter—whenever he saw her,
always reminiscing, saying 'remember, Guyanne, it's all important, all of
it; remember.' Perhaps he hoped that one day—unlike her mother who'd
followed another road, a good road, yes and he was as proud of Solange
as he was of his star fillies but a path far from what was closest to his own
heart—perhaps one day the young Guyanne would carry on his work: the
preservation and protection of 'une race, la nôtre.' She looked admiringly
at Ulric's impressive figure. "Do you think that's what it's all about, Rick?
Do you think Papa is relying on me to do something, to finish something

or maybe continue something—but what could it be, do you think? What is there left to do? What could I do that hasn't already been done?" By now, Ulric had relaxed his right hind—he could see they'd be there awhile—and he too remembered his friend Lucien, so kind and jolly, and recalled something amazing Contessa had told him when Lucien was taken ill. She'd said Lucien loved the Canadien breed so much that he'd postponed his own death.

Une race, la nôtre

LUCIEN HELD OUT as long as he could. He was waiting. Any day now, the Québec government was going to declare le Canadien an official heritage animal of Québec. He wanted to live to see it. L'Association had assured him that it was a done deal. Any day now. He'd fall into long reveries without speaking and at other times, off the morphine, he'd talk until his voice gave out.

"What—what are they waiting for?" he'd whisper hoarsely. He told his daughter that he'd been wrong about things, many things—so many he'd lost count. He thought God cruel to show him now, now that he was old and unable to change anything, a compte rendu of his wrong-headedness and mistaken assumptions. If he'd known then what he knew now; if, if—what good for God to bring him to his knees now, now as his flesh wasted away and his spirit was on the threshold?

"I will be like a man who stumbles into heaven by sheer chance, dumb luck, not knowing how he got there . . . scratching his head like a fool, gros nounours . . . . I had the stick by the wrong end . . . life, you see . . . I did good things but maybe, maybe for the wrong people—people who now hesitate—they hesitate, daughter—to claim the breed for their own after, all those years ago, telling me it was my duty, my patriotic duty, to preserve this breed for them, for us—for you, Solange and all who come after you!" he'd say again and again to his daughter. Maybe he was being punished, he'd say, because he'd laughed at the early sovereignists who came to him after the War claiming that le Canadien had to be preserved for la patrie—la patrie alone.

"Mais ces-hommes-là étaient des ignorants. They didn't even know how much had already been done to keep the breed pure, how Couture and Barnard and later, Deland—Monsieur Deland especially, daughter—who, together with some few others, understood the sacredness of their mission who—in the face of what was a diaspora, yes, the diaspora of a race whose extraordinary qualities had been bred to the Morgan and had become anonymous Canadian cousins—these men, these few, worked to recover the original bloodlines . . . . Over the years, commandeered by the British, exported by the thousands to the States, devalued by the French—this 400-year-old breed—fait au Québec, produit de chez nous—was stolen, *stolen* I say, by a covetousness that scythed away at la patrie until it had little if anything left to offer . . . was become nothing but a North American curiosity, a tourist destination! Oh what a loss, such a loss . . . and now these imbecile pencilnecks waver and ponder whether or not to claim the little iron horse as our own!"

It wrenched Solange's heart to see how distraught her father was. After a while, he'd be calm and then almost laugh at himself. All he really cared about at the time, he'd say, was being with the horses themselves: he didn't care who paid him to work with them, breed them and register them. He never did know the 'why' of his love of horses, he'd say sheepishly. Over and over again, he'd say to Solange: "Maman, sais-tu, maman used to say, 'Lucien, when a horse is sick, your hair could catch fire and you wouldn't notice.' And I'd say, 'Madeleine, Madeleine . . . some things just are. C'est comme ça, mon trésor . . . c'est comme ça.'"

Solange could barely stand to listen sometimes. She had given up a flourishing career to come home, finally homing in on values her parents had set for her long ago, values she'd tested in the big wide world and found unshakeable; finally folded them back into her life and now her father, the touchstone of this immense turnaround, was telling her he'd been wrong. Solange saw that it wasn't regret he was feeling so much as anger at his own lack of vision. She had to make him see that he had righted a wrong, that he had made things right; that the breed he'd loved so much was safe because of him, no matter what his reasons were at the time. But if he thought he needed forgiveness—forgiveness for whatever he thought he'd done, not done, not done enough of—she wanted him to have it. She wanted her father to have what he needed so he could die in peace. She phoned her cousin Darquise.

"Dis-moi pas . . . don't tell me," were Dee's first words.

"No, not yet, but soon, I think," replied Solange. "He's reminiscing a lot . . . remembering things and people from long ago . . . he isn't happy with himself though. That's what bothers me. It's so unlike him. I don't want him to go dreading his life more than his death, DeeDee—you know what

I mean. He thinks he made terrible mistakes when all he did was make the mistakes we all make, no worse than anyone—fewer than most, if the truth be told. But he thinks he failed . . . the horses, the country—everything I think—even Maman maybe. I want you to see him, Dee; I want you to talk to him. He talks a lot about the stud farm, the politics, back then. You know all about that. It's disturbing him—his choices back then, I mean. You could set his mind at ease. Come . . . come soon, cousin." They hung up without a word more.

The last story Lucien told was not about his wife, nor even his beloved daughter: it was about the night Contessa went missing.

"Monsieur Gareau, he lived not far from me . . . he had a handsome stallion, a big boy, a paint named Jericho . . . good breeding, papers and all that . . . he was a force of nature, that Jericho . . . and Achille, he was always after me to let Jericho serve Contessa . . . he liked Contessa, see. She had perfect conformation, from withers to croup, and a beautiful face. He thought they'd make a perfect baby together. It was against the rules, I kept telling him. The whole point of the Canadien stud farm was to reproduce the one breed and no other—no mixes. One night, I was out of town and Ollie called and said Contessa was gone, missing. I didn't even go home. I drove straight to Gareau's to take back my Tessa . . . I knew it was him . . . but the deed was already done. Hah . . . the walls of Jericho had fallen. I never did find out what the g-men did with that foal . . . but it must have been special, real special, with Contessa's face maybe, and Jericho's fearlessness."

Coppertone Memories

"OLLIE . . . OLLIE . . . PEUX-TU venir dans maison pour 2 minutes?" Solange was at the front door, calling for Olibade. For the umpteenth time, Guyanne and Ulric were watching Ollie tend to Ausencia's sore leg.

"Oui j'arrive. Donne-moi cinq minutes," Ollie yelled back, intent on the legwrap. He still didn't look up when he said, "You can finish, Yanne, if you like. You know what to do, you've watched me often enough . . . yes, use the palm of your right to keep the padding even—yes, like that! Oui c'est ça . . . parfait. You've got it! T'as le tour ma fille . . . t'as le tour!"

Instinctively, Guyanne stepped in to take over wrapping Ausencia's leg. She was excited and scared to be doing this, but her nightly studies in the stable with Ulric were paying off. Yanne now knew horse anatomy almost as well as Ollie did—or, at the very least, she had Ulric's down pat. Ulric was so willing; seemed to cheer her on with that amiability draughts are so well-known for. He knew what she was trying to do; he thought it was touching and told Ausencia so. Ausencia agreed, but said she was never surprised at anything people did. The mare never even turned to look when Ollie let Yanne take over, but Ulric moved closer and rested his nose on Yanne's back as if to encourage her. Yanne concentrated even more on her task, wanting to make Ausencia comfortable, wanting to reassure her friend, Ulric, and wanting to do as good a job as Ollie. Wanting—the cradle of desire, the piston of all human action—had now become part of Yanne's vocabulary. It made her feel good and that 'good' was getting better all the time. By losing herself in something beyond herself, she became more complete, more whole. Mentored by Ulric, she lost all self-consciousness and applied her whole self to the task at hand.

"Bon, qu'est-ce qui se passe?" Ollie asked as he walked into Solange's office. She had Belle on the phone. "Yes, I'm just asking Ollie now . . . you know, there's just me and him to take care of Rick and Aussie, and Contessa's away right now, but she'll be back soon. As for my daughter—well she's—" The look on Ollie's face stopped her mid-syllable.

"Hold on a minute, Belle." She hit the mute button.

"Ouais . . . pis?" she said to Ollie.

"Écoute . . . if it's about taking another horse, take it. We can handle at least ten, you and me—and Yanne's learning—she is. She's trying hard, anyway. And she learns fast, that girl. So. Anyway, c'est toi le boss so it's up to you."

With his hands on his hips and his chin stuck out, Olibade looked more like the boss. Between the two of them, he was the true horseman; what Solange knew about horses, despite her background, would probably only fit on his little finger. He did most of the work, too, so Solange couldn't make such an important decision without him—regardless of who the boss was or who the owner of Huis Clos was. Her eyes still on him as she spoke, she said to Belle:

"Okay Belle, we'll take him . . . O-b-e-r-o-n . . . three-year-old gelding . . . got it. When can we pick him up?" Ollie turned to go.

"Attends . . . attends-donc Olibade . . . oh he's still at the equine hospital in St-Hyacinthe . . . oh . . . bad, eh? Oh and what about the little pony mother and her yearling—Luka was his name, I think. Are they still at the hospital? Do you want me to take them too? Oh I see . . . that's a shame about the mother but that's great that you've got Luka."

Ollie's face darkened. "Ça se peux-tu? Who could hurt a pony for God's sake?" he said in a low voice.

"Okay, Ollie can drive the trailer over this afternoon. And let me know when the vets give the go-ahead. Right . . . You're welcome, ma belle amie . . . je t'embrasse."

Ollie was already out the door and Solange didn't follow him. All she was thinking as she looked out the window was that her daughter—her daughter, Guyanne—was trying hard. Guyanne was trying hard at something? And she was a fast learner. Really? How come Ollie knew that and she, Solange, the girl's own mother, didn't? Merde. The squirrels were at the bird-feeder again. Merde, merde, merde. She had a go at them but it was half-hearted; Belle would say that they need to eat too. The thought made her smile despite herself. She turned towards the stables. She knew she needed the curative of good hard labour and there was no better cure

CYNTHIA D'ERRICO

for self-pity than a close encounter with horse manure. She picked out the heaviest pitchfork of the bunch and began to muck out the stalls. She began to smile again thinking of Belle and her goodness to all living things. Solange wasn't at all clear on how her friend Belle's Institute worked—not the specifics of it anyway—but she knew it was a good cause, and horses had been her father's life's work, his passion. Her mother always used to say that, for her husband, horses came first. Always. And Solange knew it was important to her Belle, and anything Belle believed in, you could be sure was righteous. She'd always been one of those people who made changes happen—not overnight, like all the newsmakers Solange had spent most of her life reporting on in the news—but by dint of hard work, perseverance and belief that right would prevail. Back in college and still now, Belle—champion of the powerless—was Solange's personal hero. She paused for a minute as she fork-lifted a ripe pile. She'd caught a whiff of sunscreen from somewhere. She inhaled deeply—God, she loved the smell of horse and Coppertone. In a heartbeat, she was home again.

Mother always slathered her in Coppertone right before Papa would scoop his tiny daughter up with one arm—woup woup—and balance her in front of him, her little hands already reaching to grasp the mane. She loved the sound of her father's voice coming from somewhere behind her like the voice of god, saying, "Remarque ma fille, the strength, the power of this creature beneath you . . . feel him. Sheer power in every muscle, every sinew. And no violence in him. Non, pas du tout. Such grace, such strength . . . and no malice, no, none, pas de méchancété." And then he'd enfold her with one whole arm and say, "Là c'est ça . . . là on lui demande si on peut aller avec lui . . . wherever he's going we want to go. Ask him if we can go too—on y va!" And little Solange would crow loud, so loud, her stumpy little legs freed by the take-off, airborne like fat little commas. She could feel Marquis unfolding and folding beneath her, a reach and retreat of perfect pitch; a scoping forward, then a gathering in: reach, release, return; reach, release, return. A single, contained movement à bout de souffle. Marquis' hooves striking the ground, bringing it up around her ears. No beat discernible now . . . all below them, now just a brown blur. All three become the wind.

"Oh, I love that smell," she whispered to the water trough, inhaling deeply.

"Mother . . . everything okay?" asked the Coppertone.

"Oh Guyanne. It's you," said Solange. She put her arm around her daughter and nuzzled her hair. "I love that smell of sunscreen." Her mother looked peculiar, smiling so softly and snuffling her hair as if she were a horse. Guyanne didn't know what to say but she laughed gaily and then so did Solange. Solange put the pitchfork aside and mother and daughter walked out of the stable, arm-in-arm.

"Je me souviens . . ." she began and told Guyanne all about the Coppertone and her grandfather, Lucien, and his beloved friend, the stallion Marquis.

Where Love Resumes

THERE WASN'T A stallion on earth who could unman Olibade Ouellet. He'd seen all kinds, wrangled all kinds, gentled most. But, weeks back, as soon as he heard Solange mention the name 'Spahro,' his knees buckled and he almost went down like a girl. It was Skye, his Skye for sure. He always knew she was still around, still alive somewhere; somewhere other than in his own heart. When Solange asked him if he could drive the horse trailer over to Belle's, she found it funny that he didn't ask anything about it, about why they were lending the trailer, or how long they'd need it—or anything at all. He just nodded like he did the day she asked him to pick up Ausencia a few weeks ago. Today, his nod was so brief, it was more like a nervous tic. He'd clean out the trailer first and then drive it over, he said.

"Can I go with you, Ollie?" asked Guyanne as she watched him scrub the trailer floor.

"Not this time, ma fille. But I promise you that, next time, you'll come along and I'll show you the right way to load and unload a horse . . . ça va?" said Ollie, without looking up from his work.

"Okay and while you're gone, I'll see to Ausencia's leg and muck out the stalls," she said, smiling as she turned towards the stable. She smiled a lot these days, did Guyanne. Her soul was learning to soar. Her lips couldn't even form the phrase 'ça m'est égal' anymore. She'd outgrown the boorish vocabulary of indifference. Things were not all the same to her anymore. In fact, nothing was the same and she didn't feel the same about anything. Everything was different, every little thing and every big thing. No longer an understudy of life, always waiting in the wings, she had kicked away the lifeless props and made a space for herself, kitted up with all the essentials.

"Remember now, you promised . . . oublie-moi pas là." Ollie nodded again, only half-listening. When he'd picked up Ausencia some weeks ago, Skye never came out of the house. He knew she was there though, and that had been enough to satisfy him. Almost enough. This time, he was determined to see her, to speak to her. She couldn't deny him that. He was going to see Skye today, his Skye; as if a lifetime hadn't separated them, as if all his letters all those years ago hadn't been returned to him marked 'address unknown,' as if he hadn't spent night after sleepless night wondering where she had gone and why they weren't together. Since then, he'd let cobwebs gather in the corners of his heart, greying over what had once been his heart's desire: a life with Skye Spahro.

As he got into the cab and yelled to Solange that he was off, the sound of the truck starting up was only slightly louder than the beating of his own heart. He revved the engine, trying to drown out the traitorous thumping. Solange went outside as he pulled away.

"Did Ollie say the truck needed work, Yanne? He was revving it just now."

"No, Mother, he didn't say anything to me about it. Want to watch me wrap Aussie's leg, Maman? It's not easy, you know. You have to know the right way to do it. Ollie taught me to check all the time to make sure it's not too tight . . . See? . . . like this. Leave enough room for a finger to fit between flesh and wrapping, and that way you know it's firm but not tight . . . and . . . ." As Solange watched and listened, thrilled that her daughter was finally becoming a person, finally finally, thank God, taking an interest in something—and downright garrulous about it too—part of her was thinking about Ollie. 'Something odd there,' she thought, as she asked Guyanne another question about the wrapping, and noted Guyanne's beaming face as she talked a streak. She was relieved to be bonding with her own daughter at last, thinking about the strong bond she'd had with her own mother, thinking about new bonds and old ones. Yes, old bonds. And that led her back to Ollie and then, in a flash, to Skye. She did the math. "Ah, I see," she said both to herself and to Guyanne, so pleased with herself, completely oblivious to Solange's mental sidebar on Ollie and Skye.

It only ever took twenty minutes to get to Holdout Bay from Huis Clos Stables but Ollie stretched it to thirty. 'I'm an old man now,' he thought. 'What will she think? What should I say? Maybe nothing. Maybe everything.' How could he even speak though with a heart so full? But they'd never needed many words between them, never before, not then. Now, would they find 'then' again? Would 'now' be like 'then' for her? It was for him. And so he went on like this, until—just as when he used to climb into the corral to gentle a young stallion—as he'd done a hundred times—he grew calm, calmer, more composed by the minute, all fear gone, no trepidation left at all . . . until there was nothing left but love.

The Birds Will Tell

S KYE WAS READING—RE-READING, rather. It was her favourite part of the whole book.

> . . . Where the Bible states 'and he shall have dominion . . .' I don't think it was a license to rape, pillage, desecrate and torment. One of the roots of 'dominion' must surely be 'domus,' yet how savagely have we eviscerated the very place that was supposed to be our refuge from evil, the site at which we could, in leading sinless lives, cleanse our souls of our original sin. We have spread like a rash upon a topos meant to be full of grace. If 'dominion', at its base, means to 'be lord over', then surely 'noblesse oblige' must follow therefrom. With status must come responsibility towards others. Man may indeed be the 'favoured species' but he has fallen woefully short of the criteria upon which such favour was bestowed. Given his vulnerable physique, it would have been rather his ingenuity, inherent moralism and intelligence which, all, would be relied upon to share, protect, preserve and benignly oversee the created world and its numberless inhabitants. Yet according to Lucifer, in fact, God's preference for his creature, man, was an act of nepotism on the Creator's part—therefore nothing really more than a random whim, born of boredom . . . if indeed God knows boredom. (Impossible to know how much Lucifer knew of God's true nature before he was cast out, though Milton implies much.) Did God, then, in favouring a particular species above others, set in motion the decimation of other, lesser species? There, where in Job we read that 'the animals will teach' and 'the birds will tell', do we construe that the authors of the Bible, God's amanuenses, were

able to speak with the animals . . . like all the female issue in our family? And therefore when we read that 'there will be signs in the heavens and on the earth' . . . .

"Belle! Belle! C'est moi, DeeDee. Comment ça va?"

Skye looked up to see a youngish, dark-haired woman waving as she climbed the cemetery steps.

"Ça va bien," Skye answered, realizing that, as often happened, she'd been mistaken for her daughter, Belle.

"Oh désolé, madame!" DeeDee said, out of breath from lugging her laptop up six flights. "I thought you were Belle . . . she looks very much like you, madame. Very much."

"It happens a lot, my dear; we're often mistaken for each other, but only when people see us from a distance. Come. Come sit by me and catch your breath. That's quite a climb," Skye said, making room on the little bench for her.

"Where do you know Belle from?" she asked.

"I first met her about a year ago when she was interested in the land next door; where you live now, madame. She was meeting with Hugh—you know my cousin Solange?—well her ex, Hugh Rutherford, and we've bumped into each other here a few times since then. I know she likes to walk here because it's so quiet."

"So you must be Darquise? Belle has mentioned meeting you here on her walks. And Solange is your cousin: a very kind girl. You're working on your doctoral dissertation, I gather?"

"Yes, yes I am," DeeDee said, surprised. "Did Belle mention that?"

"Oh yes. She said she was sure your dissertation was going to be quite brilliant."

"I hope so, and how kind of Belle to say so. That would be nice certainly, but I'd settle for a strong showing. I enjoy the research part of it—it's quite fascinating—but the writing of it can be drudgery sometimes," said DeeDee, leaning over to see what Skye had been reading.

"May I ask what you're reading? That looks very old. You know I am researching local Québec history, very old stuff, going back to the 1600s, in fact. Being here, in the old cemetery, gives me quite a lot of information. It inspires me too, makes me feel connected, grounded, like I belong; like I'm a part of something much bigger than myself, something that will last forever—or at least as long as man endures. I mean, our little lifespans mean nothing in the context of human history, do they?

In the history of the earth, really. And it is in the marginalia—the stories that don't get written into the history books; the ones that are left out altogether—that the most essential qualities of the human spirit—the desire to survive, to undertake, to endure—come through. So much was achieved by people whose names never appear anywhere, as if the progress they made, their very success, depended on anonymity, an anonymity by design perhaps . . . the voyageur who fords the first stream yet leaves an account of it nowhere . . . or all the fine workmanship produced in the early centuries, none signed or even initialled, dedicated to no other purpose than 'the glory of God' . . . ."

It was unlike Dee to rant like this, for ranting is what she seemed to be doing. But somehow—and this was a rare feeling for DeeDee—she felt she had the ideal audience. "Yes, that's important, isn't it?" Skye replied, nodding. "Not enough people today understand the importance of our history—the whole of it, not just the embroidered bits, but the footnotes too. It is the past—the relentless reach of it—that makes us who and what we are, doesn't it? . . . which is why we choose to conveniently forget it, I suppose, and create futures voided of meaning, all continuity lost, all real progress compromised."

"The work you are doing is very important, DeeDee," continued Skye, as she cradled the book in her arms. "We need people like you to resurrect the wisdom of the neglected; it's a wisdom we've forced into extinction . . . like so much else."

DeeDee, thinking that she couldn't have said it better, felt that rather than having found an audience, she had been given audience. The truly amazing thing was that Skye did not sound bitter, not in the least bit, even though she'd framed her thoughts in almost apocalyptic terms. Dee's wonder at that kept her silent. Then she said: "Sometimes I feel that what I'm doing is more of a forensic study than an historical one. For example, Madame, did you know that 'Holdout Bay' is a translation of the original 'Quai Brideloup?' The meaning of the word 'brideloup' is very obscure, but according to local folklore, it literally means 'the last piece of ice to melt and give way'—give way to the incoming Spring, so to speak—the last holdout—you see?"

"That's fascinating," said Skye. "I would have thought it had something to do with wolves . . . you know, 'brider,' 'putting a bridle on a wolf,' say, as a way to control him, or as in times of crisis when we say the 'wolf is at the door,' because we feel that we are under siege. But I like your meaning better, much better. It is as if the ice resists all efforts to change its shape;

as if its own idea of itself had evolved and it was not willing to go back, to go backward and be reduced to mere liquid again . . . yes, I like that image very much."

Dee looked at her and said softly, "I expect there are people like that as well. Those who see or sense things that others don't, and can't go back—or refuse to."

Skye nodded just as a bluejay appeared and flew right above where they were seated. Skye rose to go, smiling and looking up at the bird, now circling a little distance away.

"Well, I must get back now. Sometimes, I need to skip out just to get away from the tyranny of my ringing phone, but Belle will be looking for me. She's such a worrywart, my bell-elle."

"It's been a real pleasure, madame. Please give my regards to Belle," said DeeDee, eager to see Belle again to tell her what an impression her mother had made. Of course she must have heard that about her mother a thousand times. There was something about her, beyond her obvious intelligence, her gifted insight. She'd sensed that same indefinable quality in Belle too but in a different way somehow. Maybe it was the eyes: they had a translucence to them, as if there were no interior boundary between the inside and the outside; like the chambers of crystal—but no, it wasn't just the eyes. The mother had an ephemeral quality to her, as if she were all spirit and sensibility, giving a shimmer to her as if all that was there, all that was available, had not quite been captured. As if God had set the wrong F-stop on purpose just to see if certain parts could be illumined, overdeveloped, without degrading the other parts.

Skye waved once more as she started on her way home, walking quite straight though she kept looking up at the bluejay flying in the same direction. DeeDee had never seen a bird fly that low or that close before, except maybe for pigeons in the city. 'Radiant—that's the word I'm looking for,' thought Dee, 'she's lit from within.' As Dee watched, it occurred to her that she'd forgotten to ask more about the book Skye had been reading. She had managed to notice that it was dog-eared with use, with a good quality cover though badly faded; stitched not glue-bound—clearly an antiquarian piece or close to. Dee smiled, opened her laptop and typed herself a memo to ask Belle about the tattered old book when next she saw her.

As intrigued as she was by Skye, it never once entered Dee's mind that the ancestors of this blonde, green-eyed—and very unusual woman—could possibly be part of the original bloodscape that had forged the Québec nation. This subliminal prejudice therefore blinded Dee to the further possibility that the important diary she'd been trying to ferret out everywhere—the deBeauvilliers journal—might be the very one that was being carried farther and farther away in the arms of Skye Spahro, daughter and only child of the much-sought-after Delphine.

What Only Toby Knew

THE REASON LUKA never made it to Solange's after his emergency surgeries at the equine hospital was very clear to Toby the bluejay, Justin the pinto and Cam and Penny, the two ponies: it was because of Zia. Ever since Luka's talk with Justin among the bulrushes, Luka and Zee had become inseparable. Justin had taken Zee aside to tell her Luka's story, and from that moment on, Luka had become Zee's special charge, her de facto baby. Skye noted this to Belle who immediately phoned around and cancelled all plans to move Luka. He'd be staying at Holdout Bay until further notice. Belle was adept at reading her mother's shorthand: loving friendships among the horses meant no separations except for medical emergencies, and even then, Skye would take the friend along just to minimize the patient's anxiety; a policy not always appreciated by the equine vets. But Skye's reputation was such that few questioned her methods, her decisions or her policies. No matter how unorthodox, she was always right in the end. And you couldn't argue with 'always.'

There was still the question of when to bring Ausencia back to the Institute. She'd been at Solange's for weeks now, but Toby said to Skye: "He loves her, Skye. It'll break his heart if we bring her back here, away from him." Skye said she knew that; she'd met Ulric and knew that he'd spent a lonesome life, all by himself in a pasture in PEI with a few dogs and cows for company but none of his own kind. And she knew that he doted on Ausencia, her calm and her beauty giving a grace to his retirement that he never would have believed possible. Still, she didn't want to impose on Solange longer than she had to. It was a hard call but it was her responsibility, no one else's, to see that the polo mare was brought back to full health, and—

"—but I check on her everyday as you know, Skye, and she's filling out nicely and looking much cheerier," said Toby, as he turned to groom his back feathers. Just then, Zia alerted that Ollie's truck was pulling in to the driveway. Skye winced as if someone had pinched her, and swept a stray hair back in place. "You look fine, Skye," said friend Toby. As she walked towards the truck, towards Ollie, the green of her eyes illumined by the midday sun, Toby heard her say, "We'll talk about Ausencia again, Toby. Now stay close." Wild horses couldn't drag Toby away. He knew Ollie from way back, and he knew something that even Belle, to this day, didn't know. Her father had come to pay another visit.

CYNTHIA D'ERRICO

PART THREE

Predator

AS THE NATURAL predators of equines and other hoofed equids, dogs and cats—sometime descendants of wolves, tigers and such—had had to defer in modern times to living side by side with the prey whose flesh they had once craved, their ancient lurking lust for the flank of a horse reduced by generations to a passing lick of the lips now and then, which, like their turning round and round on the expensive down of an urban bed before settling to rest, was an instinct whose purpose even they have forgotten. When, at some point in history, man made the transition from prey to predator, he began to recruit the more obsequious of these smaller predators to his service. Dogs and birds of prey would have been among the very first, followed by cats, whose pleasure in the kill had little to do with submission to men and more to do with a happy coincidence of intention.

In this sense, Volpone's name belied his character; he was more feline than canine in his profound appreciation for the kill and the drawn-out torment that preceded it. This was an irony he was completely unaware of, as he was as dim in intellect as he was bereft of character. He was what he was, and what he was, wasn't much. His mother recognised this from the first moment she'd looked into those vacuous blue eyes shortly after his birth, making her own eyes dilate with fear and her mouth form a wordless 'o' of dismay. His father discovered it when he first tried to teach his only son to play softball: the boy stuffed and shoved the ball down the throat of his father's new pet whose excited leaping had obscured his view of the finch hiding in a nearby bush he'd meant to kill with his first fastball. The boy didn't stop shoving with his thin, bony arm until the imprint of the ball could be seen as a sickening bulge halfway down the dog's gullet, seconds after the animal's jaw creaked and broke. "That'll teach you," said the eight-year-old, "not to do that again," as he walked away from the twitching, lifeless form and went to fetch a new practice ball.

There is much to be said, nonetheless, for the usefulness of such men, as history has shown and as employers like John Rash could attest to. Volpone was nothing if not fiercely loyal, a trait appreciated by almost everyone who knew him except for those whom he'd betrayed, but the latter weren't well-known by anyone—anyone of note that is. They were mostly throwaways whom no one would miss, and they'd deserved it, after all: women who'd failed to appreciate his creativity in bed, moaning in pain when he knew, *he knew,* he wasn't hurting them because he sure as hell wasn't feeling any pain so how could they be. Children who'd failed to listen when he was trying to impart some of his hard-won wisdom just because they preferred playing with some stupid toy; a toy he'd had to smash just to get their attention back on him. And he always did get their attention back: he had a way with kids. It was one of his many natural gifts that he was humble about.

His parents—now there was a show for *Maury*; don't get him started—who had failed to provide for him in a manner comparable to his peers. The very fact that he'd been born and raised in the north end of Montréal, rather than in Westmount or Hampstead, proved his parents' inadequacy and that of everyone around him. It was all really a conspiracy to keep a good man down. He knew all this before he could talk—before he could walk, even—but he also knew that not everyone had his depth of insight, especially the pill-pushing doctors. He'd accepted their failings and those of his nearest and dearest as his cross to bear. Matteo felt in a very deep way that he was a special child of God, made in His Holy Image. He wasn't colour blind. He and Jesus had the same dark chestnut hair, after all—he'd seen enough paintings for chrissake—and therefore, like Jesus, he'd ultimately triumphed over the sludge around him; the evils he'd been born into. He'd thwarted the wily attempts of the weak-willed to degrade him; those sanctimonious hypocrites who tried to make him less than he knew he was, just by being himself. There was no other conclusion really. He'd parlayed his many talents into a really good job, working with one of the top businessmen in Montréal: John Rash of Metropole Enterprises. *The* John Rash, yes. Not many had Rash's ear, but Matteo Volpone did. Not many could tolerate Rash's cold ways, his peculiar shows of satisfaction for a job well done, but Matteo Volpone could. Mr. Rash didn't make many decisions that Matt wasn't privy to or consulted on. He relied on Matt to make his morning coffee (black with sugar, not too strong, more or less regular which was hard to get just so), pour his drinks, run his errands, oversee the staff who were always up to something—that's only human nature—and just generally, watch his employer's back. He was the first to greet Mr Rash in the morning and the last to wish him a good night. Yessir, if you wanted to do a deal with John Rash, Matt 'the wolfman' Volpone was the man you needed to know.

As the son of a butcher—Matt preferred 'product renderer'—he was particularly useful, probably indispensable, to Rash—as he called his employer privately—whose abattoir holdings were a significant part of Rash's business. Abattoirs weren't plentiful in Québec where nearly fifty per cent of the beef cattle raised in-province had to be shipped to slaughterhouses in the States big enough to handle high volume, but the few that were in Québec were partly or silently or fully owned by Rash, and Matt, an experienced renderer himself, was Rash's point man for all meat-producing facilities. Since there were so few, they were easy to oversee and manage, and it helped that Matt was on good terms with all the food inspectors. He often saved them time by doing the onsite inspections himself and faxing them his reports. Overworked every one of them, the inspectors appreciated his paperwork, often kidding him about his spidery handwriting before they signed his ghostwritten reports and shredded his faxes. Matt wasn't too proud to say that he was learning a lot about business, big business, from Mr. Rash. Diversification was key, he'd often heard him say, so Rash's abattoirs didn't just render beef product; they handled a small percentage of horse—chevaline as it was called—and occasionally, bison or wapiti. See? Diversified. Matt, who was known for his great sense of humour, referred to them—the buffalo and others—as 'rank outsiders' and not just because some federal laws restricted where you could kill what. Owning 'point of origin' to 'point of distribution' was also key, so Rash was a co-owner of one of the biggest racetracks in Québec. He liked keeping a hand in established Québec traditions and harness racing was one of them. Matt often went along when Rash went to check out some young Standardbred whose breeder claimed was sure to be a cash cow on the track. Some of those horses could bring in six figures which was an excellent return on Rash's investment. When it turned out that the guy was wrong—or the horse got too injured to win any more races (which so many did, being too young to be raced at all), Matt would collect them for slaughter. And even though some American abattoirs were more efficient and often closer, Rash's policy was always 'Québec bred, Québec dead.' Sometimes it took Volpone over a week to collect them from all the different breeders. The pick-ups took more time than the drop-offs because there was a clandestine network of unlicensed abattoirs all over Québec—especially around the Laurentians but generally everywhere. The quaintness of tradition—'l'abattage au bout de la pelle'—was just too easy and inviting for local farmers who had neither the means nor the inclination to pay for the transport of animals who could just as easily be killed onsite by bludgeoning them with the tractor shovel or running them down with a tractor. They often bet with their neighbours which hapless creature would be the proverbial 'deer in the headlights' and simply stand still, immobilized, as the oversized cudgel slouched towards them, and which would run madly to escape a fate not foreseen yet sensed in an instant. The problem of carcass disposal—which these farmers never thought of in terms of disease transmission—was never considered at all, so out of ignorance or carelessness, these rogue farmers simply deposited the carcasses at the edges of their property, usually in an open field, and let the local wolves feed and grow fat on the entrails. To the farmers' way of thinking, it was nature's way of cleansing what, for them, was an inexpensive and traditional way of dealing with the unwanted and the unserviceable. Rash, always sensitive about these things, didn't want to know details; of such matters, Rash would often say his one weakness was his fondness for animals. For his part, Matt Volpone couldn't say the same.

CYNTHIA D'ERRICO

Other Predators

"BUT I DON'T understand. Why would a person get up and just sit on my back—what's the purpose of that?" asked Luka.

"I'm not sure myself," answered Justin, "but Zia's told me that we are service animals, and what makes us valuable is that very thing, odd though it may sound; that we can be mounted and ridden and then sort of instructed to do things—tasks, Zia calls them. I came to Skye before anyone actually sat on me, but I remember some time before I met Skye, my owner threw a strange thing on my back, with little bulges all through it, like dusty rocks, and with rough scratchy skin. It wasn't very heavy, but it was so scratchy. Zia said it was a burlap sack of potatoes. When I bucked it off—it wasn't supposed to be there—he took a whip to me. That's when I began to be afraid. But Zia says you get used to it, the feel of a person on your back, always moving, and every move an instruction to do something."

Luka was just about to ask more about what 'service animal' meant, when Zia came up to them. She was going down for a snooze. Both he and Luka knew to stand guard. Zia had said she'd smelled coyote nearby, though as far as was known, there were no coyotes on the island, except for some who once in a blue moon made their way over from the western region. Coyotes or not, someone always has to keep watch. Every herd animal knew that.

After a bit, it was obvious that Zia was dreaming: she was back there, back in the transport van. She couldn't understand how this had come about. Like the ten others she was stabled with, she had been standing in her stall as usual, wishing she had the space to lie down and mostly wishing that she would be out of the dark smelly stable and grazing very soon. Then she saw her owner with another, darker man. Then she and the others were all led out to this big trailer-truck; one so big and dark inside that she couldn't see where it ended. They all caught the scent immediately. Most of them balked even before being loaded in. Once lashed inside, they could see and smell pieces of decaying body parts and entrails. Smears of blood and saliva, yellow and green, covered the walls. The stench of gore was stifling. The roof was so low, they couldn't raise their heads, forcing their noses level with their knees. When Zia's friend, Maya, was loaded in, she tripped over something and fell badly; it was an entire hoof just sitting there, rocking back and forth with all the commotion. Maya, close to foaling, had broken her leg in the fall. She got crazy, trying to get to her feet but was unable to get a grip on the slimy floor. Zia and Duke tried to help her, pulling at her mane and tail, but to no avail. She stopped thrashing after a while and just sat where she had fallen in the goo and slime, spent and exhausted. At first, there was plenty of room; there were only the ten of them. But the truck kept stopping and picking up other horses; some stallions, too, and that wasn't pretty. But soon there was no room to flick a tail, much less fight. And they were all fighting for air as it was. Night fell, then light again, then dark. By the next light, the misery of thirst had taken over. Of the forty-eight souls on board, eighteen were dead or dying, some so mortally injured they wished for death; others, if their tongues could reach, licked at the wounds of their fellows, whether out of pity or thirst, impossible to say. Maya had been trampled early on and was long since dead, flies feasting on her broken bloodied leg and whatever fluid spurted feebly from her womb. Days later, as the trailer slowed and pulled in to their final destination, Zia knew then that the suffering had just begun.

She opened her eyes and saw Justin and Luka, right where they'd been when she'd closed her eyes. She inhaled the fragrance of the grass and the marshy river water, not so far off. She sighed and sat up, still resting but wakeful. She felt she should remind them of the foreknowledge of suffering we're all born with, gulled into forgetting by the endless tumbling of day into night: the lullaby of a lie we're born to fulfill. The way of all flesh. Instead, she stayed quiet and the three of them loitered in the peace of the pasture till dusk, not a coyote in sight.

A Livewire Tenderness

"WHAT ARE YOU looking at, Mr. Trottier?" asked Belle. Chano had been staring out over the St. Lawrence towards Beauharnois for some time.

"I was just thinking that it's a pity we don't have any sand dunes here, like they do around Tracadie Bay in PEI. Dunes are nature's way of protecting shorelines from storm surges, among other things."

"What about these marshes here? Do they help at all?" asked Belle.

"Not really. If anything, these provide riparian habitats that we're trying to preserve; to save from drying out when the sea level drops. Last year, water levels dropped in the freshwater reach—that part of the St. Lawrence fed by the Ottawa River and the Great Lakes—to an alarming degree. They hadn't been that low since 1960. When that happens, when sea levels go down, land plants invade, unfriendly ones, ones that the seabirds can't feed on; then their migratory and feeding patterns change as a consequence and—well in short, the entire area's ecosystem is altered. It's like a domino; it ripples right through the system, affecting all the flora and fauna in a given area—and that in turn impacts surrounding areas."

"I have no doubt that, since the industrial revolution, our lifestyles have much to do with these sea level fluctuations. You could scrapbook our mindless neglect. It's criminal, really. I'm sure that's how SARA became so important . . . ."

"Yes, SARA. They do essential work, bringing together a wide range of people, experts and others. But the consultation process takes long and it takes much too long before it trickles down to the man on the street. By the time we've identified a species at risk, it's almost gone. We now know that overfishing is decimating certain species, and out in the west, entire bird species have all but disappeared—some estimates go as high as eighty per cent. Here along the seaway, we need to worry about shorelines like this one being vulnerable to upsets, marine clay erosion—and overall bank erosion. In and around Montréal for example, erosion rates run between one to three metres a year."

"That affects available drinking water too, doesn't it?" said Belle, as they began to walk along the shore.

"Not just availability but quality of water—and bank erosion is only part of the problem. Over seventy per cent of Québec's population lives and works along our shoreline. People settle along shorelines for practical—but incredibly short-sighted—reasons: whatever we need to dump, we dump it into the nearest waterway. It's like sleight of hand: we think we make our garbage and waste and chemicals disappear into the water, as if our rivers and waterways had some magical tonic in them that just dissolves all the flotsam and jetsam man's lifestyle produces. They don't and we know they don't, yet we keep doing it. Our little island is a template of how threat scenarios caused by loss of sea ice up north, climate warming and increased storm rise would transform Islanders' lives and livelihoods. Just the loss of these marshes along your shoreline would be one link in a chain reaction. That cemetery next door is a tourist attraction which generates money, not just for the municipality that owns it, but for the surrounding businesses that exist because of tourist spending. If that natural cascade of ledges were to one day fall back into the St. Lawrence—just sort of slide back down and rejoin the seabed, it wouldn't just destroy a main industry here; it would spread contaminants into the river and into the marine bed, in one fell swoop. There are pollutants approved for land use that should never go into the water supply and since the 'verglas' last year, we see mounting evidence for an increase in landslides . . . ."

Chano stopped for a moment and looked over at Belle's bright beautiful face. Somehow this woman had expanded his comfort zone. He didn't know how. It was a bewildering thing and it made him fall silent.

Belle looked up at him. "Please go on. You were talking about the effects of the verglas, the Ice Storm . . . ."

"Yes . . . last year's Ice Storm showed how milder winters impact bio-systems, very destructive ones, and give them a wider area to devastate. A phenomenon like the verglas can make it easier for destructive insects to live out the winter and establish themselves further south. They can affect livestock, tree farms, and all sorts of agricultural and forest products. Studies are in the works on the gypsy moth migrating further into the south of Québec, as we speak."

Belle stopped and smiled. "You certainly don't seem to be someone who stayed in his own cubicle with blinders on. You've strayed pretty far from your field."

"Well I'm not a specialist yet," replied Chano, "and what got me started in the sciences—and what keeps me at it—was the enormity of—"

"—how everything is connected; every big thing and every little thing . . . even the most pusillanimous creature that crawls on the earth . . . ."

"Yes, exactly, and how every act of creation carries within it the seed of destruction."

"That sounds like Rachel Carson to me," said Belle. And then together, they said: *"Silent Spring."* He felt her laughter thread through his like a welcome rain on a humid day.

"Surely your curriculum is too advanced to include Carson's work?" Belle said, eyes sparkling. Chano replied with a quote: *Islands are ephemeral, created today, destroyed tomorrow.*

"You amaze me!"

"Some memorized *Flanders' Field* . . . others, Poe's *Raven*. I was mesmerized by Carson's connections between so-called advances in agricultural pest control and damage to the environment . . . and ultimately, the dangers to public health. We all owe Rachel Carson. Thanks to her, DDT is forever banned. Without her work—and later, de Laet's and others—the EPA in the States, Environment Canada and even SARA—wouldn't exist. Maybe I myself would be locked up in a lab somewhere, concocting even more deadly mixes of pesticides."

Belle shook her head. "Oh I can't see that at all. You and the outdoors go well together. You seem to thrive on it, I think. You look very . . . fit. But you're right about Carson . . . . She had a lot to contend with in her day. They called her an 'alarmist,' a 'bird and bunny lover,' but she saved untold generations from the short-sightedness of pesticide manufacturers and governments with terminal tunnel vision." Not really knowing why, because he didn't actually know what Belle's mother did as an animal communicator, Chano knew she was thinking of Skye as she spoke. Maybe, he thought, there was something of value there, in the work of the Institute, something of great value, just as Carson's research ultimately proved to be in the sixties, and he and his colleagues were just too thick, too stubborn, to give it a second look. Deciding not to go there just yet, he said instead:

"As for being fit, I never wanted to work at a desk job, in an office somewhere in a building where the windows don't open. I love the outdoors, being outside. I need to breathe, to feel the wind and sun. I guess between the field work and the in-house research, it all gets balanced out." Belle turned back then. Chano began to drag his feet.

"I guess your research has taken you all across Canada. That must be wonderful. You must know the land like the back of your hand," said Belle.

"Well, I only see shorelines mostly, and my work has really centered on Québec so far. I was in PEI for a while, and I may be called to the Verchères region soon, but I, well, I thought I still had more to do here. Verchères is at the opposite end of here, quite far, quite . . . a distance from here, but I, so I . . . ."

Belle began to feel that awkwardness or whatever it was that she sensed that first day they'd met, so she changed the subject.

"You know, when we first moved here, I met an islander walking in the cemetery, my friend, DeeDee—"

"Oh yes, you know DeeDee, don't you. She told me she'd met Ms Spahro and—and you." He reddened.

"Yes, and we often meet each other walking next door. Where do you know Dee from—oh of course, you're both at the University together, aren't you?"

"Actually, it was Dee who vetted my letter to you, to the Institute, I mean. I'm not a very good speller."

"Oh, I can imagine that DeeDee is an excellent speller," Belle said, laughing. "She strikes me as someone who'll go far in the academic world. I like her very much."

Belle could see Chano and Dee together; a nice match. Both were passionate about their work, both highly educated, and both really good-looking. She looked at Chano, trying to guess his age. He was quite a bit younger than her, and only a few years younger than DeeDee, she'd wager.

"Yeah, Dee's great."

By now, Toby had arrived, made sure Belle saw him, then perched on a nearby branch and waited. Belle knew Skye wanted her. Daylight was fading fast as she turned to go.

"It's been a pleasure talking with you, Belle—a real pleasure," said Chano, feeling bereft already.

"Same here," said Belle. "We'll talk again, I'm sure—as long as your work keeps you here. I'd be very interested to know more about your findings and what you learn about our shoreline."

"Oh, I'd be happy to give you updates as often as you like," replied Chano, who, without thinking, was following her as she made her way towards the house. He stopped when she turned and waved, her features silhouetted in the dying light. He chided himself for not being more, more . . . oh damn. For the first time in his life, Chano wanted no distance between himself and a woman—this particular woman, who, every time she walked away from his personal space, left his gravitas vacant, stripped him of longitude and latitude. In between this visit and the next and the next, he did nothing but spin forlorn until she was back with him, situating him deep in an orbit that centered on her.

He walked back to where he'd left his kitbag and instruments. Since he'd been at the Institute, he'd kept clear of the horses as Belle had instructed—though in PEI, he'd grown fond of a big Belgian who was expert at frisking his pockets for carrots—and he'd been reluctant to tell her about even that. She might think he was trying to insinuate himself into the Institute somehow. He'd kept away from the house, as Belle had further stipulated. Despite her visits, they hadn't even shared a cup of coffee. 'I'll have to ask Dee what she thinks. And Dee knows her. There must be a way to . . . .' He didn't know what he wanted except that he wanted everything about her, everything she was. Damn but wanting was an aching sore thing. Still, as he packed up for the day, he had to admit it was nothing like that personal wrecking ball he'd carried with him these past few years, lacquered with the debris of prior liaisons; ones he'd madly run from in the end, as if they were glue traps for the unwary. This livewire tenderness inside him was nothing like those, and it had taken him over, balls to bones; he felt like a man possessed. Once he'd mounted his kitbag onto his back, he watched the very last blur of daylight slip under the horizon. He'd stop by Dee's after his shower and beg her for advice.

Belle wouldn't say she was as smitten with Chano as he was with her—no, she wouldn't say that, not really—but there was an energy and a passion in him that she found attractive—magnetic, even. And they certainly seemed to share the same values. Attention to the environment, for Belle, naturally streamed into her work with animals: the two were strands of the same worldview. Yet it wasn't the first time she'd met someone with values so close to her own who, like her, had chosen work imbued with those values so that every workday, every project, was an affirmation of what they believed. But Belle had long ago given up on any kind of romance: it was too late for all that now, and anyway, she had no time to devote to it even if it did come up. 'Too late, no time' was the chorus of a song she'd sung since she was in her late twenties that she couldn't forget—or give up if the timid truth be told. Still, it had been a while, so for the moment, she permitted herself to bask in the way he'd looked at her when he thought she wasn't looking.

As she walked up the drive, she saw Skye talking with Ollie and a young woman. She hadn't seen Olibade since he'd picked up Ausencia, and again, as she looked at him from a distance, she had the feeling she knew him from somewhere. Something about him was so familiar, but for the life of her, she just couldn't place him, and she'd never been to LaGorgendière where he'd spent most of his life, so it wasn't likely they had met before. Still . . . .

On ne Mange pas Son Ami

O LLIE HAD KEPT his promise that the next time he went to Skye's, he would bring Guyanne along. He didn't need much of a reason now—if any at all—to visit Skye; their first meeting when he'd delivered the trailer had been more than he could have hoped for. All that she'd meant to him he could see reflected in those eyes, as iridescent as he'd remembered them, and she just a later version of the only woman he'd ever loved. She took his breath away. Still.

As soon as she'd laid eyes on her old and faithful lover, Skye's concerns about her senior looks vanished as utterly as if they'd never been. Wordlessly, they had embraced, each sliding into the fit that had eluded them for years, like puzzle pieces sliding into long longed-for places. They rested in each other's arms as if they'd both finally reached the only safe place they knew, one known only to them.

Guyanne was surprised by the warm reception Belle gave her when she was introduced as Solange's daughter. Glad to meet Solange's girl at last, Belle wanted her to feel as welcome as her mother would have been. Aware by now that there was some history between Olibade and her own mother—though Skye hadn't yet said a word to her about it—Belle steered Guyanne towards the ponies.

"You must come and meet our friends, Yanne," said Belle as they walked arm-in-arm towards the pasture.

"I heard that you have a real champagne mare here. Is that true?" asked Guyanne, eagerly.

"I've read about them . . . well I mean I'm learning about them—horses, I mean. And I'm trying to memorize the colours—roan, bay, sorrel—and the breeds, too. We have a Belgian, Ulric the Red, from PEI . . . ." Yanne's voice trailed off as they came upon Zia, in her sentry stance, with ears pricked towards where Skye was walking hand-in-hand with that man. Zia didn't trust men at all. Someone had to keep watch; if not she, then who? "She's so beautiful, and her colour—it's so . . . perfect." Guyanne quickly pulled a notebook from her vest pocket and read aloud:

> *Palomino, Dun, Silver Dapple and Grullo are just a few of the colors that are created when a base color and a dilution gene are combined.*

"Oh she must be classic champagne! Was her sire or dam black? *'Black plus the champagne gene produces a classic champagne colour . . . highly prized and exotic.'*"Guyanne looked again at Zia. "She looks almost like a palomino—except all shadowy. It's almost as if somebody poured varnish on her!"

Belle smiled broadly at the girl's keenness and said, "We're not exactly sure of Zia's breeding beyond that she is a Canadien. But we know it was her unusual colour that saved her from being slaughtered. The abattoir owner happened to spot her just as she was about to go into the stunbox—hundreds of horses are terrorized forward into a narrow alleyway, sort of funnelled, single-file, towards what's called a stunbox—so the owner singled her out, thinking that, if she did have the champagne gene, he'd use her for breeding rather than have her slaughtered. Our volunteers got her just before the results of the DNA tests he'd had done on her were ready."

The shock on Guyanne's face was a look Belle was familiar with. Learning that horses were butchered for meat left many people feeling raw and lied to, like suddenly finding out that your neighbour had barbecued your retriever or microwaved your cat. Like so many others, Yanne was clearly unaware that, whether for meat or other reasons, horses were slaughtered at all. The very idea was horrifying to the young woman. Yanne was as white as a sheet so Belle downplayed it.

"Come and meet Luka. He is doing very well now after some surgery . . ." Belle continued with deliberate vagueness, " . . . but he's still very shy of people."

"Was he—was he going to slaughter, too?" asked Guyanne in a low voice, still white-faced. Solange had told her daughter that the Institute rescued horses, but somehow, up to this very minute, Guyanne hadn't comprehended, had never fully processed what they were being rescued from. Ausencia, after all, was an expensive polo horse. There were no

CYNTHIA D'ERRICO

signs of abuse on her—no overt ones, at least . . . though it occurred to Yanne with a jolt that, if there had been, would she have known enough to recognise them? She had blithely assumed that Ausencia had been retired by her owner the same way Ulric had been by his. She suddenly remembered that Ausencia too had been on her way to meat when Skye intervened. Of course, yes, Mother had even told her so, the very day Ausencia arrived; the day she, Guyanne, had let Aussie stew in that hot, steamy trailer. It just hadn't registered; she just hadn't paid attention as with everything else back then, back when the world and everything, everyone in it were, to her, nothing but meaningless ciphers. 'Poor Aussie,' she thought, reliving how she'd ignored Ausencia that day, ashamed of her own thoughtlessness . . . .

"Guyanne . . . are you okay? Your colour has gone from white to red—you're all flushed." She looked feverish. Belle felt Yanne's forehead.

"Come over here and we'll sit for a bit. Why, you're almost the same colour as our Luka over there," Belle said, ushering Yanne towards the shade of the big willow in the yard. Luka who'd been watching from as safe a distance as he could without getting too far from Zia saw Zia turn and slowly follow the two women. Mostly, Zia was following the sound of Belle's voice as Belle spoke quietly to Guyanne; Zia always found Belle's voice as soothing as Skye's. Besides, Zia wanted to meet this young person; every visitor to the Institute was of interest to Zee, and this one seemed to be getting special attention from Belle for some reason. Zee needed to know what that reason was. Keeping one ear cocked in the direction she'd last seen Skye go, she walked right up to Guyanne, now sitting on a log under the willow with Belle's arm around her. Zee lowered her head, almost into Yanne's lap. Guyanne immediately put her arms around Zee's neck and began quietly to cry.

"I'm so sorry . . . I'm so sorry that . . . that such things are done to you all . . . it's not right, it's not right . . . I'm ashamed of us, ashamed for all of us," Yanne sobbed incoherently. Zia stood very still as the girl hung on to her neck, clutching at her mane in an agonized distress. Like Belle, who fell silent each time she witnessed similar epiphanies time and time again, Zia, in her stillness, bore witness, too.

Luka, afraid to approach any closer, was still some distance away when Justin came up beside him.

"What's going on, Luka? I hear a funny noise, a sad kind of sound," said Justin.

"I don't know exactly, but I don't like that sound either," replied Luka nervously, "and I wish Zia would get away from there. There's a stranger there and another one, a man. I saw him walking with Skye a while ago. I . . . I hope he hasn't hurt Skye."

"Oh no one would ever hurt Skye—how could they? Anyway, they'd have to get through Zia—and me—first. I'll just go check with Zee and see what's up."

Justin made his way over to where Zee's scent led him. As he approached, Belle said, "Look, Guyanne. Here's someone special for you to meet. That's Justin coming over to see you. Justin is very friendly, very sweet. You'll like him; everyone loves Justin."

Guyanne looked up slowly from the wet tangle she'd made of Zia's mane. Her tear-filled eyes still clouded, she wiped them clear. The most beautiful horse she had ever seen was walking calmly towards her. His head was low, angled to the right as if he were listening for something, but the closer he came, the more amazed Guyanne grew. She blinked her eyes clean until he was next to Zia.

"Ohh," was all she could muster. Always a leader, Zia immediately moved to herd Justin. Justin stepped immediately back. "Zee," said Belle, "let us visit for a bit." Zia looked at Belle, then lowered her head to graze.

"Justin is blind, Guyanne, but you wouldn't know it, would you? He has all the confidence in the world, our Justin . . . and," she continued, stroking Zee's nose, "he has Zia to thank for it."

"Blind!" said Guyanne, unable to conceive that this stunning creature was anything but perfect. "But how can this be? He's so . . . so perfect. It can't be." She passed her hand over his eyes; his left eye reacted a little, his right eye not at all. "How did this happen?" And then, passionately: "Who did this to him? Who could do such a thing?"

"What's important is that Justin can manage—and manage as well or better than most. Animals have a much keener sense of smell than we have, and much better navigation skills. When Justin came to us, Zia—everybody's auntie—took him under her wing and taught Justin things that only a horse can teach another horse. He does very well, and we're not sure, but we think that some sight in his left eye has come back. Not only is he hardly aware of his handicap, but he's never hurt himself, not seriously anyway, and . . ." Belle paused as she saw Guyanne shaking her head in disbelief, " . . . and he is absolutely fearless. Fearless, Guyanne. He knows he is limited, but it never stops him; in fact, he's always investigating something or other . . . aren't you, Justin?" Guyanne was almost afraid to touch this glorious creature, as if he were a figment of her imagination like a giant centaur or a unicorn.

Belle turned to Zia: "Shall we play, Zee?" Zee threw her head up and whinnied. Justin answered, paralleling Zee nose to tail instantly. Zee turned suddenly to the left and cantered away—and so, remarkably, did Justin. As she avoided or jumped over dead branches, whirled around trees, stopped on a dime, changed direction, halted for an instant to graze; then, as if on a whim, took off at full gallop, Justin mirrored every move like a shadow. It was an exquisite duet, lyrical and masterful; the pair revelling in a playful possession of time and motion. Guyanne was moved beyond words.

"We've all seen a flock of birds take off at the same time. There is no song, no alert, nothing obvious beforehand—to us, anyway . . . and yet, they all, all together, take flight at the very same moment, and head in the exact same direction—and in perfect formation. It's just the same here. So whatever replaces Justin's sight—and it's certainly beyond our ken—serves him well."

Speechless, Guyanne ran her hand from Justin's withers to his croup, taking in the whole wonder of him, his perfect symmetry. He was indeed a big boy, over 17 hh, wide hooves—almost the spread of that of the big German breeds—a strong neck set high on a proportioned, not heavy base, a lovely topline, and a strong backside, powering well-muscled hind legs. Justin turned as if to look at the young woman standing by his flank, so close that he could feel her body heat. He leaned into her, relaxing against her long, deliberate strokes. "Hello, Justin," said Guyanne. "You're . . . you're . . . magnificent. Do you know that? Do you have any idea how perfect you are?" She stroked his nose with two fingers. It was as smooth and as soft as velvet. He nibbled at her hand, tickling her palm. In the event that she might have carrots somewhere on her person, he was advising that he'd be happy to relieve her of them.

"Was Justin on his way to . . . ?"

"Yes. All the horses here were rescued from abuse or slaughter. Justin was only a year and a half when he developed an eye infection. His owner didn't bother to have the eye checked by a vet. For less than ten dollars, a simple ointment would have curbed the eye infection and he would have been fine. Instead, neglect led to blindness. Of course, that made him no longer rideable; no point in breaking him to saddle, although some horses, even racers and eventers, are blind in at least one eye to some degree . . . so he was slated for the nearest abattoir. By that time, he was also grossly underfed but still, the owner would have gotten thirty-to-forty-cents per pound for whatever he weighed at the time. Pennies are cold comfort for the cold-hearted."

Guyanne rested her forehead on Justin's neck, sadness and anger welling up in her like a mounting geyser. She felt like her heart was going to burst from the pressure. She wasn't a religious girl, but she felt that if there was a god, then surely he'd be incensed to see this wondrous creature of his neglected and abused and then sent to a grisly death. For an instant, she almost longed for the days when she saw nothing, felt nothing; nothing touched her; when nothing had the power to twist her insides like this, making her gorge rise. But she couldn't go back; it was all a vague memory now, not-feeling. And she couldn't un-know what she now knew. Belle smoothed the girl's hair and said: "Don't worry, Guyanne. Wherever they are, we are. And they know we're watching . . . all the time. We have eyes everywhere."

Zia, privy only to the quiet energy now taken hold, bumped Guyanne in the chest; the two horses crowded her, nuzzling one and then the other, and all together, the three of them schmoozing looked like one of those horsey magazine pull-out posters. Guyanne didn't seem to notice when Belle, with a shining smile, began to walk back towards the house. '*My* work at least is done. She's quite at home now, very much at home, I'd say.' But the pretty postcard Belle left behind belied what was at that very moment being forged deep in the young woman's being, in a place where the darkness of man had just become visible to her. Here, in this quiet field, standing under a weeping willow, Guyanne's purpose had found her: it was by turns licking her hand and nuzzling her cheek. Something had shown itself to her, to Guyanne Deschambault Rutherford, heir to horsemen over many generations, and she recognised it for what it was. 'You see, I do remember, Papa—I remember it all.' Well out of earshot now, Belle turned back only for a moment when the wind picked up. She watched as it brought the willow branches down low around the trio in quick genuflections, as if in benediction. At that very moment, what was being borne by the nimble wind was the murmured promise of a young woman, renewing an ancient family passion: 'I *will* protect you.'

First Contact

IT HAPPENED SO fast that even Toby hadn't had time to alert Skye. Belle, who had just left Guyanne with Zia and Justin, had no time to think. She had stumbled badly when the earth shuddered, and had looked up just in time to see Chano, who'd been running towards the house, go down himself. Still down on one knee, Belle scanned quickly for Skye's whereabouts. Her heart was racing.

"Mother!" she called out. "Mother where are you?" Nothing.

Then: "She's over there . . . behind the house!" It sounded like Ollie.

Belle ran and found Olibade cradling Skye in his arms as she lay on the ground.

"Mother . . . Mother, are you all right?"

"I'm okay, Belle . . . I'm okay. I must go to the horses." But Skye was still dizzy, not going anywhere in the next few minutes. Chano appeared from the side of the house and said: "It was a shift, a random tremor. Everyone okay?" He was looking at Belle brushing off her jeans.

"I think so," said Belle. "Where is Toby, Mother, and why didn't he—like he usually does?"

Her balance restored, Skye sat up, her look intent, inward. After a minute, she said: "It's all right. Zee said everyone's okay; she hasn't seen Toby but Guyanne is with them and she's okay too."

"Omigod . . . Guyanne!" Belle said as she turned and ran back towards the pasture. Now on her feet, Skye turned sharply and looked at Chano.

"I was coming to warn you, Ma'am. An anomalous reading came up suddenly on my meter and, and I thought . . . I thought everyone needed to know . . . for the horses, I mean."

He turned immediately to go but Skye put a hand on his shoulder, saying:

"Thank you, Mr. Trottier. We have our own alert systems here but . . . thank you anyway."

Chano nodded uncomfortably, aware that his contract forbade him being so close to the house.

"Perhaps you could do me another favour, if you like: you could perhaps see if my daughter needs any help with our guest. She's a very young woman and probably scared. Perhaps you could explain what just happened, scientifically I mean—the young people today place all their faith in science—maybe that would make her feel better. Would you mind, Chano?"

Chano exhaled and smiled and said he'd go find Belle right now, and yes, he'd be happy to be of service to Belle and to Skye. As Skye and Ollie watched Chano canter to catch up to Belle, they turned to each other and smiled.

"Ah oui . . . il y a quelque chose qui se passe là sans doute," said Ollie, with a wink.

"Sans doute," replied Skye, resting her head on his shoulder as they walked slowly towards the house. Before they'd opened the back door, Skye came to a dead halt.

"Toby . . . where have you been?" Toby was soaring just beyond the porch.

"I was too high up and too far away, Skye. You wouldn't have heard me. Are you okay?"

Ollie looked over at Toby and then at Skye. He said: "I'll go make us some tea . . . you come in when you're ready and have a rest."

Toby continued: "I did warn you before we moved here, Skye, that this island was unstable; its foundation is all clay and that—"

"Yes, you did, my dear friend. You warned me the very first day Belle told me about Holdout Bay. But this island is no more unstable than anywhere else on earth. And whether I live here or anywhere else, I can't escape my own body; its sensitivity to the earth has always been intense. Every time mother earth shrugs—even if a plate fidgets—my inner ear goes. And her unease is growing . . . . These spells of mine are increasing. It's as if she's slowly dismantling herself, but picking up speed as she goes along. This last one was almost more than my human frame could bear. We've insulted and abused the very ground we walk on, Toby, and soon, we won't have a leg to stand on or anywhere to stand it on if we do."

"But Skye, remember Delphine and the quake of '29? It took everything out of her. She only lived long enough afterwards to give you life. Maybe this was a warning . . . something big is about to happen here, where you are—maybe to you yourself, Skye . . . . Maybe you should tell Ollie and Belle, and maybe we should move away from here," replied her friend, perched in that military pose so typical of the bluejay. Skye looked in the direction Chano and Belle had gone.

"No," she said, "Belle is very happy here. I can't uproot her and Zia and the others just because of what may or may not happen."

"One more thing, Skye—Belle heard me. I was still a good distance away when I told her where you were—her first thought is always of you, Skye—but I know she heard me and that's the very first time. She thought it was Ollie answering her. That means it won't be long now, doesn't it?"

"Ah, finally . . . that's wonderful. Some of us come to it later in life than sooner, and often it's triggered by a trauma of some kind; sometimes just a little event but an intense one. And Belle has always been so preoccupied with other things . . . but that's good, that's very good. You're right: it won't be long now. Thank you, Toby. And as for the other thing, I'll tell them; don't worry, my boy."

Skye stroked Toby's back reassuringly and then went into the house. The blue jay sat where he was a long while, now brooding with his chin tucked into his chest, fretting for his special, his longtime friend, Skye Spahro. He knew Skye well. He knew she wouldn't tell them everything . . . not everything.

Not a Rash Decision

FOR DAYS AFTERWARDS, the news was full of what some people called a quake, others called a tremor and what Skye knew was yet another tremulous warning. Journalists scrambled to find experts to interview, most of whom assured the public that only a quake measuring 6 and above was considered worth worrying about and this one had been just above 4. The human interest stories almost all focussed on the queer behaviour of pets hours before. One woman said her dog who had just whelped gathered up all her pups and deposited them in the bathtub before jumping in herself and trying to close the bathtub door with her teeth. Leashed dogs bit through their leashes while some of the more nervous among them chowed down on their own paws until they were raw and bloody. Heart attacks claimed some caged birds who'd behaved just like canaries in a coal mine minutes prior. Cats of course disappeared, their fallback position in times of stress being always 'every man for himself.'

It's not that it had never happened along the Gulf before. In fact, the earth shimmied and shook all the time. Western Québec was a seismic zone well-known to geologists, though it wasn't as active as the Charlevoix-Kamouraska region. Most of the time people felt nothing at all, and, in the big cities, this minor twitch on the seismograph hadn't even disrupted traffic flow, much less the good china. Comparisons made to the 1988 Saguenay quake, which measured 5.9 on the scale and had a reach of over 400 km, were just plain silly; the quake in '88 had been the biggest in eastern North America in half a century. That one had levelled an impressive tower in Montréal East, exposing its clay foundations, and brought down some of the weaker railway embankments. Overall, the damage done in '88 was so random as to make it seem like a one-off. But last year's verglas, the Ice Storm of 1998, was still fresh in Quebeckers' minds, and with all the hype about Y2K and the year 2000, psychiatrists and psychics were busier than ever.

DeeDee as usual was circumspect about the whole thing. She'd been walking on campus at the time, thinking of paying a visit to Solange, calculating the distance between the Université which was at the inner end of the island near the little bridge to the mainland, and where Huis Clos was, on Pointe-de-la-Méduse, at the island's far end jutting into the St. Lawrence. She saw the tallest campus building, La Tour, seem to shimmer as she felt her own balance go. She managed not to fall, so she waited half a minute to see if an aftershock was coming, and then moved swiftly to help other students who'd fallen or whose fear had overwhelmed their good sense.

By the time she got back to her dorm suite, it was evening. Her housecat, Tawser, had scooted over to a younger student's dorm room just down the hall and only needed feeding and Dee to sympathize with his very vocal complaints since it was clear the world was coming to an end and what was Dee going to do about it. Dee thanked the young student, fed Tawser more than his usual and then listened to her voicemail which was full of messages of concern from relatives and friends. She returned all but one, took a shower, poured herself a glass of red and then picked up the phone again.

"How did you get this number, Rash?"

"Aw, DeeDee . . . is that how you greet an old friend? I was worried about you, sweetheart."

"I'm fine. I thought you understood the last time we met, John. I thought I'd made myself clear."

"Well that's the thing, my dear Darquise. You think you're fine but you could be more fine with me. C'mon now, my love, let's make nice. Here I had my staff spend hours—well almost a full hour anyway—looking up your number and you don't even appreciate it. Now, is that a good attitude to have? That's always been our problem, love . . . you never learned to appreciate me whereas I—"

"—Don't call me 'love,' Rash—in fact, don't call me at all. Don't make me change my number again just because you can't get over yourself."

"Well don't call me Rash . . . because you know how that excites me. I can feel it now . . . spreading all over you like a very sweet, warm rash, giving you goose bumps all over. Remember?"

His voice deepened.

"Darquise . . . you know the story about Adam's missing rib? Well that's how I feel about you . . . like you're that missing part of me, a piece of my personal puzzle that I've been looking for, for years. I'm sure part of you, down deep, recognises that, and whatever went wrong between us—well, anything is fixable. Our connection is strong, so strong, Darquise . . . I can feel you from here . . . I can—"

All Dee could feel were her white knuckles gripping the phone.

"—John . . . . I don't know how to make you understand. You've mistaken me for someone else. I don't feel that way about you—I never did. And all I remember telling you is that it's over—in two languages. Leave me be, John. I mean it!"

Dee hung up, determined not to let any of this faze her. She began dialling Solange's number.

John Rash sat back and closed his eyes, enveloped in the scent of her. He wished he were still a smoker because this was one of those times he'd have inhaled deeply.

"Well at least she talked to you; that's more than you expected."

"Yeah. A good start, I'd say—or, better yet, a new start. That's really what I want."

"And now you have her new number, you can pick up where you left off."

Rash looked at Volpone coldly. The man never listened. "I don't like where we left off, wolfman—that's the point." Rash got up to pour himself a generous bourbon, neat, and waved Volpone away as if he were a bad idea.

Dee's shaking hands had made her misdial. She put down the phone and went to dry her hair. She'd go see Solange first thing tomorrow, sans faute.

Blood Will Tell

WHEN THE EARTH trembled, Solange was busy de-trailering Contessa who'd just returned from a show in Ontario. Contessa was no show horse but her lineage and her status as one of the few remaining LaGorgendière broodmares brought invitations from all over Canada. All she had to do was be present, this classic black Canadien; a calm, cool veteran, biddable and bombproof, Lucien's 'Tess-ah' and Marquis' true love.

Once off the ramp, the usually unflappable Contessa reared so suddenly that Solange instinctively let her go. And go she did, at a speed Solange hadn't seen from her since Marquis the old stallion had died. To this day, Solange didn't know what had made her so instantly free Contessa or what was exchanged between them in that milli-second it took her to rear, but whatever it was, it had probably saved Solange from having a bad fall herself. She'd grabbed hold of a nearby fence and steadied herself against the tremor that came not a full minute after Contessa had taken off.

"C'est Solange . . . est-ce que ma fille Guyanne est chez vous?" she said minutes later into the phone.

"Don't worry my dear," replied Skye, "she's okay. Belle is just bringing her in now."

Skye passed the phone to Ollie. "Non, non . . . ça va . . . inquiète-toi pas. Are you okay? Did you check Rick and the others? . . . if Aussie fell, it won't help her leg . . . oui, we're leaving now . . . here's Yanne."

"Oh Mother," said Yanne excitedly, "wasn't that something? . . . no, I'm okay . . . are the horses okay? . . . the most amazing thing, Zee, Zia, you know the champagne mare? She herded me, Mom! Just as if I were another horse, like part of her herd. I fell, you know and then . . . no, no, just a little bruise—anyway, she kept at me to get up, she kept circling and nudging me and pawing the ground, and then . . . oh okay . . ." Ollie touched her arm, "yes, we're leaving now . . . . Yes Belle is fine, and . . . yes, so is Skye . . . . It wasn't a quake, Mom. Chano said it was a shift . . . . oh Chano? . . . He's a scientist . . . okay, we'll see you soon."

Solange put the phone down, relieved. But she wasn't crying because Guyanne was unhurt; she was crying because she hadn't heard her father's voice for a very long time and Guyanne had sounded just like him. 'Call it what you will,' she thought as she reached for a tissue—a family fetish, a latent gene—her girl had equines in the blood on both sides of the family, and from the changes Solange saw in her daily and genes like that, well . . . . She sniffed again—she hated crying—who knows what she could accomplish . . . eh, Papa? And the thought of her father made her cry harder.

'I guess it's true what they say: blood does tell . . . eventually,' Solange thought, calm now as she looked around the house to see if there was any damage. She wasn't worried about the horses. She knew their sixth sense for these things had led them to go as high up as possible. They'd be at the far end of the east pasture where they'd feel safe. That's where she would go if she were a horse. She'd wait for Ollie and they could bring them home together. She went into her den and looked through the papers from the Ontario show Contessa had just come from. The name 'Jericho' caught her eye.

JustInTime out of Contessa #3456 by Jericho APA #0278-4r (retired) Owner: les écuries Gareau & fils enr., Cap Rouge, QC

Disbelieving what she'd just read, she quickly scanned the list of Horse Associations: APA was the Association of Paints of the Americas. Jericho had been a paint stallion, she remembered. Lucien had said approaching Jericho was like coming up against a wall of air. Fearless and wild, he was a force to be reckoned with. Solange sat down, laughing and shaking her head. So that's what came of Achille's kidnapping of Contessa . . . a foal named 'just-in-time!' 'Oh Papa . . . j'ai trouvé le bébé de Tess-ah . . . notre bébé perdu.' Yes, they had coupled just in time, Jericho and the gentle Tessa, only a few hours before Lucien arrived to snatch his purebred Contessa back from that daring sneak-thief Monsieur Achille Gareau.

Still, Solange knew enough about the horse industry to know that cross-breeding was a serious offence, akin to pirating, and Achille must have had to pay a heavy fine to Agro-Québec for absconding with one of their purebred Canadien mares. The whole purpose of the stud farm at LaGorgendière and its predecessors at St-Joachim and Cap Rouge was to produce Canadien stock, pure and unadulterated, and thus keep the breed alive and thriving. She wondered if she could track down the foal now. He or she was on this official list as registered issue of Contessa, but that couldn't be from the Registry of Canadiens; the foal—filly or colt—must be on the APA list somewhere or some other pinto or paint association's list. Even if the foal had developed more like a Canadien than a pinto or paint—maybe even had come out the classic black colour of the Canadien—Agro-Québec would still never have entered it in their Registry. Horse breed registries are as sacred as bibles. She remembered her mother Madeleine spending long hours at night transcribing in her flourishing hand the bunched-up notes Lucien would hand her in his hurried scrawl after supper, saying, "bon voilà mon trésor . . . nos biens de la saison." Every two months, a bespectacled young man would come to pick up Madeleine's neat logbook, and nod approvingly at her entries, inscribed in that careful Catholic slant. They in turn would be transferred to the Registry, *La Race Chevaline Canadienne,* in Québec City, with a copy sent as a courtesy to the feds for 'le bureau de Docteur Ford'—short for Dr. Rutherford who had been the first incumbent of the Office of the First Veterinary General and Livestock Commissioner—the same Rutherford whose great-grandson Solange had married and who was Guyanne's great-great-grandfather. Solange always knew when the young government man was due because Maman would always cook ci-pâtes, a traditional Québec dish—its aroma would fill the house—and the young man would invariably stay to dine despite his feigned protests to the contrary.

As she heard Guyanne running towards the house from the van, Solange decided she'd do some digging to try and find this JustInTime, the illegitimate fruit of Contessa's adventure with that handsome rogue, the stallion known as Jericho.

An Undiscriminating Attention

" COLIC IS THE very devil in horses," Guyanne read to herself from her book on horse ailments and remedies. *The pain and fear experienced by the equine is intense and must be taken very seriously. Severe colic can lead to death. Symptoms of colic can resemble those of other illnesses, such as kidney stones and inflammation of the liver. These and other possibilities must be discounted by a qualified vet before treatment for colic commences.*

Guyanne pulled out the big logbook she'd made labelled, *Equine Registry, Huis Clos Stables* (Owner: Solange Deschambault), Isle-Saint-Jean-Baptiste, QC, which had section tabs for *Ulric the Red* (formerly of PEI), *Marquis* (deceased), and *Contessa* (retired), and a special section labelled, *Institute Rescues,* beginning with, *Ausencia* (Argentinian polo horse). Each section recorded the breed, age, colour, height (in hands high), weight, markings, provenance (if known), registration number (if any), lip tattoos (particularly common in owned Thoroughbreds), lineage and progeny (if known). Guyanne had also recorded femur-to-stifle and topline measurements, and other ratios that she'd recently learned about with captions under photos of each horse. Ulric's section opened with: "Next to elephants, draft horses are the strongest mammals (land)." So far, Ulric's section was the most complete due to their many nights' study in the stable.

Guyanne intended to make good on the promise she made that day in the pasture with Zia and Justin. She was determined to learn first about the horse industry and how it worked, and then follow the breadcrumbs into its netherworld of horse abuse. She prepared new sections following *Ausencia* (Argentinian polo horse) with the tabs, *Justin* (Overo Pinto) and *Zia* (Champagne Canadien), ready to be filled in with data on her next visit to Skye's. Then she flipped back to Ausencia's section, wrote a sub-heading called *Illnesses,* carefully noted the date and time, and began copying, *Colic is the very devil in horses* . . . . She didn't hear DeeDee enter through the back door.

"Hello Guyanne . . . how are you doing?" said Dee warmly, surprised to find her young cousin so absorbed in what seemed like homework.

"I see Madame Spahro out there with Solange and Ollie . . . qu'est-ce qui se passe?" she asked, after helping herself to some coffee and looking out the window.

"Well when we got back from Skye's yesterday," replied Guyanne, continuing to write in her logbook, "me and Ollie after the earthquake, I mean, Mom was up in the east pasture with Ulric and the others, and Aussie—that's our polo mare—was lying down and sort of agitated, and she didn't want to get up. Ollie right away said that it looked like colic and that colic is very bad for horses. We finally managed to get Aussie on her feet and then Mom told me to run on ahead and phone Skye right away to tell her because Ausencia is one of her rescues. Poor Ulric was so upset; he's just crazy about Ausencia."

"And Ulric is . . . ?"

"Oh Ulric is a retired Belgian that Papa took in for one of his friends." With obvious pride, Guyanne brought her logbook over to show her Ulric's picture. Dee was impressed by the sheer size of him as most people are, but beyond that, Dee's interest in animals, generally, was limited to her housecat, Tawser, and that only because cats were so clean and low maintenance. She was more interested in how meticulously Yanne had set up the logbook. As an historian, collating, cataloguing and recording were right up her alley. Dee suggested a few improvements as well as ways to research the lineage of different breeds on the internet while Guyanne, thrilled that her older cousin liked her homemade registry, avidly wrote down all her suggestions. As she wrote, Dee noticed that Yanne certainly looked healthier than she'd ever seen her, and that her skin had cleared up nicely. She could see Solange's fine cheekbones in her and she smiled at the thought of how relieved Hugh and Solange must be at these welcome changes in their daughter. Since it looked like Solange wasn't coming in any time soon, Dee decided to join her and the others outside. Guyanne said that, in the meantime, she'd put some fresh coffee on for Ollie who was a big coffee drinker. Her mind racing with the events of the past 24 hours, including all of DeeDee's ideas which would make her logbook look more professional, more like a real Breed Registry, Yanne went back to copying. *Severe colic can lead to death . . . .*

The reason for Dee's visit was two-fold. She wanted to give her cousin the happy news in person. The notice had finally come from l'Association du Cheval Canadien that the province had set the date for officially declaring le Canadien a national heritage breed of Québec—a status her uncle Lucien had died waiting on—and she also wanted to tell Solange that John Rash had found her again, despite her best efforts. As a well-known journalist, Solange knew a wide range of people from different social strata, including some as powerful as Rash himself, and Dee was sure that through one of her contacts, her cousin could persuade Rash to leave her alone once and for all.

Outside, Ollie was leading a horse in large, meaningless circles, it seemed to Dee; but as the faces of Ollie, Solange and Skye Spahro came into focus, DeeDee saw that it wasn't the time to impart news of any kind, happy or otherwise. She joined the group quietly, almost creeping, keeping a watchful eye on the big one—Ulric she guessed from Yanne's photo—even as she noted that he was wholly engrossed in Ollie walking the other, fine-boned horse who seemed to be the worse for wear. Solange looked at her cousin briefly and told her she'd asked Guyanne to stay in the house 'to let us know when the vet arrives.' DeeDee understood immediately. It took only minutes before she became part of the tableau of support wishing Ausencia well again, so moved by the sight of this very sick horse struggling to keep to Ollie's shoulder. Captivated, she watched Skye whose eyes were like a flicker show of the mare's pain. And it was gruelling; in fact, Ausencia's pain was so intense that she couldn't even reply to Ulric, much less hear Skye. Her barrel was distended, and now and then she tried to kick at the classic rumbling sounds issuing from her own belly. All she wanted to do was lie down and pedal which both Skye and Ollie knew would make matters worse. Ollie kept walking her slowly and each time it looked like she was about to go down and roll, he and Skye coaxed her to stay on her feet and keep moving.

Despite her faith in Ollie's experience as a horseman, Skye had asked a dozen questions when she'd arrived: had they changed her feed? Were they giving her concentrates of any kind? Was she turned out most of the day? Was she getting enough water? Had she started cribbing? When they'd found her, how bad was she thrashing about? Ollie answered everything patiently. His experience with colicky horses had taught him to take it seriously, even mild cases. He'd seen mild cases turn on a dime, especially if torsion set in; then the pain preceding death was so acute that only euthanasia could relieve the horse's suffering and assuage the horseman's helplessness. Colic was the bane of every horse lover he ever knew. Though they both agreed that it was probably the quake that had unsettled Ausencia, Skye believed in being thorough. She had already done a walk-through of all of Aussie's grazing and stable areas, checking for any toxic materials, natural or unnatural, synthetic or biological, that the mare might have ingested. But there were no bushes harbouring blister beetles and none of the bad clovers or locoweed about. This was Lucien's place, after all, and he and Ollie would have been too careful, too experienced to miss any hazards of that kind.

Ulric couldn't understand why they just wouldn't let her lie down. As a draught breed, he wasn't as susceptible to the gastric disorders that plagued a lot of the finer breeds, especially race and show horses. He stayed as close as he could to Ausencia as Ollie walked her, trying to give her company, poking and nuzzling her and urging her to feel better, to please get better.

"Why can't she lie down if she wants to?" he'd asked Skye.

"Walking relieves the pain," Skye replied. Or some of it, she thought, beyond Rick's hearing. She'd just taken Aussie's temperature again and it was low. Shock might be setting in. They'd phoned the vet two hours ago—the banamine wasn't working—and Skye could see the mare was getting tired. She walked over to Ollie. Ulric followed close behind.

"We have to let her rest a bit. Let's see what happens. If she just lies down without thrashing or pedalling . . . ."

Ollie lifted Aussie's lip. "Her gums are blue-ish."

"Her temp is low too, Ollie."

They shared a look which Ulric saw but Ausencia didn't, absorbed by this relentless inward turmoil and yes, fatigued beyond reason.

"The vet's here!" Guyanne yelled from the porch. Solange grabbed Dee's hand and they both ran to the house.

Where Love Begins

WITH AUSENCIA SICK, Belle knew Skye wouldn't be home for as long as it took to either make the mare better or end her pain. Toby didn't sing much whenever Skye was away, which made Belle think he must miss her terribly, so she thought it was a lucky thing that they couldn't actually communicate the way he and her mother did because that would have made her feel even worse for him. Still, in the way that most people talk to their pets, Belle included Toby in her plans for the day.

"Shall we go visit Zia and the others and then take a nice walk along the shore, Toby?" She heard the bluejay answer with 'jay, jay, jay' so Belle took that as a 'yes.' He, as well as she, knew that Chano was working somewhere along the shoreline and though she was too old to need a chaperone, his longstanding habit of looking after Skye's daughter when Skye herself was absent kicked in automatically.

It wasn't that she didn't have paperwork to finish, or, as Toby noticed, that the weather was fine for a walk; in fact, it was beginning to rain. But to be perfectly honest, Belle had had to revise her view that she wasn't as smitten with Chano as he with her. She'd tried to parse it—"to smite" means to strike with great force and usually without warning—and she had felt a little light-headed when they'd first met, as if she'd just received a bump on the head. Since then, she would start out for her usual walk through the cemetery and would somehow find herself strolling along the shore, standing alongside Chano as he worked, like a truant skipping class. They talked and they didn't, and when they didn't, there, in the deep of their quiet, was a lush peace that filled her senses. Belle was in love and she knew it.

Zia, Luka, Justin and the two ponies, Cam and Penny, were all together, standing under a big maple, talking about the recent quake. Zia, as usual, was leading the discussion. She nickered hello as Belle approached, and with the exception of Luka, they all closed the distance between themselves and Belle eagerly, the ponies trotting in the lead. Chano, who tended to look towards the house more than was really necessary these days, could just catch flashes of Belle's saffron hair, with only that powerhouse of a pinto completely blocking her from his view from time to time. He hoped she was on her way to visit him, too, where he was working, straddling the two elements, earth and water; two elements, separate and discrete, yet forming a union as the waveless water met the shore, dishevelling the pebbles and dampening the sand. He hoped to close the distance between them in that very same way, bring her to and into him. He had to speak. He looked up again. She was still with the herd. He watched her bring Justin's head down close to her and begin rubbing his ears. Chano fervently wished he were a horse. He forced his attention back to his laptop and re-read the last paragraph . . . again:

> Somewhat like the Charlottetown soil [op cit], there are loamy deposits marking the fine topsoil in this region. However, unlike Charlottetown soil, heavy mineral preconcentrates are found, presumably originating in sediment effluvia which have travelled downstream from the St. Lawrence maritime sub-region, an area active in maritime transport and harbour activity.

"I hope the drizzle isn't interfering with your research," said Belle, speaking softly so as not to startle him. As he raised his head, he took in the whole of her with one fluid sweep. The intensity of his gaze felt like a tractor beam, dragging her forward. His daring took her aback only for a moment; she stood fast. Justin came up behind her.

"Justin . . . what are you doing here, you silly boy? You followed me, didn't you—or my scent rather," she said, sounding nothing like herself. 'Just in time,' she thought, relieved to bring the reality of sound into that scary space filled with Chano's mute appeal.

Chano got to his feet quickly and stood as close to her as he dared. "Could I?" he asked, "Would you mind . . . ?" But he wasn't even looking at Justin. So what was he asking exactly? It sounded like a plea. Her legs seemingly turned to iron, Belle took a clumsy step back, which put Justin's sizeable head between them.

"Oh yes, yes, please. He's very friendly."

Chano cupped Justin's face in his hands, kissed him right on his stripe and then covered his whole head with slow, broad strokes, never taking his eyes off Belle. Justin, always up for cuddling of any kind, lowered his head, his own eyes half-closed. Belle's mouth opened and closed, and then, steadying herself on Justin's shoulder, she reached over and rested Chano's hand on her cheek. As he pulled her to him, she poured herself into his chest. The drizzle turned suddenly into a hard, beating rain, saturating the sand, and no one, not even Justin, seemed to notice or care.

Fair Price for Fair Gain

A S A CHILD, John Rash's favourite superhero was Superman which is why he'd named his holding company Metropolis—Metropole, in French. He did think that Lois Lane was a tease, though, and that Superman would have been much better off with Lana Lang. He disliked false modesty in women, in people generally, and he felt that Lana, though conniving, was much more honest about her ambitions than the virginal Miss Lane and really should have been rewarded accordingly.

Honesty was everything to Rash. He'd built up a multimillion dollar business on the premise of 'fair price for fair gain' which applied as well to the many hostile takeovers he'd successfully managed. His two marriages had failed precisely because his wives had failed to grasp the concept that marriage was like a hostile takeover—exactly like, in fact—and that what was being paid fair price for was a complete erasure of self, of needs, or anything else that conflicted with his values, his plans or his comfort. Wasn't marriage a sacred bondage after all? They should have realised when he'd flatly refused to sign a pre-nup that they certainly were not getting alimony; he'd directed his lawyers to see to that before the minister pronounced. Logically, from a business point of view—which was the only point of view Rash ever adhered to—there was no fair gain in support payments to someone who had disappointed you so badly, someone who had not only failed to meet your expectations, high though they may be (no, he would *never* apologize for having high-minded ideals), but who had clearly misrepresented herself from the get-go. That was just plain dishonest. His disappointment was so great that it almost made him lose faith in his abilities as a businessman. Almost.

He took solace in the fact that there were honest people out there, like the businessmen, bureaucrats, and so many others he paid off on a regular basis, who were very clear, blunt even, about what they needed to give him what he wanted. They worked so hard behind the scenes, as it were, for so little credit and needed so little, especially compared to what he wanted, and after all, he was a 'giver,' not a 'taker.' Every opportunity to show his magnanimity was a gift, he felt. His relationships with those people embodied the very essence of 'fair price for fair gain.'

One of the reasons he'd located Metropole Enterprises in Québec was because Québec business, more than that of any other province, was steeped in the very same ethic that he practised every day of his business life. He'd explained to nervous investors that that was the very reason big business was so regulated, over regulated, in Québec: guilt over corruption bred more restrictions and the restrictions bred more corruption which was just more discreetly carried on. It was like a dog chasing its own tail, he'd say. A time-honoured Québec tradition as respectable as fur-trading in the old days; part of what made Québec distinct. The very thought of it made his face flush red with patriotic feeling. He didn't need to speak French to feel a deep appreciation for how special his homeland was. 'Special,' 'rare' and 'unique'—anything that made Rash look twice or made his head turn, would fire up his interest. Especially since, as a rich man, he'd already had everything out there, everything commonly available anyway, so he was always on the lookout for anything different or unusual. If it turned out to be something he could make money from, so much the better. He'd always felt his aesthetic sense was highly developed—or so he'd been told at least—so for a while, he dabbled in the art world; collecting and then selling prized objets d'art at inflated prices—absurdly inflated prices when the artist in question died or had a jihad put on him, which sometimes happened. It was almost too easy. But his art consultant's salary cost him almost as much as a Ming vase so he decided to stick with what he knew and not rely on the expertise of someone else. What he knew best was human nature and its vices—and betting on horses was both, wrapped with a bow. What he liked about horse racing was the minimal investment and the high returns. He didn't mind horses at all; they were easy on the eyes and exciting to watch. The horse industry in general was a zero-waste proposition: this was one animal you could take from birth, exploit all its qualities—speed, strength, tractability—through breeding, racing, eventing, calèche or companion service, and then profit from its flesh when it had outlived its usefulness. You had to respect the horse. He was more than a beast of burden. He was a full service animal from birth to barbecue—no part of him wasted, no quality left unmined. Other herd animals, like cows and sheep and what-have-you, didn't come close to providing society with such full-spectrum utility. Of course, views of the horse varied wildly, depending on which branch of the industry you had to deal with. He knew how to play breeders—often holier-than-thou purist types—by sighing in with their love of the animal and all that cultural icon stuff. He read all the horsey magazines just so he could speak their language. Building camaraderie was an essential element in business. He didn't consider his dissembling deceitful; he just felt breeders were a tad short-sighted when it came to the economics involved, probably blinded by their adoration of what was essentially a fast cow without horns. You had to be alert in business; think of any given industry as a continuum: from point of origin to point of distribution. You could stand a purebred stallion at stud and make a small fortune selling his semen, then his offspring; and as the broodmares approached their best-before dates, you could dispatch them to the nearest PMU facility—and not only make a profit there too, but contribute to the wellbeing of menopausal women, themselves saggy old broodmares past their prime. Rash shied away from calling himself a philanthropist, but still, he tried to do his part.

Pity about the PMU foals though, born deformed or defective. He always felt there was a potential market there for genetics or eugenics or something like that. There might be a Seabiscuit or a Rio Grande hidden away among those splay-legged babies. That was a sideline he meant to give some attention to one of these days. That's how he'd found Zia, after all—at one of his own abattoirs—just by paying attention, by always looking out for the special, the unique. You couldn't help but spot that incredible champagne coat even smeared and gouged as it was. He'd had her pulled from the alleyway just before she reached the gate to the stunbox. If it hadn't been for that idiot, Volpone, they wouldn't have lost track of her. She or any of her babies, if they carried the colour gene, could have made him a small mint—the market niche for designer breeds was growing. He was so mad, he'd nearly fired the stupid bastard. He did end up firing the manager of La Petite Vallée, though, for talking to those crazy animal people. But he had need of a man like Volpone. He was useful for certain kinds of tasks and despite being as dumb as paint, he was able to close off deals with—there was no other word for them—with obstructionists who failed to appreciate Rash's way of doing business. What Volpone was really gifted at was making it so that nothing was traced back to Rash. Though in so many other ways Volpone lacked finesse, he was some kind of idiot savant when it came to messy situations. Rash never asked what he'd done to whom or how he'd done it. In business—especially big business—you had to delegate and Rash was content to delegate troublesome loose ends to someone whose footprints seemed to disappear behind him. As with all his employees, he didn't trust him as far as he could throw him; he knew there were some things the wolfman did that had nothing to do with business and everything to do with his own bizarre compulsions—really dark ones from what Rash gathered from his many sources—but he allowed it as one of the few perks of a very demanding job. Again, even then, Volpone never left a trace, and that was the important thing. Rash was also aware that Volpone had an almost womanish obsession about pleasing his employer which, alone, guaranteed his loyalty and his silence, and cinched him tightly enough in Rash's sphere of operations such that Rash overlooked his boast that he was 'the boss' right-hand man.' Everyone he told was nobody that mattered anyway. In his own way, Volpone was special, a one-off, so Rash kept him on.

He'd tried to add another one-of-a-kind to his collection: Darquise Brucy. When he'd spotted her, he couldn't take his eyes off her. Her look nearly melted him on the spot. A rare beauty indeed. He did everything he could to please her. He'd spent thousands of dollars sponsoring one of the most prestigious charity functions in Montreal. Just for her, just because it was her pet charity. Didn't that tell her immediately what kind of man he was; what he stood for? He'd thought dozens of time of offering to marry her, but she wasn't buying what he was selling. It puzzled him a great deal. But he liked puzzles, and this was an especially comely one with delicate features and legs that went on forever. Oh those legs . . . he wanted them back. He could still feel them wrapped around him like a cummerbund made of silk, snug along his sides, pulling him down and close, manoeuvring him in, deep, deeper. His neck straining, he turned his face into the pillow to clear the sweat off his brow and then took himself in hand. After a bit, he got out of bed and went for his morning swim.

Entr'acte

FROM OBSERVING OLLIE and Skye, Solange knew that Ausencia was getting worse and the vet's prognosis was bound to be grim. She didn't think Guyanne needed to see what was sure to be a dismal solution. She had a few quiet words with Dee. Guyanne, still transcribing the notes on colic into her Huis Clos Horse Registry, jumped at another chance to visit the Institute with Dee. Dee said Belle was probably home and Guyanne could learn a lot about horses from Belle. Guyanne was thrilled at the thought of seeing Zia and Justin again. With them alone, she'd shared a life-altering epiphany; one she was convinced Papa Lucien had led her to. What there was to do, she could do. Yet deep internal changes go by intervals, like that space between taking a step—that momentary suspension in air—and actually landing your foot on new ground. And because she dwelled still in that entr'acte, everything she was reading about colic and its dangers hadn't really registered as relevant to her new purpose. Blind to fatal consequences, she went with DeeDee to visit Belle, her registry tucked snugly under her arm.

Belle, who'd been holding the fort, was happy to see them, especially Dee whom she only ever encountered on the cemetery grounds where they'd first met, and lately, that hadn't been very often. As she hurried over to where the horses were, Guyanne barely stopped to wave to Belle. Dee was surprised at the broad stretch of land the Institute sat on as Belle took her on a quick tour.

"No one would ever guess that all this," said Dee, with a sweep of her hand, "sits right alongside the cemetery beyond that line of trees. I had no idea and I'm sure very few others do either. It's almost as if we all think the island ends at the cemetery and what lies beyond it is all water; as if those natural ledges continue under the river itself, on and on, like an underwater walkway leading to—who knows—maybe another world." Belle laughed.

"It was nothing so enchanting that sold my mother on this place, I'm afraid. It was—as it always is with Skye—the privacy of it. The trees and marshes on all sides are like a privacy shield of soft, but dense greenery, just as effective as high fencing. But you're right about there being an underwater walkway of sorts. The way Chano explains it, the underwater flooring—made up of submarina clays—stretches all the way over to the nature reserve across the way, les Îles de la Paix, and it's all shredding—just flaking away like the crust of a pie. The constant waves made by watercraft, big and small, have put too much pressure on the shorelines, and the rapid rising and falling of the sea level doesn't help either. He says the shoreline right where we're standing is degrading ten times faster than anyone expected."

"A sobering thought. I know there was a lot of talk at the uni after the tremor," DeeDee said. "Some said that if the tremor had been a little stronger, it could have destabilized the sea floor—which I understand is made of many layers, like the plies of a tissue—and that would cause the shoreline to slip and slide under—maybe up to five metres." They both stopped and looked down at the bevelled sand where the still waters licked at the shore. It was hard to believe that such a prim crease of land could suddenly slip into a watery oblivion.

"He's not here today. Busy elsewhere," said Belle quietly.

"Ah," Dee nodded, as she searched her friend's face.

"With all that," Dee went on, "Chano's told me he loves working here, just loves it . . . he'd never given much thought to how idyllic, how beautiful our little island was, he said, until he came to work here. He said it's funny how you never expect to find what you're looking for in your own backyard. And though his own backyard may be deteriorating, at least what he salvages will be something or someone that he didn't even realise he was looking for. So often, a salvage operation is also a rescue, a rescue of oneself."

"Yes, it's like stepping through the looking-glass, isn't it? We never know what we'll find there; and sometimes it's just us so topsy-turvy that we don't know ourselves . . . and for Chano, that world—teeming with life, all different kinds of life—biota, as he calls it—that world is more real to him than his own. I think, for a long time, it was the only world that held any meaning for him with its little dramas of potential extinction, migratory changes, breeding habits . . . . It's safe, impersonal, with no particular vendetta or grace—just nature following an inscrutable design of its own; an agenda it shares with no one—all of it much easier for him to fathom than the world of man . . . . He's like a scuba diver who only surfaces now and then to report his findings—give us all a 'heads-up'—and then returns to his work of measuring the measureless. His work consumes him but I don't think it really touched him until now—touched him inside, I mean."

"You understand him well," Dee replied. Belle's face was aglow. She knew she didn't have to say it; the truth is no less the truth for not being said, but as she looked at her friend, she knew she wanted to say it, wanted it to be framed in words—words she thought she'd never say.

"I love him."

"I know."

Nothing more was needed because all that was necessary, all that was true, had just been said. DeeDee was happy for both of them, especially Chano whose high standards had always worried her. It's a small lonesome space, that seat of judgement. But it was obvious to DeeDee that the thunderbolt which had struck Chano when he met Belle had snatched away that narrow pedestal. He had tumbled into that state of grace called coup de foudre. Science had found religion, and its name was Belle Spahro.

"So what will happen now?" said Dee, squeezing her friend's arm.

Belle shook her head in the way of a lover who still can't believe her luck and hasn't thought beyond it. Laughing, they linked arms and finished their walk in a comfortable silence.

When they got back to the house, DeeDee suddenly remembered.

"Belle, I've been meaning to ask you about a book Skye was reading the day I met her. It was a very old-looking book, a journal or diary of some sort—"

"—oh you must mean my grandmother's diary, I'm sure. Yes, Mother has it with her often. She reads it over and over. It seems to give her comfort. Wait, I'll find it for you so you can have a look," said Belle.

"I've never really read it myself . . ." yelled Belle from upstairs, " . . . but I really should one day. It was written by my maternal grandmother, Delphine," she said as she handed it over to Dee.

"Delphine? Your grandmother's name was Delphine?—not Delphine deBeauvilliers, by any chance?" Dee's amazement crested as Belle answered:

"Yes, actually. DeBeauvilliers . . . Mother is part Québécois."

DeeDee sat down in one smooth fluid movement, possibly to avoid sliding down. As she turned the pages carefully, Belle sat across from her and watched the play of emotions on her friend's face go from shock to delight. Finally, DeeDee looked up. "I have been looking for this diary for months. I can't tell you how surprised—how thrilled I am to be holding this in my hands. Belle, this is a very important document; it records the history of an important family in Québec—one of the first families to come over from France, here to our island; one of the first jeaniste families . . . ."

After DeeDee expounded enthusiastically on the value of the diary—not just to her own doctoral research—but to Québec historians in general, Belle said she thought Skye wouldn't mind if Dee borrowed it for a short time, if only to make a copy—as long as she returned it in the same condition, frayed and dog-eared though it already was. Belle's offer to Dee was more a kneejerk courtesy than anything else. Inwardly, Belle was still digesting her surprise that her mother had probably been born on Isle-Saint-Jean-Baptiste—underlining once more, as had happened other times and in other places, how little she knew of her own mother's background. All Skye had told Belle was that she knew the island; she never elaborated and perhaps Belle, always so busy, had never really asked. With her spirit taken up with this very full internal monologue about her own mother's birthplace—which also explained, she realised, how Skye and Ollie knew each other—there was no thinking room for Belle to consider that Skye might very much mind her daughter offering a personal, a family, heirloom up to historical scrutiny by strangers; and though it did of course occur to DeeDee, her desire to study the book overwhelmed her good manners. It was an historical record she coveted and she just couldn't help herself.

Soon after, when DeeDee and Guyanne were taking their leave, it began to rain. As the three stood outside still talking, Yanne stuck her registry, now filled with even more information on Justin and Zia, in Dee's briefcase to keep it from getting wet. Good thing, too, because, once on their way, the heavens really let rip.

A Secure Herd of Two

AUSENCIA HAD HAD bouts of colic before but never like this. She didn't know what to make of pain so overwhelming that it made every breath a struggle. She deferred to the ministrations of the vet and the others although it seemed to her that, by taking her temperature, fussing around her gums, putting tubes up her nose and giving her rectals, they were missing the point entirely. And she particularly wished they would leave her backside alone. The pain was in her belly, nowhere else. It felt like someone had set fire to her innards—its exact location a mystery even to her. It was somewhere even she couldn't get at, though every time the pain would flare up, she'd kick at it anyway. If she could dislodge it just a little, she thought, maybe she could get some relief—if it was an obstruction, that is—like a hoary cumulus of feed that had balled itself into an implacable mass. If it were something twisted, then maybe a kick would un-twist it. 'A kick from a horse can solve a lot of problems; why not this one?' she thought. This inner flaming wasn't at all like the heat of a hot iron branding. She could barely remember the pain of that permanent embossing of her skin. It probably had hurt too but she was sure it was nothing like this live fuse inside her. She wished she could just expel it but none of her exudations thus far had made even a dent in the pain.

Though completely turned inward on her problem, Ausencia was aware that Skye was trying to speak to her; she could hear a kind of static whose volume increased whenever Skye came close to her. But she couldn't make any sense of it. Even most of what Ulric was saying was indistinct. His voice seemed to come from far away, as if he were talking through damp cheesecloth. But if there was anything positive about this whole awful ordeal, it was having Ulric beside her. He pulled on her mane and continually nosed and nuzzled her, just stepping out of the way when people got between, and never far away so Ausencia could always see him there, urging her to get better, to lose that fiery ball in her belly once and for all; his alert ears a lesson in perfect, unbending devotion.

She'd had a bad moment when she saw Solange come out of the stable with a lead rope. Solange thought it best that Ulric stay out of the vet's way and meant to stable him for the time being. But Skye wouldn't hear of it. She knew that, if anything, Ulric's presence was a help to the sick mare. They'd just have to work around him as they had been doing. He wasn't in the way, anyway, she'd explained to Solange, and she repeated, separating them would make things worse. The vet exchanged a look with Ollie but said nothing except that he wished horses were capable of vomiting. Ausencia heard nothing of this; the cheesecloth had thickened. It was all just pantomime to her now. She was relieved though to see Solange drop the rope on the ground and Ulric stay where he was, near and steadfast. She tried to nicker to him; to say how glad she was that he wasn't going to leave her all alone with just people around her, but she had no breath for even that.

If Ulric could have taken on Ausencia's pain himself, he would have, and gladly too. He'd had a good life in Prince Edward Island, as far as that went, and through it all, he'd been able to tolerate his loneliness, making friends with the cows and the dogs even, and especially enjoyed the cats who were so quiet and calm, like he was himself. His retirement, up to when Ausencia arrived, had been okay, too. Ulric's easygoing nature embodied the adage, 'bloom where you are planted.' He'd heard stories from others since and had come to understand that, for a service animal, he'd been fortunate, very fortunate indeed. In short, it was Ulric's way to always make the best of any situation he found himself in. But knowing Ausencia had stirred memories of a primitiveness deep inside him: a quorum of insights—fear, longing, loneliness and despair—which his sanguine nature had up to now shielded from him. He'd quickly realised that Ausencia too had been lonely in her lifelong service to a gamesman, deeply lonely, and had been permanently marked by that, and had never—despite all the demands made on her in the world of men, demands that made some horses forget they were horses—gotten over being a mare without a herd. An unthinkable thing. The poignancy of that, of how deep her well of loneliness was, touched him to his very soul; made him want to lift her up and out of that well, and enfold her in companionability—a safe and secure herd of two.

CYNTHIA D'ERRICO

As he watched her suffer, Ulric's helplessness amounted to a suffering of its own, and though he had every faith in Skye, she would not talk to him. 'Not now, dear boy,' she'd say, before blocking out the rest of her thoughts. So like every other domestic, he'd been reduced to carefully observing her body and facial language, and to a lesser extent, Ollie's. What he read there made his huge heart recoil in anguish: for the life of his beloved girl, they were losing hope. It was then that Ulric the Red came undone.

Ex cava veritas

DEEDEE WAS IMPRESSED by the genealogical tree the young Delphine deBeauvilliers had sketched into her diary. It was painstakingly done with no erasures suggesting that Delphine had probably re-drawn it several times on penny paper before she'd got it just right and then copied the final version directly into the diary itself. Everything about this journal excited DeeDee, especially the range of time it covered: from Dr. Alcide himself arriving in 1672 up to Delphine's own marriage and the birth of her daughter, Skye Spahro (née deBeauvilliers). The girl's grandmother, Odile, who'd lived to the age of eighty, had been the repository of family stories stretching back generations; a living time capsule of the history of a prominent Québec family. DeeDee couldn't believe her luck; it was an historical gold mine. She turned the diary over reverently and opened it to the first page. Even the Preface, a jewel of concision, gave her shivers:

> *Herein I faithfully record the true lineage of the family deBeauvilliers as has been solemnly recounted by my grandmother, Odile Eusèbe Marie Beaudet (née deBeauvilliers) born 1822 (dD), Isle-Saint-Jean-Baptiste, Lower Canada; on this, the eighth day of the month of May, in the Year of Our Lord, eighteen-hundred and ninety, at Québec City, in the Province of Québec, of the Dominion of Canada.*

'Not bad for a ten-year-old,' thought DeeDee, which was how old Delphine was when the ageing Odile had the foresight to make the girl her scrivener. Odile died ten years after her granddaughter began keeping the diary but clearly the old woman saw early on that the girl had a sufficiently fastidious nature for such an undertaking—unlike Odile's own daughter who had died giving birth, unwed, at the age of twenty-eight. This too had been duly noted in the diary, without comment, without recrimination and with no trace of sentiment. Yet the young girl must have had feelings about the fact that her own mother had lived a foolish, even dissolute, life by the standards of the day. If she did, she kept those thoughts out of the diary—its early entries anyway. For the young Delphine, as for her grandmother Odile, the diary was strictly intended as a record of events—births, deaths, marriages, even recipes—some opinions and thoughts, yes, but only on religious or community matters; nothing personal or at least nothing as personal as in this age of the glorification of intimacy and Brazilian bikini waxes.

But DeeDee had only just scanned the diary's contents so far. She could see that the young Delphine's childhood scrawl gradually matured into the confident flourishes of an adult hand. That gave her hope that, along the way, the adult Delphine had discarded Odile's officious agenda in favour of one more open, more revealing.

She looked again at the Preface and noticed something:

Odile Eusèbe Marie Beaudet (née deBeauvilliers) born 1822 (dD)

Now what could 'dD' mean? As she looked through the family tree, she saw that all the deBeauvilliers women had that same designation by their names. Only the women; not the men. None of the deBeauvilliers women had been 'filles de roi,' women ferried across an ocean to be wives to the settlers of Nouvelle France, so it certainly wasn't anything like that. And she'd come across allusions to clandestine groups before now—like the secret society, Saint-Sacrement of the Altar, dedicated to purging New France of its Protestants—but the puzzling out of their occulted acronyms and palindromes had long since been deciphered by better historians than her. In any case, what she'd learned so far about the deBeauvilliers, starting with Dr. Alcide himself, was that they were unlikely to be involved in sects or cults. It looked like a bibliographic notation—bibliographers had their own glyphs for describing book covers, types of paper and all that—but this diary had been untouched by archival experts, residing solely in the hands of Skye Spahro all this time, so . . . ? And why did it appear only beside the names of the women?

Ex cava veritas. DeeDee felt that chill again. God, she loved her work.

Ulric Undone

T HE VET DIDN'T often see a case of colic as bad as Ausencia's. He thought, as he often had before, that both the Belgian and his patient knew what was coming just minutes before he opened his bag to prepare the fatal dose. Horses always seemed to know better, know more, know it sooner. At that same moment, the Belgian lowered his head to kiss his suffering friend, and the mare, who hadn't raised her head in several minutes, brought her face as close up as she could to meet his loving muzzle. The effort had cost her but the vet had no doubt that of all her earthly efforts, it was the one, possibly the only one, that gave her peace. As he injected the palliative poison, he said softly as he always did: 'you go have a nice rest now, girl.'

Afterwards, only Skye remained, there in the rain-soaked pasture, while Ulric called and called for his beloved friend, pausing only to nose and nuzzle her motionless form and pull roughly on her mane as if he thought there might still be some mistake and maybe she was only sleeping and if he could just get her up on her feet, everything would be fine again and none of this would be true. His plaintive cries tore right through Skye who, though she had been through loss a hundred times, would never, as long as she lived, get over her grief at each and every one. Olibade, in an effort to persuade Skye to come in and rest, brought Contessa out; the sturdy Canadien mare whose own spirit had been diminished by the loss of Marquis two years ago. Ulric immediately trotted over to her, keen to tell her all that had happened and all he was feeling, and paced in noisy distress alongside as Ollie led her to where Ausencia lay. Ollie could have sworn Contessa was listening intently to Ulric, her eyes and ears at full attention, nodding as if in sympathy; Skye knew for a fact that she was listening—and intently, too. When Guyanne, fresh from her visit at Belle's with DeeDee, arrived home, she found Ulric and Contessa standing vigil over Ausencia. Whether or not she was in shock was hard to say because she immediately went to get the dogs for protection—coyotes, if there were any about, would come at night though Ulric's sheer mass might deter them—brought out the rifle and a sleeping bag, and without a word, joined their vigil which would go on until Ausencia's body was collected at daybreak.

As Solange watched from the window, her astonishment turned to admiration of her daughter, her Guyanne, showing so many virtues all at once and at such a sad dénouement and without a trace of sentimentality: a vignette of strength of character which her mother had longed to discover some day in her only child; the young woman she was only now getting to know. Deciding not to wait for Olibade who had driven an exhausted Skye home, she went out to kiss everyone good night, chief among them, the grieving Ulric and her surprising daughter. Then she, limp with fatigue herself, went back to the house and collapsed on the sofa.

Fear and Grace

G UYANNE BECAME AN adult the day Ausencia died. During the vigil with Ulric and Contessa, she came to grips with who she had been and who she wanted to be. And she realized that intention wasn't enough; it had to be powered by attention. She thought about the dozens of times teachers, her parents, even her few friends would say with a frown or a glare: "Guyanne, pay attention!" Attention or the lack of it had been her one distinguishing feature; everything else about her nondescript, punctuated by 'ça m'est égal'—the last resort of the uncommitted. She didn't have attention-deficit—not in the clinical sense—but she finally understood why 'deficit' described the problem better than deficiency. Deficiency implied a flaw; a deficit was a sorry interruptus; a gaping space, in a canvas otherwise whole. Attention was a state of wholeness, of fullness, which could not hold itself together if it was also in a state of lack. But she was no linguist. All she knew was that when Ausencia was suffering, she had paid no attention. Scribbling away in her registry, she'd missed the whole point. She'd paid attention to completely the wrong thing. Like the orchestra continuing to play as the Titanic sank, full attention discriminates. Aware of the tragedy about to be, the musicians chose to pay attention—not to the fear that it bred—but to the grace that comes when fear releases its grip—that moment when sinew and spirit collide, and spirit wins out saying 'I accept.' 'Yes,' she thought, 'Yes, that is the difference.' She, on the other hand, had been oblivious—like Nero fiddling—a blindness unworthy of someone who had already had the benefit of heredity, wealth, instruction. But the heredity of man was imbued with imperatives which had more to do with awareness and less to do with accidental privilege. She knew that her inattention to what was going on around her that day was a terrible lapse back into the old Guyanne; that pre-Ulric girl whose skin she'd shed the night Papa had handed her a signpost—the day she'd met Justin and Zia and had her eyes opened to that dark space where man and animal face off. A discriminating attention was the descriptor for the difference between the Guyanne who was and the Guyanne to be. She resolved to do better; to be aware, alert, and though she only had dim views of what they had to be protected from—the details were still gray and dark and unknown to her—she would forego fear and step up to that further state. In the world where fear deferred to grace, 'I accept' and 'I will protect you' were kin.

She got dressed and spent twenty minutes looking around for her Registry then gave up. 'It'll turn up,' she thought. She went downstairs, intending to prepare an early breakfast for Solange and Ollie, determined to be free of fear and full of grace.

Finding Your Bliss

IN HIS OWN way, Matteo Volpone had made a study of human nature and had concluded that everyone had a passion. He'd had this really smart girl once, a real egghead, and she'd said that this writer or shrink or something, had called it your personal daemon. Volpone liked that. Most people called their passion a hobby, which Volpone considered reductive, like they didn't have the balls to do what they really liked; living instead lives of quiet misery, forced to indulge their passion or daemon in stingy allotments of time, usually alone or in secret, each hobbled in his own way from using his personal gift in the way his nature craves; in the way his nature, left to itself and its own devices, would bring the gift to fruition. For others, for people like him, their passion was an avocation. Ah/voh/kay/shun . . . Volpone sounded it out. He liked that better than 'hobby'; it sounded classy, like a word someone from college would use. He'd tried to phone that girl to try his new word out on her, but her phone was disconnected, and he didn't know her last name. Of course. Names didn't figure in one-night stands. Hey it wasn't as if he knew the brand of the tissues he used to blow his nose; he just called them all kleenex. Kleenex was kleenex.

Lately, he'd gotten really interested in this idea of 'following your bliss' which, to his way of thinking, was connected to your passion or your daemon. After all, he was a man of ideas. His mind was always working, always working, so he'd thought about it quite a bit. What is bliss if not satisfying that daemon that lived inside you, the one that you had to hide sometimes because your joy indulging him was so intense that you didn't really even want to share it; so fulfilling that there were laws against it. As if the law was there to protect everybody—c'mon—he'd heard of Rand. The Fountainhead was the biggest spurting phallus he'd ever heard of. What a guffaw. He knew that men were not created equal—some were better and smarter. Look at him; look at Rash. And women, hell, women weren't even in the equation. Wasn't he a member of sixteen sites, a member in good standing by the way, six of which were into s&m and the really hot stuff—the snuff films? What is bliss if not taking one's daemon to its highest expression? That'll bliss you out, alright—all over her face—watching it glom on, like Spidey's webs, in every direction. He liked to aim for the eyeballs so he'd pin their eyelids open with his thumbs first. Some squawked, like it wasn't a turn-on to see all this juice coming at you close up and then feeling its wetness dirty you all over; then sorb into your skin, become part of you. That was true love, true intimacy. The peace that follows from letting that daemon inhabit you, completely and utterly, and leaving its mark, like the Z of Zorro, on a girl or whatever . . . well now, that's all good.

He'd had some trouble deciding if the avatar of his personal daemon was Marvel's Wolverine or Edward Scissorhands. On the one hand, he loved that Wolverine had knives sheathed into his skin that he could pop out at will. It was complete and utter self-containment—no reaching for a bat or a knife or a gun—just complete self-reliance, timed by one's own sense of threat—and threats were everywhere and constant, weren't they. That was something he could have really used when he was learning to butcher at his father's shop. But as he matured, he saw that Scissorhands was an even better avatar than Wolverine who randomly slashed away—thoughtlessly, sloppily even. There could be nothing random—no gratuitous slicing—in the sculpting of body parts. Scissorhands, like Volpone, was an artist; his precision slashing was the application of intricate, calculated moves that produced elegant results. And elegance was everything. When Volpone was younger, he'd often stayed late at his father's butcher shop to practise carving into the viscera of the smaller animals—some dead yes, but others not quite, like small dogs and cats who'd strayed in, looking for food. He'd coax them in with food and then deftly slice across the throat. Exsanguination went faster when the heart was still beating, and he didn't have all night to wait until they bled out. He was a natural at time management, always had been. There'd been lots of strays and they were there for the taking, most too sick and hungry to fight back much, though there'd been the odd feisty one whose neck he'd had to wrench first to get anything done. He had taken a course in taxidermy too when he was in his late teens just so he could perfect his craft, and so really, when he looked at it objectively, his avocation was science even though he wasn't a quote-unquote scientist per se. He used the same work methods as they did—although sometimes he'd had to sacrifice complete antisepsis since he was working out of a butcher's shop and not a laboratory; he experimented on the same animals they did, and he always had one control animal and one non-control so he could assess the results, which he copied directly into a hardbound notebook he kept strictly for that purpose.

In a nutshell, Volpone concluded that his daemon, his bliss or whatever you chose to call it, was a profound preoccupation with the circuitry of life which in part was the reason he preferred eviscerating living creatures rather than dead ones. You cannot learn about life from cadavers, as the great Dr. Chopra once said. So in time, he evolved beyond what was available at his father's butcher shop—its minutiae mostly concerned with already rendered flesh—and graduated into John Rash's world where opportunities for growth were limited only by squeamishness or a lack of vision. Sometimes, the depth of Volpone's understanding amazed even him. He was able to scale such great heights, he believed, because despite having an inquisitive, even beautiful, mind, he also paid close attention to who and what was around him. And that wasn't just because his daemon led him into areas shunned by mainstream clones and their draconian laws; it was because paying or not paying attention meant the difference between freedom and the loss of it. At work, where he spent all his time—it was more than a career; it was his life now—paying attention meant everything. Paying attention to the needs and wants of his employer had kept him in a job that most people couldn't even handle. More, paying attention meant teasing out his employer's desires without his having to even ask. Volpone had always been gifted at sifting the chaff from the grain, distilling truth from reality and—crucial in his work with Rash—reading character.

Like now. He knew that Rash had gone to some lengths to get that snobby French girl's phone number; in fact, it made Volpone think about that time with that fancy horse, that mare that Rash said had a special gene, for colour or something. It was the only time Matt could remember Rash raising his voice to him, stopping short of, well, he didn't know what. At the time, if he hadn't known how indispensable he was to Rash, he almost thought he was going to hand him his walking papers. He chuckled at the very thought of Rash letting him go. But he knew he had to make good on that. Rash was a bit anal about things he wanted, like that mare. Or that girl. He could start with her. Yeah, he'd start by finding out her address. He knew enough people in enough places.

CYNTHIA D'ERRICO

Questionable Goings-on

VOLPONE COULDN'T BELIEVE his luck. He'd managed to kill two birds with one stone and now he was going to present his boss, Mr. Rash, with the results, proving once again that he was the one and only wolfman. Yes indeed. Indispensable. Waiting while Rash finished a phone call always gave Volpone more time to exalt himself.

"From what I see here, the regulations on those bloody machines are curbing revenues—and turning Blue Bonnets into a huge tavern for losers. It's going to be another Toe Blake's with state-controlled gambling . . . . We're getting into a mood akin to prohibition . . . you know, gambling isn't a virtue, it's a vice. It's a thing that can't be over-regulated because once it is, it loses its fizz. Let's stop trying to paper over this crap. It could bring the industry to its knees . . . . Well then, what is happening to the money? Where's the cash going? If you don't know, find out who does . . . . Follow the cash, senator, follow the cash . . . yeah . . . get back to me."

Wordlessly, Volpone handed him the ripped-out page and waited for what he knew would be, even for Rash, a big reaction. Rash sighed as he handed Volpone the phone, took the paper and came to a dead stop on his way to the bar.

"You found her? Where is she?"

"She's at Université Jean-Talon, room 528." Volpone thought he might like a drink at a moment like this, but he didn't drink.

Rash looked at him as one looks at a wall. "Yeah? They have stables there, at the college, do they?"

"Oh you mean the horse? Oh she's at this Institute, one of those animal shelters. See . . . here at the top . . . right there, Institute of Nature Communications . . . right there."

"Huh. I know that name from somewhere. And you found Miss Brucy—Darquise—too?"

"Right."

"And you got this from Darquise's dorm room?"

Volpone knew better than to answer.

"What would Darquise be doing with a Breed Registry—and why would an animal shelter even keep a Registry?" Rash said aloud to himself.

"So what do you need me to do now, Mr. Rash? Do you want the girl—"

"—right now, all I want is time to think. Hold my calls for half an hour. That's good work though, wolfman . . . good work," said Rash, as he gingerly picked some lint off his silk shirt.

Full of himself and his own cleverness, Volpone left, preening himself on having created such excitement in the usually imperturbable Mr. Rash, and already working out what he was sure his employer wanted done next; something he always knew before Rash did himself—well, almost always. He'd start by getting that old nag back for him. Rash sat back and read carefully. As soon as he'd seen the Institute's name, he knew it was all about the champagne mare. His mare. His property. The mare was a loss he wasn't prepared to take at the time, but he'd had to swallow it because that woman—what was her name again . . . something to do with birds—had outsmarted him with paperwork. She'd had the mare picked up before he'd even got confirmation of the colour gene—and as it turned out, she did have the gene. It was downright theft is what it was. He recalled his ire at the time as if watching a slide show of past events. He'd driven to the slaughterhouse himself because he'd had a feeling, a bad feeling, about this woman. But the mare was long gone by the time he got there; his witless fool of a manager showed him papers in perfect order releasing the mare to this Institute as if—as if it were okay. Stupid son of a bitch. And then later, with his lawyers, finding out he had no legal recourse, he did a slow burn. He hated adversaries like this, bloated with their own self-righteousness; worst of all, smart enough to cover all the angles—the legal ones anyway—and savvy enough to befriend certain bleeding hearts in the media. Whereas he, Rash, had to rely on ignoramuses like that manager or pods like Volpone. You just can't drill through the wood with people like that. He sighed. Oh well. Nature of the beast.

His reverie on failure, a mild but irritating one, ended when he reapplied himself to this new information. Now he knew where the mare had gotten to, and more important, now he knew where the Institute was. There was no address but it had to be in the west end since the thing was found at the university just past Ste-Anne-de-Bellevue. Always learn from your enemies. She—Spahro was the name he remembered now—had beaten him by paying fastidious attention to the paperwork; the law. She'd done everything by the book. So he came full circle back to his first thought: what was an animal shelter doing with a Registry? Are they selling off the horses they're supposed to be rescuing, profiting from sales that are unrecorded, unknown to the federal Charities Directorate? The Directorate would pull their license in a hurry if it had evidence of such goings-on. Grinning, he scanned the page again: proof was already in hand.

Something I've Been Meaning to Tell You

BELLE HEARD SKYE come in when Ollie brought her home in the middle of the night; the afternoon downpour had left the air moist and thick so Belle was restless and partly awake, anyway.

"You all right, Mother?"

"I couldn't save her," said Skye, removing her damp clothes in slow motion, like a drunk or a dreamer.

"Let me help you."

Skye didn't object. She let her daughter prepare her for bed, and for sleep too, she hoped. She wanted to be unconscious. She just needed sleep and the next day, she'd be fine, she knew. With only the moonlight scoring the darkness, she looked around her room: a storied chamber of woeful images and faces that kept vigil only in the dark, coming to life as soon as her eyes closed. There were those kinds of sleeptimes, marred by memories waiting to pounce, but not always and she prayed, not tonight—she was bone weary.

"It was my fault."

"Colic is rarely anyone's fault, Mother. You taught me that."

"She should have been here, with us."

"The tremor upset her and the tremor was here as well as there. Stop it."

"All I could do, all I can ever do, is hold out my hand to them in the dark, let them know I'm there—that someone is there—"

"—Mother—"

"—who loves them . . . and make sure that their friends are with them. Ulric . . . he was her greatest comfort."

"Skye . . . she was on her way to slaughter when we got to her—when you rescued her, Mother. You saved her from all that. A sport horse used to people for companionship, for trust, for everything—why, the gruelling transport alone would have killed her. She would have been DOA and then thrown among rotting carcasses in a back field somewhere for the wolves to feed on after years of faithful service."

Ausencia died with care and respect, surrounded by love, not like the countless slaughtered whose only reprieve from misery is death. But it was still hard on Skye, she knew. She looked at her mother, at that small frame lying in a bed much too big for her, and kissed her softly on the forehead.

"There's something I've been meaning to tell you, my bell-elle."

"That's fine, Mum . . . you can mean to tell me tomorrow. I'll be here."

"Yes. You always are, Belle. Always, my Belle is with me . . . ."

Belle left the door slightly ajar, in case. 'Tomorrow,' she thought, 'tomorrow, I'll have something to tell you, too, Mother; how will you take it?' Then she went into her bedroom and phoned Chano. Despite the hour, he sprang awake at the sound of her voice.

"Belle . . . everything okay?"

"We lost Ausencia today."

"Oh no . . . Ausencia . . . ?"

"One of our rescues. A polo mare. Skye is . . . well, she needs some sleep."

"Anything I can do, anything you need . . . you know, anything . . . I love you, Belle."

"I know . . . I love you too . . . but there's nothing. Tomorrow . . . ."

"I'll be there . . . around two—or earlier, if you want."

"No, two is fine. Do what you need to do. I'll be talking to her tomorrow."

"Good . . . I mean, right . . . I can be there with you when you . . . tell her how much you mean to me . . . how I want to make my life with you . . . us, to make a life together—"

"—No, my love. I'll tell her myself, alone."

"Okay . . . Belle?"

"I'm here."

"I don't breathe right without you."

"I know . . . . Go back to sleep. I'll see you tomorrow. 'night."

Then she went downstairs to see to Ollie. But he was already down, half on the sofa and half off. She gently lifted his legs and covered him well. Once upstairs, lulled by the soft staccato of his snoring, Belle fell asleep instantly.

What Zia Knows for Sure

T HE NEXT DAY, as she came downstairs, Belle heard Skye talking
on the phone.

"We have a two-year-old Quarter Horse stallion, two mixed Arabs,
both in their twenties, and a Rocky Mountain Pony in his late twenties
that need fostering . . . it'll just be for a month or so until I can find them
permanent homes . . . yes, they're in pretty bad shape. They're at the equine
hospital now here in Québec but I need a firm yes from you for fostering
before I can confirm with the head vet there . . . yes, we're having the
stallion gelded—as soon as he recovers from his injuries."

Belle poured herself some coffee and glanced at the papers on the
kitchen table. It was as she thought: the CFIA violations report on the
Gravel Slaughterhouse in Saskatchewan had finally been written up. The
Canadian Anti-Horse Slaughter Coalition had sent an undercover in and
produced incriminating video which finally shut down an abattoir that
was like a training ground for sociopaths. The Canadian Food Inspection
Agency kept claiming that everything at Gravel was up to code but even
local abattoir operators had insisted it be shut down. It gave them a bad
name, the operators said; bad enough they had to deal with the saturated
fat scare in beef and mad cow disease. It took nearly a full year after the
video came out for the CFIA to act.

"No," Skye continued, "we don't know whether they've been tested
for trichinella or not, much less bute and the steroids. Even though
they're American horses . . . how do we know? . . . we know because
they have USDA feeder tags on them which means a kill-buyer at an
auction somewhere in the US bought them specifically for slaughter in
Canada . . . . Tagging them as feeders makes Customs think they're going
to feedlots to fatten them up. The owner claims she can't recall where she

bought them but she wasn't bright enough to remove the feeder tags. She probably made a deal with the trucker on the q.t. Canada isn't as stringent as the US in requiring those tests before slaughtering horses—especially racehorses—for human consumption and since we sell their flesh to overseas buyers—yes, mostly Japan and France—our best guess is that CFIA lets their food agencies worry about it . . . . Yes, a big oversight, I'd say, especially since even trace amounts of bute in human food can be fatal . . . . Right. I'll send you copies of all test results our vet will be conducting—including those required by Ontario law—beforehand . . . . We'll be in touch shortly, within the next 48 hours. Goodbye and thank you—oh and Charlotte, remember: the court case against the owner is pending so . . . mum's the word."

As Belle sipped her coffee and began reading the report, she wondered if Skye remembered saying that she had something to tell her. Skye said, "Turn to page six."

> *Ante-mortem protocol inspection: Only one stop gate (fanny gate) was closed behind eight horses in the alleyway leading to the knockbox. Employee was whipping horse closest to the knockbox to make him advance. The horse moved backward away from the whip until all eight were so crowded that the last horse attempted to jump the alley wall. It got pinioned atop the wall and because of its flailing, finally fell to the other side, breaking two legs and apparently fracturing its pelvis, unable to stand. The animal was not removed until the other seven were processed. It succumbed to unknown internal injuries; exsanguination seemed to be primarily oral. Its blood and other fluids were allowed to dry, thereby unacceptably contaminating the external alleyway area.*

Belle, who, like her mother, had read—and seen—worse, never got used to such horrors, but she said: "Still, we got them, Mum. CFIA will have to close them down. And we'll get the rest of them . . . too many consumers know now, and they're horrified—if only because they realise how easily the food they eat is contaminated. As for the brutality of it all—"

"—we won't stop, till it stops," said Skye, who felt rather than saw that one horse whose desperate leap for freedom separated him from the rest; the one who decided he'd rather die his own way than be savagely whipped before he was skinned and eviscerated half-alive.

"Mother, how did it go with the fosterers? Are they still interested?"

"Yes. But I'll tell you more later, when we write up the police reports. Belle . . . ?"

"Hmm?"

"What do you think of Olibade?"

"Ollie? I think he's great, Mum. He knows as much about horses as you do—and even a few things maybe you don't know. Although obviously you know things that he couldn't know—"

"—He and I, Belle . . . he and I were very close when we were young. Very close. I've never been closer to anyone—except of course for you." Skye put her hand on Belle's arm. Belle looked up from the report.

"I know. I can tell from how you look at each other that . . . ." replied Belle quietly.

"It was a long, long time ago. But you see, things were different then, and I had work to do and Olibade, well Ollie wanted different things from what I wanted, what I felt needed to be done . . . ."

Belle looked away and in that minute, flashed to Ollie's eyes, and for the very first time, realised why they were so familiar. She had her father's eyes.

"He's father, isn't he, Skye? Olibade is my father. You told me that my father was dead. Why, Mother? Why didn't you tell me?"

"Belle . . . even he didn't know. No one knew . . . ."

"—does he know now?"

"No, I wanted to tell you first . . . but Belle, try to understand. It was a different time then. And Ollie was more—well not different, like me. I was afraid that if I told him, he would insist that we get married. And I, well you know me Belle, I had another goal, another aim, that I couldn't ignore . . . so I left. I couldn't give you up and I couldn't stay either, so . . . . My only regret, my bell-elle, is that sometimes I think I've held your whole life hostage to my calling, a calling that I had, but maybe not one you would have picked for yourself—the very thing I was afraid would happen to Olibade, I sometimes fear, I sometimes think, I imposed on you."

Belle, usually a quick study, able to process things rapidly and come up with an answer, was struck dumb, as if she'd known since the day she met Olibade who he was yet unable to commit to the fact of it, flying as it did in the face of nearly forty years of fatherlessness; of a day-to-day reality that now her own mother was telling her wasn't real at all, had never been real. She wanted to bang this new fact on the table to see if it was solid, was true, before she could put together an answer; an answer to something which, really, she thought now, was unanswerable. She didn't know any other kind of life. Apart from her college years, she'd never been separated from Skye; had always worked with Skye in horse rescue. Even during those lean college years, she'd spent all her free time working to improve the lives of others: the disempowered, the abused, the marginalized. It was what she had always done . . . impossible to say whether she'd have done any different if her mother hadn't been an animal savant; had been instead a lawyer, a homemaker, a saleswoman. And since she didn't know what it was to have a father, how could she tell if any damage had been done; if she'd been lacking something, missing the influence of another parent? It was like finding out you were adopted and nothing, no one you thought was yours, really was, and all the beliefs you had lived by were based on fiction—a family fiction that had suddenly put up a sign that read 'gone fishin.' Belle felt like she'd just discovered she was standing in quicksand in the very place she thought she had been most solid. Who she thought she was turned out to be nothing but a fabrication.

But Belle loved her mother. She looked at those marvellous eyes, now limpid pools of anxiety, and decided she could not say how she felt one way or the other, so she patted Skye's arm and then got up and went outside. Skye watched from the window as Belle walked down towards the horses, terrified that her daughter, whom she'd brought up never to be false to anyone, was, in her own mind and heart, accusing her own mother of that very sin, with each step she took, with the sure-footedness of an infantryman—left, right, left, right, liar, liar, liar, liar. When the phone rang, Skye answered as eagerly as if it were her daughter calling, even as she watched Belle walk further and further away from her.

"Skye, it's Solange. Something has happened—"

"—not to Ausencia?" Skye had already worked things out with the vet.

"No, no . . . but it's something that you need to know about. There was a robbery, some vandalism, at DeeDee's the other day. Something was taken and it has to do with one of your horses."

"One of my horses? What do you mean?"

"Well, my daughter, Guyanne . . . she's been working on this Horse Registry for our stable, you see . . . breed, age, and other information on each of our horses, and she—I didn't know she was doing this, Skye . . . . She had a whole section on the Institute rescues. It was innocence on her part. She doesn't really know what the Institute does. She just didn't know that she couldn't do that . . . leave a paper trail, I mean."

"I see," said Skye, sitting down quickly. "So . . . the thing that was stolen, it was information on my rescues—where they are and who we got them from? Is that all they took? No valuables? No other items?"

"No. Dee said nothing else was missing. It seems like it was someone who maybe owned one of your rescues and wants him back—maybe a racehorse."

"Solange, how did Guyanne's Registry end up in DeeDee's dorm room?"

"Well that's the funny part. The day Ausencia colicked, Dee came to visit and drove Yanne over to see Belle while we were all with Ausencia. Apparently, Yanne brought the Registry with her over to Holdout Bay and then it started to rain, so Yanne stuck the book in Dee's briefcase to keep it from getting wet, and then forgot about it till she went looking for it the next day. Dee herself didn't know she had it until she found her place all upside-down and the book lying open with a page ripped out. It was all just by chance that the Registry ended up at Dee's."

"Solange—"

"—I know. This is very serious, isn't it? Guyanne is right here. Will you speak to her?"

"Yes. No—listen, both of you. I have to find out which horse they were looking for. Tell Guyanne to come here to see me. Right now, if she can. She must tell me what was on that missing page."

"Yes, Skye. I'm leaving now. Skye, I'm so sorry, I—" said Guyanne, through the speaker phone.

"—we can make it right, my girl. But I need to know which horse or horses they were looking for so I can have them moved right away, right now—today. Don't waste time, Guyanne. Leave now."

Even before she'd hung up the phone, Skye was calculating how many rescues there'd been in the past six months. At least sixty, she thought, but none of their previous owners had caused trouble nor were any pending court cases. It must go further back—maybe last year, maybe two years ago. She reviewed the names and cases of Standardbred pacers she'd placed in the previous year. No, even if some of those were problematic, those trotters had been placed very far away and since Skye never documented their new locations anywhere, they'd never find them—unless, in talking to Belle, Guyanne had recorded some locations. There were those six Thoroughbreds but they were too old to be valuable . . . there was that one Thoroughbred filly, though, a great-granddaughter of the Derby winner, Unbridled—she'd be worth her weight in gold for breeding . . . . Skye rubbed her temples. She knew she had to calm down and just wait until Yanne could tell her whose name was on that missing page—and how much information and what level of detail.

After all these years, it never ceased to amaze her how—despite the Institute having full and irrevocable legal rights to all her rescues—there were still some scofflaws out there who didn't give a damn about any of that. And of those, there was a percentage who only wanted the horse back to spite Skye. Still, she thought, if it was someone with an axe to grind, they would have taken the whole book. There was a whole sub-culture of horse abusers out there and they all knew each other and all covered for each other—just as long as the horses made them money—whether from exhaustive overbreeding, overworking, over-racing, or for the few dollars they got from the knacker's—really, just pennies per pound for the shadow of an equine, usually starved to a third of his normal weight. She knew quite a few who'd run a jumper or eventer into the ground—the great warmblood, Anvil, was a case in point—and then use the money they got from his slaughter to buy another and do the same thing to that one and the next, endlessly, as if horses were used cars you could just keep trading in right before their tranny blew for another, slightly younger model. So much for the historic, the iconic value of the horse. We are fire itself, after all, consuming everything that comes our way, she thought. Abuse was a perpetual torment to Skye, her deathless compassion the rock she heaved and toted ceaselessly up a sisyphean hill. And though the tome she carried in her head and in her heart was a heavy one, she couldn't forget, dismiss or discard it—even if she wanted to. But she didn't want to. Not ever. If she did, she would cease to be who she was; and if nothing else, Skye Spahro knew who she was and what she was on earth to do. And as always, as now with this new threat, death, that smarmy backbencher, was afoot. Ubiquitous lurker, ever only a step or two behind her. As she watched Belle drive away, she saw DeeDee pull into the driveway.

"Madame, I just heard . . . about the Registry . . . what was on that page, I mean." DeeDee was carrying another book; one that Skye instantly recognized.

"What—?"

"Yes, this is Delphine's diary. Belle lent it to me the same day Yanne's Registry was mistakenly left in my briefcase. I thought . . . I should bring it back for safekeeping, in case the thief returns to the scene of the crime."

"It must have been awful for you, DeeDee, to enter your own place and find it violated," said Skye, taking back the diary she hadn't even known was out of her possession.

"The worst part was my cat, Tawser. He refused to come out from under the sofa for two days. The man must have terrified him. Or worse, meant to kill him. I think I would have hunted him down myself if he'd done that," replied Dee.

"DeeDee, have you read the diary?"

"I have. I know it's a personal family diary, Skye, but Delphine was a meticulous recorder of events, important historical events, much like Catharine Parr Traill, and . . . . I sincerely hope you didn't mind my borrowing it. I did have second thoughts but my passion overcame my good sense, and it seems, my manners."

"I won't lie to you, DeeDee. I am not happy that Belle lent it—even to you, who I know would use it with all due respect and discretion . . . but if you read it then you know about the—"

Guyanne came through the screen door so fast, she nearly tripped over the armchair.

"Skye! Skye, I'm here. And I can tell you exactly what I wrote on that page—it was about Zia, only Zia—I have it all in my notebook. I write stuff in there and then transcribe it into the Registry."

"Zia? You mean that information was on my Zia?" Skye couldn't believe what she was hearing. This made everything worse, much worse. Skye sat down in the armchair with such a blank look that Guyanne went to fetch some water. DeeDee said: "Zia? Zia is the name of this mare? I know that name." Skye, her mind racing, looked up at her.

"Is this a horse with unusual DNA; a special gene for something?"

"Yes," said Skye, who, as she answered, got up and apparently spoke to Toby who immediately flew off in the direction of the herd. "Zia carries the colour gene for champagne or cremello, as it's sometimes called. It's considered very desirable by certain breeders. It's especially rare in the Canadien. Why?"

"Then I think I know who did this. For a short time, I dated a man, a very rich businessman who was big in the horse industry—"

"—John Rash," said Skye, her voice strained but clear. Dee, surprised, simply nodded.

"Damn," Skye muttered, "how can he still want her after all this time?"

"I'm so sorry, Skye. It's all my fault. I didn't know that the horses here were . . . I mean, I knew but I . . . I didn't understand . . . ."

"Maybe it's not the same horse," said DeeDee, patting Guyanne gently on the arm.

"No there's no mistake," said Skye, energized anew, knowing she had to act, and quickly.

CYNTHIA D'ERRICO

Guyanne was about to tell DeeDee what Belle had told her about Zia the day Guyanne met Zia and Justin, but she stopped herself. She was, now more than ever, aware that the trouble she had caused was very serious. But no one could foresee the danger Skye herself was in—except that is for Zia who was coming at full gallop screaming for Skye and about ready to fly up the verandah and bust through the front door. Her panic and fear were justified, for of everyone there, only Zia knew the madness that was Matteo Volpone.

PART FOUR

Love will Keep

SOLANGE KNEW ABOUT Skye and Ollie, and she knew about Belle and Chano, but she didn't know about Ollie and Belle. So when her dear friend Belle showed up the same day she'd sent her erring daughter to tell Skye all that was in the Registry related to the Institute, she was beyond surprised to see her. Belle pulled into the driveway like a trucker and then just sat there staring blankly at the windshield. Solange went out to meet her.

"Are you coming in, or are you just here to admire the view?"

"Where's Ollie?" asked Belle from the driver's seat.

"Ollie? Ollie could be anywhere—in the stables, or in one of the pastures," replied Solange, studying Belle's face. "Maybe . . . maybe not even here . . . picking up feed somewhere or salt licks or something."

Belle didn't answer.

"He's not in the house anyway. Come. We're all alone."

Solange listened as Belle dropped her whole heart onto the kitchen table, without interruption, without comment, not so much like the good reporter she'd been trained to be, but more like a friend who felt every emotion her beloved Belle was experiencing as if they were her own.

"Does Ollie know?"

"No. I don't even know if I want to him to know—but if I do, I think I should tell him, not Skye—I'm not a child anymore," replied Belle, in a tone just a shade off petulant.

"No . . . but you're his child . . . his and Skye's. It might be better coming from her. And it hit you like a ton of bricks . . . who knows how it will hit him? Ollie isn't as young as he used to be. Losing Ausencia hurt him more than I ever would have imagined—an old horseman like him—he's seen everything. You'd think—" Solange stopped as they heard someone drive up.

"Ah," said Solange, as he walked onto the verandah, "so this is the dashing young scientist."

"I hope you don't mind, Madame Deschambault," said Chano, as they shook hands.

"Not at all. I've heard so much about you. It's a pleasure to meet you at last," replied Solange, who never thought she'd use the words 'dashing' and 'scientist' in the same sentence. She looked at him looking at her friend and decided then and there that she couldn't wait another minute to go check on the horses.

"Who knows where Ollie is, eh. I'll be back in a little while so make yourselves perfectly at home—and Belle?—don't leave without saying goodbye."

Chano had come looking for Belle after showing up at the Institute at 2 o'clock and finding her gone. Skye had walked down to the shore to meet him, Guyanne and Dee in tow, and told him what had happened—itself an indication of how perturbed Skye was. Belle couldn't believe that Skye had told him.

"I can't believe that Mother would tell you before telling Ollie—and only hours after telling me. That's so unlike her," said Belle, still unsure as to how she felt about it all.

"Ollie? What does Ollie have to do with that missing page on Zia?" replied Chano. In the time it took for Chano to explain to Belle and Belle to explain to Chano, Olibade had returned from wherever he'd been. They heard him pull in. Belle didn't mean to sweep past him as they crossed paths in the driveway, but she was in a hurry. She'd introduce herself—who she was to him and he to her—some other time. Right now, everything she loved was under threat and in that instant, Belle would realise later, she had her answer. Chano and Solange watched her rush away and exchanged a look. As Chano made a move to follow her, Solange deftly stopped him.

"No, let her go. Just for now. Her mind is full to bursting with this news about Zia . . . and Ollie . . . . She has a lot on her plate just now, but don't worry, her heart won't forget you . . . and your love, I expect, will keep."

Chano, his own mind racing, slumped into the nearest chair. Solange set the coffeemaker and sat down across from him. If she'd learned anything as a journalist, it's that people wanted to talk, needed to talk—they didn't need much coaxing. Forlorn as he looked, she knew he'd talk when he was ready. She waited patiently; it only took as long as the brew cycle.

"You see, what I'm asking of her is a big change—a sacrifice even. She and her mother—the work they do, they do together—it's inspiring, essential work, and I'm asking her to leave all that and come with me, be with me. I've been called to Verchères and then to Sorel—there's a lot happening along these shorelines. Bellwethers, we call them, warning of what is likely happening all along the Québec coastline . . . bank erosion is accelerating, much faster than we'd thought, and not just along the shorelines: whole islands—like the îlots running all through the Sorel archipelago—are sinking. Right here, right across from our island, Îles de la Paix where the national reserve is—and its 240 hectares of marsh that provide staging areas for wildfowl—is under a twenty-year death sentence. Foundation floors for land masses, especially little ones, like yours here, on Pointe de la Méduse, are threatened. That means that the random tremor that we just had—if there's another, even slightly stronger one—the quay and the bay shoreline will slip underwater and . . . ."

As he spoke, citing fact after deadly fact, Solange was thinking that, probably for the first time in his life, this young, dispassionate scientist was no longer seeing just a string of collated data, but holding, in his mind's eye, a new image—a different one for him: the heartstopping face of his Belle.

"Yes," Solange nodded, "I've read the reports. The situation is dire for our little island, isn't it? Being so close to the highly urbanized Lake Saint-Louis shore and to the spewing factories of Beauharnois has put Isle-Saint-Jean-Baptiste in harm's way. And you want Belle to leave with you, is that right?"

"Yes," replied Chano, working his hair again. Solange waited then tried again.

"You're a Trottier, aren't you? One of the first families of Isle-Saint-Jean-Baptiste—like my cousin's, Darquise. The Brucy's and Trottier's were original landholders here, weren't they? I understand DeeDee and you both attend Université Jean-Talon."

"Yes." She tried yet a different tack.

"You know, I saw that there was a pinto there at the Institute. Do you know that horse's name? . . . I meant to ask Belle but . . . I only caught a glimpse of the Registry before my daughter tore out of here like a tornado—I didn't even know Guyanne was keeping a Registry. Poor girl, she was so heartbroken that she was the cause of all these problems—I barely had a look but I did see 'pinto' on one of the pages."

"Justin," replied Chano, "His name is Justin and he's—well, exceptional. He'd make anyone's head turn, even someone who didn't like horses or didn't know anything about them. He has a sort of . . . presence, I guess. I know very little about horses except for the few I met in PEI."

"Ah, Justin . . . Justin, is it?" she murmured. Jericho had had presence.

"I probably shouldn't even be telling you this . . . ."

"Please don't worry. I'm one of Skye's fosterers and my lips are sealed."

She looked out the window to the row of firs where Ulric and Contessa were standing together, and sipped her coffee soundlessly. 'It seems the season for children finding their long-lost parents,' she thought.

"Come," she said, putting her cup down decisively, "you said you'd met horses in PEI. Well, you must know Belgians, then. We have a retired Belgian here. His name is Ulric—"

"Rick? Ulric the Red?" Solange smiled and nodded as she pointed through the window. 'A pleasant surprise,' thought Solange, 'is a quick restorative when that slippery slope of hard decisions, no foothold in sight, has become one's whole world.' Chano didn't believe in signs even though his life's work was all about studying signs, but he found it more than a coincidence that the one horse he'd befriended—or who'd been good enough to befriend him—was now living a short drive away from Belle's. He asked if they could bring carrots. As they left the house and walked towards Ulric and Contessa, Solange felt he would be all right. She'd talk to Belle when things calmed down. She also made a mental note to phone a few friends after her guest left, some highly placed friends, who, better than she, better even than Skye, could deal with Mr. John Rash and his obsession with a champagne mare named Zia. Some things, as her mother often said, were not for the asking: ça ne se fait pas, she'd say with the moral certitude of a priest . . . 'and some things,' thought Solange in that same steely vein, 'no matter how coveted, are not just for the taking.'

Zia Refuses

THE PROBLEM WAS, Zia refused to leave Skye or the herd. It was her herd, after all, she told Skye, and they needed her, especially now that that horrible man had found them. The horrors that Zia witnessed and suffered at La Petite Vallée Slaughterhouse she would never forget, could never forgive. Images of unrelenting suffering had lodged in her blood and bones, and the dark-haired man, the man they called the wolfman, was the worst of the lot: a visiting devil who'd browse the holding areas for victims and do unspeakable things to them, keeping them alive and screaming as long as he could. After his third visit, two horses—one a young stallion—dropped dead of heart attacks at the mere scent of him. The smell of blood and gore and guts on him was strong. He was a foul decanter of gruesome endings; deadlier than a predator, crueller by far. Even the white-haired abattoir manager was afraid of him. Zee wasn't letting him anywhere near Skye or her herd. Skye would have to think of something else, that's all.

Skye walked back to the house, deep in thought. She'd separated herd members before; they never liked it and she didn't like doing it. But it was unavoidable when even a court-ordered injunction couldn't keep a crazy owner or one of their flunkeys off Institute property. Only the Sûreté could handle them and Skye usually got a heads-up beforehand. She thought back to the time of Zia's rescue and how her volunteers described a man, with dark hair and blue eyes, who was the scourge of La Petite Vallée. He was despised by the abattoir workers and so hated by the manager himself that, in the end, he'd secretly abetted the rescue of Zia and a few others. To most of them, slaughterhouse work was just a job, like any other. There was no reason to waste time and energy torturing animals who were half-dead on arrival anyway. The manager knew Volpone was favoured by

Rash, the big boss, so he tolerated him. But what finally did it was the day Volpone walked over to a mare going into labour and began twisting a tree trimming pole deep into her vagina. The weight of the foal doubled her meat weight, yes, but, as Volpone explained, no need to have the foal alive. It was double the slaughter work, he knew, but he'd do these two himself, no problem, and resumed his sweaty twisting with a grin. The manager nodded and walked away, muttering, "t'es malade dans tête touais," went in to his office, shut the door, and dialled the volunteer's number.

"La Canadienne brouillée . . . t'la veux-tu toujours?"

"Oui certain, toujours."

"Bon . . . ce soir après minuit. Emmène la van. Elle sac' son camp."

Worried that Volpone or even Rash himself might come after them before the paperwork went through, the volunteers drove through the night and well past daybreak to deliver Zia to Skye, to safety. Skye, who'd rescued horses with eyeballs gouged out and legs dangling without batting an eye, took one look at Zia, fell to her knees and covered her face with both hands. 'Yes,' thought Skye, the dark memory making her green eyes spark, 'I'll just have to think of another way.'

What DeeDee Knew
Almost for Sure

MORE THAN A bit shaken the day Zia—throwing her head wildly—mounted Skye's verandah, the porch creaking under her pounding hooves, DeeDee drove home feeling a new tenderness for her little cat, Tawser. Unlike cousin Solange, Dee wasn't familiar with the powerful language of horses, and Zee's dramatic display confirmed in Dee's mind that she was more comfortable with smaller mammals, dogs and cats, and of those, the smaller the better. Yorkies or Siamese—anything that fit the cradle of her arms—was big enough for her. As she turned in to the parking lot, she suddenly remembered Skye's words just before Guyanne arrived—the girl's whirlwind entrance an opening act for the wild horse on the verandah. Skye had begun to say, '. . . then you must know about the . . .' '—the what?' thought Dee. She felt sure it had to do with the mysterious notation 'dD' appended to all the names of the deBeauvilliers women. Dee had developed special instincts after so many years spent examining ancient documents in hermetically sealed archive rooms. Call it seasoned intuition, intelligent speculation—it had won her research scholarships over more favoured candidates with better grades. She'd read most of the diary; it had to be that.

Though she'd meant to, she'd never had the chance to tell Skye that she had made a copy of the diary. Just for her own use for now; permission to disseminate would come later. But thinking back to Skye's reaction, she wasn't sure now whether she should even tell her. If she asked her to destroy the copy, she would in good conscience have to do so; but the fact was, the diary was a real find, a fountainhead of information that would keep veteran historians busy for a decade at least. And she'd be lying if she didn't admit that the diary would put her on the academic map—and the cultural map as well. Diaries like these, long believed to exist in two out of five patriots' homes, mouldering away amongst moth balls and lavender in an old steam trunk or chest in the attic, were rarely found, and when on occasion were, had become too damaged and illegible to communicate anything of note. Historians were reduced then to mere bibliographers, examining the age of the paper, the type of binding used—deducing from a worn artifact only cold data about ancestral crafts and livelihoods, and nothing about day-to-day ancestral life itself. Bringing Delphine's diary to light would do for DeeDee what the Gulf War did for Christiane Amanpour, would do for historians what Amanpour did for foreign journalism.

Dee knew she shouldn't even be thinking such things. Belle was her friend and though she didn't know Skye well at all, their meeting that day in the cemetery gave her an insight into who this woman was—not to mention her startling ability to calm a 1000-pound horse with just a look, and her lifelong devotion to a lame-duck cause in a province known as one of the worst offenders in North America. Then Skye's own words came to her, about exhuming the wisdom of the neglected; about not letting it become extinct. Surely, then, Skye would agree with her that the diary belonged in the public domain; that if, as she herself had said, it is in the past we find the tools for a better future, then what better, what nobler use of the diary than to publish it? Tawser was at her feet, meowing 'pick-me-up.' "Mais qu'est-ce que tu veux, mon bébé, mon petit don de Dieu, hein? . . ." DeeDee scooped him up into her lap and cuddled him close.

What it all Comes Down to

NO-ONE KNEW SKYE better than Ollie Ouellet did, and he knew that she was crazy. Crazy like a kamikaze pilot, crazy like those angels who spend all their time dancing on the head of a pin. Crazy like a saint. He had to make her see sense. When he pulled into her driveway, he could see from her stride that she'd determined on a plan of some kind, probably the very one he'd have to talk her out of.

"Ollie, Ollie, have you heard? Someone's after Zia—my Zia—after all this time! It's Rash, I know it. He's incorrigible, that one. Even after all the paperwork went through, all the legal stuff taken care of, he still—through the lawyers—he still tried to buy her from me. As if that was going to happen, after all we'd gone through to save her and to have that bloody place shut down—it's still running, you know. And now, and now Zia refuses to leave. I've tried to explain it to her, but she's adamant—"

"—Skye, Skye," said Ollie, blocking her way, "she's a horse, Skye. Horses don't make decisions. She doesn't know what's good for her—and neither do you, my love. You have to move her somewhere else because I know you: if they send someone out to get her, you'll get hurt trying to stop them. I know you. That can't happen, Skye. Skye, look at me. Look at me. I can't let that happen." Skye turned to face him, her eyes as flinty as shot-glasses.

"Have we just met? Don't you know by now that I would never let anything happen to these horses; they're my friends—friends under my protection—my protection, Ollie—they have no one else, only me and each other. And you should know better, Olibade: horses do make decisions—every minute of every day—their survival depends on it, even when—especially when—their survival depends on obeying the bit. Just because we don't understand doesn't mean a process isn't going on; a process that involves love and loyalty as much as fear and all of the primitive emotions we stupidly think is all they're capable of. I'm so sick of trying to bring people beyond their limited experience of the world—of trying to make them see that the human experience of the world, of the human senses, is not the only way of being. Our interiority is not the only kind out there. But we just can't get over ourselves, can we? At best, we humanize them—a sentimental conceit that shows how petty we are. At worst, well . . . . Either way, it's a grotesque failure of the imagination, and it's a vanity we can't afford to pander to anymore. It's killing us."

She began to stomp away, then wheeled around.

"I understand why Zia wants to stay: she loves me, she loves the herd. It doesn't matter who or what we love, Ollie: it only matters that we love—and it's her loyalty—despite the threat to herself—loyalty, a virtue we think only people have, that makes her want to protect us . . . . How, Olibade, how can I do any less for those I love than a horse is willing to do?"

"Willing, yes, but capable, no," said Ollie, desperate now. "Do you think one horse, all alone, would be able to stop—to beat—a thief, a poacher, at his own game? And do you think, Skye, you—standing alone against the world—do you really believe you can, you can . . ."

"If you don't try something because you think you'll fail, Ollie, then you already have failed. And Zia, who's seen the worst of it—and all those like her—they're the ones who've taught me to always try . . . to keep on . . . no matter what. I may not change the world, Ollie, but my small piece of it will always be safe. What I think I can do is of no matter—that's only the flash of ego we all indulge from time to time, but what I manage to do with the resources I have, that's what counts. And that's what keeps me going."

"Ollie," she continued, sitting on the porch steps, "when we were young, you seemed to think of me as someone who could do parlour tricks on demand, like a magician or maybe a freak. But have you ever thought what it's like, seeing into the minds and hearts of creatures so unlike—and yet so like us? Did you ever stop to think what it's like to have this ability to . . . to connect deeply to these animals, to feel their pain—all of them, all around us, all the time?" Skye suddenly felt very tired, as if she'd been crying. "They're with me all the time, Ollie. It's a gift from God, a don de Dieu, yes—but the world of man makes it a burden."

"You're wrong, Skye; I never thought of you that way. I knew how special you were. I was so proud of you. Always. But I can't imagine what it must be like to be you. And no, I don't understand it, and no, I don't understand everything you say though I know here, inside, it's all true. But it was that very thing—this miraculous thing that you were born with, that made you, you—that kept us apart. How could I not resent it, Skye, even a little? And what I am, who I am, Skye, that's who most people are; we can't hear what you hear, understand what you understand. Even now, can you see how hard it is for me—a horseman all my life, grooming, taming, breeding, vetting them—loving them, too, Skye—can you see how hard it is to accept that you've let a horse, an old mare, make a decision that places you in harm's way? I'm just an old farmhand, my love . . . and all I know is that I love you, I've always loved you, and I won't lose you again. I can't . . . . If you please, Skye."

Skye looked at that face, that face she loved, now creased with worry, even his laugh lines now crumples of anxiety. So earnest always, her Olibade. Not a shadow of guile to be found. Always the same. Her Ollie of old, always the same, now as then.

Skye sighed. Then she said: "You know Belle is our daughter?"

Ollie was still only a moment and then nodded slowly.

"I knew it as soon as I laid eyes on her. She's a beauty. And so smart . . . like her mother—and her name—Belle, like 'Belle Bayonne.'"

"Yes," Skye managed a smile. "She was born on the eighth of May, the same date as our famous Québec mare. That was for you, Ollie . . . and for me too. I've always loved our Canadiens."

"That was the reason, Ollie—the only reason."

"You didn't want to tie me down?" Ollie said, surprised.

"No," replied Skye, "I couldn't let myself be tied down. I had to make a decision between who I was and what I needed to do, or letting that go to—to—become instead—to—"

"Oh my love," Ollie took her in his arms, "did you really think I would have stopped you? Did you really think I wouldn't have followed you, wherever your gift took you—and with our baby? Oh my Skye . . . ."

Perched quietly on the edge of the awning, Toby had heard everything. Or at least, Skye's part of the conversation. 'A burden,' he thought, turning it over in his mind, 'a burden.' He'd never looked at things from Skye's point-of-view. People were hard, he knew; he'd had enough run-in's with them. But he'd never thought how hard it must be for Skye: just to be Skye, just being herself, had cost her something in the world of man. Bluejays, after all, are what they are, at all times, in all places, with little variance. A cow doesn't neigh and a horse doesn't moo. That was just the nature of things. But Skye, well, what was she? Human certainly, with her own very definite character, but with something more that strained definitions of human sentience; of what was available to human perception. And that extra dimension of being had kept her separate from the rest of her fellows who could accept, say, an extra toe or a lazy eye or congenital deafness, but not the gift of inter-species understanding. He had to think more on this. Toby thought best when in flight so in an instant, he was airborne.

Someone else had been eavesdropping. Belle, home from Solange's as soon as Chano had told her the news, had been in the house all the while, waiting for Skye to come in. Tears streamed down her face. 'Oh mother,' she thought, 'a burden, a burden . . . you never said . . . not a word . . . I never knew, I never knew.' After a few minutes, she took a deep breath, wiped her face clean and went outside to formally meet her father for the first time.

Toby Makes a Decision

You can kill all the bluejays you like . . . but you must never kill
a mockingbird.

Harper Lee, *To Kill A Mockingbird*

THOUGH NOT A great reader of classic American fiction (in
fact no reader at all), Toby was nevertheless aware of the poor
reputation of bluejays. As nest-robbers—in fact, one of the finest cannibals
in the avian world—bluejays are feared by other, smaller birds whose eggs
and young make for a nutritious feast. Though, when called for, he could
be an adroit liar, Toby would never deny such a self-evident truth. As one
of the more upright of his kind, however, he would have been hurt to
learn that bird fanciers referred to his sort as, 'one of the noisiest and most
obstreperous creatures' alive. He could never agree with such a statement
as he considered his talent at mimicry—he could mimic the cry of a hawk
perfectly for example—one of the most useful gifts God gave him. And
though he most often cried hawk to roust the parents from their nests so
he could feed, he also, at least some of the time, used it to warn his smaller
fellows of the nearness of a predator, like a hunter or a feline. Hunters
especially made such a mess preceded by ear-shattering noise; at least the
cats went about it all quietly if gratuitously. Toby dipped his beak in a
nearby water trough. The beak of the bluejay (cyanocitta cristata cristata)
owes its generous length to his relationship to the crow and the magpie
(pica pica hudsonia). From its apex, the beak curves cleanly downward,
which, along with what appears to be an underbite, gives the azure-striped
bird a very severe look indeed—one might even say forbidding. Even the
straggly tufts hiding the nostril, being much less dense in the bluejay than
in the magpie, give the impression of a military moustache, well-suited to

the warrior crest at the bird's crown, topping off what is overall a military bearing. In short, the jay always appears battle-ready, and, at first sight, his bewitching but fierce beauty always makes one wonder: 'friend or foe?'

At the moment, Toby's storied beak held something which he clearly wanted Belle to take, and for the life of her, Belle couldn't make out what the dickens it might be. He waited patiently while she squinted. Toby knew all along that Skye had no intention of telling Belle or anyone else for that matter about what was coming. She'd said she would but she hadn't, and after fully analysing 'burden' when aloft, he'd decided she was tired; something he knew human beings fell prey to from time to time, and something that, in Skye's case, was probably closer to battle fatigue. Things were going on—as a keen observer of human behaviour, he knew that—but none of it had to do with what he felt was essential to Skye's safety, and since he couldn't converse with Belle as readily as with Skye, this was the only way to share what he knew. Once Belle reached for the thing, he flew up and away. It was a crumpled page of newspaper. She began to read:

> Long before 'tsunami' had entered the common vocabulary, vying with 'holocaust' to describe a disaster of epic proportions, Canada as a nation experienced its first early in the 20th century. The Laurentian Slope earthquake and the South Shore Disaster (aka the Grand Banks earthquake and tsunami) of November 18, 1929, hit Maritimers around fish culling, quay docking or supper time, depending on where you were at 5:02 pm, Newfoundland time, 20:32, universal time. The epicentre was 250 km south of Newfoundland, measured 7.2 and was felt in Montreal and New York. The quake claimed 200 cubic km of land, impoverishing forever the area known as the Laurentian Slope. As the land buckled into the seabed, twelve transatlantic cables were crushed, severing energy and—tragically—communications with the mainland and the world at large. But what was to come was far worse. Two hours later, a tsunami hit, reaching as far down as South Carolina and as far across as Portugal. The narrow bays along Newfoundland's Burin Peninsula were especially vulnerable: from Port au Bras to Taylor's Bay. The tsunami, with waves as high as thirteen metres, claimed twenty-seven lives, a death count later revised when a young woman succumbed to injuries sustained and died four years later in 1933. As unimaginable as the damage was, it was made even worse by a white-out blizzard hitting the region the very next day. Over

forty villages in southernmost Newfoundland were decimated, with homes, livestock, and whole communities demolished.

Belle looked up to see Skye watching her from inside the screen door. "Mother was there," said Skye. "She wrote about it in her diary. It's in the final few entries, about when the big water hit Newfoundland in '29 . . . seventy years ago now . . . a quake, tidal waves—and a blizzard—all at once . . . what the Indians in British Columbia call the battle between the Thunderbird and the Whale . . . . That one was centuries ago; in 1700, I think . . . . Four years before she died, Mother was visiting a friend who'd left Québec to marry an islander up there. They were supposed to meet at the local hotel—I can't think of the name—but it was in Kelly's cove right in the heart of the peninsula where all the worst damage was done. I found that article a few years ago, and it filled in a few of the gaps for me . . . about what Mother went through and why she suffered so much before she died." Skye looked up but Toby was far beyond anyone's line of vision. "I can't think why Toby wanted you to see that."

"So—" began Belle, but Skye had already disappeared into the house. 'No more secrets, mother,' thought Belle. And she meant it. She picked up Delphine's diary on the desk, kept it close under her arm as she put on the kettle, and then began to read. From the beginning.

Guyanne Makes a Request

INVESTIGATIVE REPORTERS ARE a breed apart: one part whistleblower, three parts bloodhound. Ferreting out malfeasance—whether by individuals or industry—requires a criminal imagination minus the criminal intent. In a nutshell, that's how Solange's mind worked—all the time—and it had served her extremely well in her career. It was as simple as two simple questions: how far will so-and-so go to obtain what he wants, and how confident is he that he'll get away with it? These always kindled speculation in her mind which she followed up on—either by gumshoe or armchair research—and led her to prove what often turned out to be the worst-case scenario. That's why when Solange finally had a good look at the Registry, she zeroed in on the last and most damning section, 'Breeding Potential.' As if channelling John Rash, she explained to Skye, Belle and Guyanne what Rash's first line of attack would be, and why it would be through the Charities Directorate. With his resources and contacts, she said, that's the first thing she'd do if she were him. She didn't bother mentioning a close second would involve trying to bring DeeDee over to the dark side; that wasn't in play right now. This was just triage.

"There's just one thing, Mother. He stole that page, from DeeDee's home, out of my book. It's my property. Doesn't that mean that if he produces it in court, his lawyers have to tell where it came from?"

Belle and Skye turned and looked at Guyanne as if she were a two-year-old who'd just won the national spelling bee.

"Enfant prodige!" said Solange, putting her arm around her daughter and giving her a squeeze.

"That's exactly right! And Rash knows that . . . which is why he's going to bypass the system and use his contacts. I only know Rash by reputation but in a way, that makes it easier for me to figure out whose shoulder he's most likely to cry on. In fact, I already have an idea who that might be . . . ."

Belle looked at Skye, who'd been silent throughout. Without taking her eyes off her mother, she said: "This is wonderful of you, Solange, to want to help but . . . but we have a pat response to threats like this—"

"—not this time," Skye interrupted, "This time, Belle, we're staying put. Before we came to Holdout Bay, before you even found it, you said things that made me think very hard about how I went about my work; how the abuse of horses had to be taken more seriously and how we could only do that by grounding the Institute, making its work visible . . . ." She looked over at Solange. "So," continued Skye, "we stay and we fight. However, I still have to persuade Zia that she must be moved from here temporarily—just until we deal with the relentless Mr. Rash and make him understand, once and for all, that not only can he not have Zia, but he can't have any of them, and that wherever he goes, I go. I'll always be just a few steps behind him—and all the rest just like him. That precious duty I will never give up, as long as there is breath in my body."

Solange leaned over and kissed her cheek. But Skye hadn't shared the main reason she'd decided to stay and fight. She couldn't spirit Belle away—not now that she had found Chano and he her. She knew her daughter was in love and she would do nothing to jeopardize that. Besides, a little bird had told her that Chano was being assigned to another region, so it wasn't just Zia she had to persuade to leave; it was Belle. And unlike Zia, Belle had to leave for good, to live her own life, not her mother's; leave and be with the love of her life, the man of her dreams. Skye wanted this badly for her daughter.

As she headed outside, Guyanne followed her. "Skye? There's something I've been meaning to ask you . . . ."

Call Waiting

O NE OF THE perks of being a pillar in the business community—and by extension, a high-profile charity donor—was being able, in most cases, to bypass the comatose bureaucrats and all the red tape just by making a phone call. At the Charities Directorate, Rash's name wasn't on a list of premier donors anywhere, but it didn't have to be. He was often featured in the Social Notes of both English and French newspapers, sometimes gussied up in tenue de gala; other times, crouched down in spotless, creaseless jeans, smiling into the face of a young child. So he wasn't worried that he wouldn't jump the queue; it was more that he didn't really know anything about the inner workings of the Directorate except that it was charged with assigning or removing the charitable status of any organisation, and that it was an arm of the Canada Revenue Agency. He and the latter had always managed to stay out of each other's way, and he wanted to keep it that way, so he had to think through how to go about what he wanted to go about. And what that was, was the downfall of Skye Spahro.

It wasn't personal. Little in business is. If there was any personal animus here, he'd say it was hers. After all, she'd gone out of her way to cheat him of a lucrative gene pool, and she'd made a point of making a fool of him by using the ignorance of his own men against him—and not just against him but against Metropole Enterprises which as everyone knew was an engine of philanthropy. And why had she come after his abattoirs—though, true, he did own most Québec slaughterhouses, one way or another. What with holding companies and silent partnerships, it was complicated. But more to the point: how did she know that a champagne Canadien was even among the mangy lot, that particular mangy lot, ready for processing? And somehow she'd found out before he did. And why did she save only Zia the mare, and leave the rest? After all, on a good day, one abattoir could turn over eighty equines; that's a lot of horsemeat. Why not try for a few more? If it could only salvage one animal at a time, the Institute couldn't be a very big outfit. That was another thing. When he'd tried to get the horse back through the courts, he couldn't get any information on this so-called Institute. Yet it was clearly well-regarded. He shook his head as he recalled even the judge showing deference to the Spahro woman as she produced the required legal documents with all the 'tees' crossed.

He came back to why only the one and not the others. This was, at the very least, circumstantial proof that she only 'rescued' equines which could make her a profit. He knew a little about horse rescue outfits: there were plenty in Ontario and the Maritimes. They always 'rehabilitated' their rescues and gave them away—or sold them to so-called good homes. So re-homing and selling rescues had to be something the Directorate accepted—if the organisation was clear from the get-go that that was part of its mission. What he didn't know was whether the Institute worked the same way. Even if it did, was breeding at a rescue—using Zia, a viable mare with a desirable colour gene—acceptable? Wouldn't that put it on a par with regular stables whose principal source of income often came from stock breeding? That alone would give the Directorate pause. But he had no proof of that. He only had that ripped-out page which was suggestive but nothing more.

He could go the other way. It was a charity like any other; charities were always greedy for money. He could make a donation—a big donation which, in his experience, often opened the doors to those highly visible, self-righteous organisations, the kind that always snubbed big business but were content to tax shelter their profits if the numbers crunched were generous enough. But he had a feeling that this woman wouldn't be that easy to seduce. In and out of court, she had eyed him as if he were the spawn of Satan. Worse, unlike so many other self-styled do-gooders, her look conveyed no fear and no judgement, as if he were part of the landscape—here a judge, there a lawyer, there a few chairs, here Satan, there a window—nothing more: just part of the decor of the banal; the everyday canvas of modern western culture. Her levelling gaze had cowed him a little at the time. He resented that feeling.

The memory made him twitch a little as he realized that he couldn't circumvent one small fact: the page was fruit of a poisonous tree, acquired during the commission of a break-and-enter. Unless, of course, he could get the luscious DeeDee to cut out the coyness and play ball. The purloined paper had come from her dorm room after all which meant she knew something about the goings-on at the Institute. A solution finally began to take shape in his mind as, mildly irked, he left a message for the Senator. Apparently, the Senator's private line was otherwise engaged at the moment. The honourable member was happily reminiscing with his goddaughter, Solange Deschambault, who had called to ask a big favour.

Flight or Fight

ZIA WASN'T HERSELF. The smallest sound made her skittish. She wasn't eating much and when she did, her head bobbed up and down like a jack-in-the-box as if she were waiting for something, or someone. Justin, who by nature and necessity, was sensitive to such changes, took note but said nothing. He felt it had to do with that day Zia went careening towards the house, so hysterical and overwrought only Skye could calm her down. He'd seen Zia overreact before—for example, when Luka first shied away from her—but he'd never known her to lose her cool like she did that day. And since she hadn't told him anything about it, he was as much in the dark as Luka and the other ponies. He continued to observe quietly with just a little more attention than usual.

Like now, he heard Zia address Luka in that peremptory tone she'd adopted ever since:

"Where are you off to now?"

"I was just going to see Justin for a bit," replied Luka, chewing submissively.

Zia looked across the field at Justin. 'Yes, he's big, he's strong; but I've seen that devil put down bigger ones than him,' she thought.

"He's too far. I don't want you that far from me. Visit with him later."

Justin decided to abandon his patch and began to make his way towards them.

"There . . . here he comes. Remember—stay close." Zia snorted and turned her back slightly.

"What's the matter, Luka?"

"Nothing," the young pony replied, head hanging.

Justin knew that Zia's protectiveness towards Luka had gone into overdrive, and Luka, getting older and bolder by the day, was beginning to feel stifled. It didn't do to discourage the natural curiosity of the young. True, some mothers—themselves nervous nellies—did, and ended up raising scaredy cats who shied at the wind and balked at limp logs of lumber. Yet Zia was the one who'd taught Justin to be fearless, to sniff the unknown before judging it a threat: investigate first and then decide, she'd said. A panicked horse endangers himself and others. Always remember, she'd told him: panic is your enemy.

Justin walked over to Zia and, without a word, began to groom her. She jumped—so unlike her—recovered, and then relaxed.

Finally she said, "I know what you're thinking."

"You know me so well, Zee . . . that doesn't surprise me."

"You don't understand—none of you can. You haven't been where I've been, seen what I've seen." Zee began to groom Justin back, carelessly, anxiously; a little roughly he thought.

"True, Zee. I've lived most of my life here, with you, with Skye. I don't remember much except what I've seen here—in fact, I don't know much about anything. But now our Luka there—well, he's been through stuff, scary stuff from the sounds of it, and because of you Zia, he's beginning to get through it . . . because of you Zee. So far at least . . . ."

"I won't say it was nothing, what he went through . . . . It was far from that. But what I know is coming, what is coming this way, Justin—coming our way—well, I—I have no words for it . . . and I can't let Luka—or any one of us—face that—that demon if I can help it!"

"Does Skye know about this? Is it a cougar . . . coyote?" He two-stepped heavily, his senses now on high alert.

"Skye knows, yes, but in a way, she doesn't know, she—no one—knows the half of it . . . . It's not a common predator, Justin; it's worse than a predator. I don't know . . . I don't know how to . . . ."

Zia stepped away suddenly, exasperated. "It's a man, Justin. A man who is more than a man and less than a man . . . a killer . . . a, a devil."

A devil who is more than a man yet less than a man: it sounded like a riddle to Justin. He didn't know what to make of that, but if being blind had taught Justin anything, it was patience. And from the look of Zee, his patience would have been rewarded. But he felt a swoosh of air as Zia wheeled round. Someone was approaching. Justin, ever calm, stayed where he was. Zia, on the other hand, danced and snorted; a display of dominance so elegant—and from a mare, not a stallion—that Yanne's mouth fell open.

"It's only me, girl." She could almost hear Zia's disdain so she pulled back her hand. Yanne stopped where she was, a good twenty feet away. She waited. They would come to her when they were ready. Zee continued her display for a bit, then became almost as still as Justin, except at that very moment, Justin, remembering Yanne's voice and the lovely massage she'd given him, ambled over, halting just a hairsbreadth' short of her heart.

"There are things going on, Justin," said Guyanne, inhaling deeply as she began to stroke his forehead.

"And I'm to blame . . . . I have to set things right. I have to—well I'm not sure what I have to do . . . what needs to be done . . . but things must be set right again. You all must be protected . . . ."

And so she rambled on in a stream to Justin and to Zia, who was standing a little ways off and, for those few moments, was back with Maya and Duke and the gray-haired manager and the devil-man.

"—so that's what I'll do. Skye said I can stay here and help and learn and if anyone tries to take Zia away, or you, Justin, or the others, well then I'll go to court and I'll explain about the Registry and how it was just mine, for me, and was just a learning tool . . . and that it was stolen and then everything will be all right . . . everything will be as it was and all of you will stay here, safe with Skye. And if that doesn't work, then . . . then I'll find another way . . . . I *will* find a way."

The change in tone from disquiet to determination registered with Zia. To her, this meant 'stay and fight.' Of all the options under consideration, Zia, herd leader, couldn't agree more. Zee began to have hope that they could keep the devil at bay and Guyanne felt certain that the law would set things right and guarantee everyone's safety and security. They were wrong of course, and as the hopeful little band watched Skye walking towards them, only Justin whinnied hello. What silenced Zia was what Skye carried in her right hand: a halter with a lead.

As Zia trotted over to meet Skye (and question the halter), a pair of binoculars followed her. The dense cover of trees between Skye's pastures and the cemetery had caught Volpone's attention as he scouted out Isle-Saint-Jean-Baptiste. He hadn't been able to find the damn place—in fact the little island seemed to be nothing but trees and grass and more trees. But then he came up to the semi-famous cemetery with its little flagstone churches—the new one and the old one from the 1700s—all of it looking like manmade thumbprints indenting a grand natural surround.

If he'd been driving too fast, he'd have missed it, but the impressive wall of trees along its west side caught his eye. Just like a tourist, he'd stood at the top of the staircase cemetery and looked over the water and across to Beauharnois. Then he heard it—faint, but unmistakeable—the whinny of a horse. 'Gotcha!' he mouthed as he jogged back to the pickup to fetch the binoculars.

Save Changes

GUYANNE'S MIND WAS like duck soup. The day after Skye had agreed to have her, Guyanne, come and stay at the Institute, Guyanne had a) informed her mother; b) decided to bring Ulric with her who was still so sad and without whom Yanne would have felt a little lost; and, c) written to her father, Hugh, to tell him she was changing residence though she was not at liberty to give him the address at the moment ('I don't mean to be mysterious, pops, but there it is—for now anyway. Trust me or if that's too much to ask, check with Mom and you'll see it's all good. Either way, it's a done deal.'). Hugh, who'd been regularly in touch with Solange, who all along had been sharing with him her delight at their daughter's rejuvenation, was in no way about to rain on his daughter's parade. Like his ex, he was relieved and thrilled to hear that his daughter was taking life by the horns, finally.

What Guyanne didn't know till much later was that Chano and Ollie had met the day Belle sped home from Huis Clos Stables and Ollie had offered to drive Chano to Verchères thence to Sorel and beyond—which meant that, once Guyanne left, Solange would be left alone with only Contessa and the dogs for company. She also didn't know—in fact, no one did beforehand—that Skye not only had persuaded Zia to move—as it turned out, to Solange's—but she had convinced Belle that her place was with Chano: Belle should leave immediately and meet up with him in Sorel, nothing to worry about at home; everything was under control and Yanne and Toby would be there to help, with Solange, and even DeeDee, as back-up.

Toby was all agog, not knowing what to make of such dramatic changes. That day, that remarkable day Zia agreed to be haltered—something that took more doing than words can convey—Toby had been flitting among the firs and the few cedars that abutted the cemetery. He'd seen the binoculared man and alerted, causing all the finches and sparrows to flock away with much ado in droves, hosts and other impressive avian formations. Skye, addressing Zia most earnestly, stopped in mid-sentence, turned and looked. It was a wary look. Toby flew over right away to give assurances that the dark-haired man was no more than a birdwatcher.

"No worries, Skye. Just a birdwatcher. No harm, no foul," he'd said as he took in the unusual combination of Skye, Justin, Luka and Zia with the young woman from Huis Clos. A sceptical Skye quickly herded everyone and led them towards the barn, towards home—barn and house both beyond Volpone's line of vision. As distance swallowed the little group, his perspective diminished until they seemed to disappear—in fact did disappear entirely. But no fool he. He knew where there are horses, there's a stable, and there where a stable, horses. And he didn't need binoculars to recognize that mare—her funky coat stood out a mile. He walked back to the pick-up, smiling and shaking his head. The blonde had haltered the nag which meant she intended to move her, hide her somewhere. People were so stupid. Did she think that would stop him—him, Rash's right-arm—from taking back what rightfully belonged to Mr. John Rash, to Metropole Enterprises? Huh. Now that he knew their prime location, he could track everything from there. Easy peasey. She'd try to move the mare early morning; all he had to do was follow the trailer or its tracks: so much rain lately and only one boulevard led to and away from here. He could camp overnight; there was even a B&B nearby he could stay at. Instead he drove home fully intending to return at sunrise, sure in his own beautiful mind that the blonde wouldn't make a move before then. It wouldn't be the first time the wolfman had mistaken female beauty for sloth.

A Ride on Horseback

W HEN ULRIC SAW the trailer brought out and being cleaned, he naturally assumed it was for Contessa; if a breeders' show were going on somewhere, she'd naturally be invited. But now that profound loss had touched him—something he might never have known if he'd finished his life in PEI, alone and herdless—he understood Contessa's mourning like never before. They had bonded over their shared grief: he'd miss her. Contessa, more accustomed to partings, said not to worry; she'd be back soon. So when Guyanne entered the stable, it was Contessa who was hoofing the stable floor, not Ulric.

"Not today, Tessa dear. It's Ulric I need," said Guyanne, as she led Ulric out.

Ulric looked back at Contessa, their surprise punctuated by four upright ears.

"I know," said Guyanne, "but it's just for a while. You'll be with me at Skye's, a wonderful place with lots of pasture and other horses to make friends with. We'll be together, Ulric, you and me. You'll like it, you'll see."

Solange was to be the driver though she wasn't sure this was such a good idea. She'd assumed of course that it had been cleared with Skye; she and Skye both knew that introductions into a new herd were filled with tension—it was as bad as breaking into a clique in high school, with favourite mares vying for dominance. A lot of strong-arming went on. She'd feel better if she were there on the spot, in case Guyanne needed help or Skye did, especially now that Belle and Ollie weren't around. She shook her head in a rerun of the amazement she'd felt when Ollie had told her that he was going off with Chano to Verchères. Just as the driver, he'd said nonchalantly, as if it weren't a transparent attempt to get to know his daughter's lover better. Ultimately, she'd thought it was a great idea, although she knew his absence would double her workload—be, really, a baptism of fire for the prodigal daughter of the master horseman, Lucien. She thought she would find comfort in Guyanne's knowledgeable presence; her daughter had apparently learned horse husbandry by osmosis. But no, the girl was off to Skye's and taking Ulric with her, which again Solange thought was a great idea, grateful that that left only Contessa to see to. Frankly, she felt Contessa would know best what's to be done and when, and would find a way to let Solange know. One thing she'd never forgotten in all her years away was how to read a horse; something Lucien had schooled her in before she'd reached the age of reason.

Solange had just closed up the house when both she and Guyanne heard an unmistakeable clip-clop coming from just outside the driveway. Skye and Zia had arrived; Skye riding bareback, Zia bridle-less. Skye slid smoothly to the ground and Zia turned aside to graze. Finding mother and daughter speechless, she gave them a minute before she went straight to the point. "Solange, I need you to keep Zia here for a little while." Not just Volpone but everyone, including Skye, knew that there was only one road leading to and away from Holdout Bay, making passersby easy to spot. So Skye and Zia had set off in the night and walked from there to Pointe-de-la-Méduse where, apart from two other fermettes, there was only that tidy sprawl of land called Huis Clos Stables. They'd kept to the side where the mud had slowed them down a bit which explained Skye being barefoot, her caked boots wrapped in halter straps. She'd only brought the halter along for show in case they got stopped. When Skye had tired, Zia took her on her back the rest of the way. The first to find her voice, Solange entreated Skye to come in and rest, have some tea and of course, yes, she'd be happy to keep Zia if that's what Skye needed, but Skye's attention was elsewhere.

"Ulric says you're taking him with you to a nice place with plenty of pasture, Yanne," she said, "but that can't be right."

"Apart from Ollie, everything I've learned, I've learned from Ulric, with Ulric and so—"

"—do you mean you never asked Skye if you could bring Ulric over?" said Solange, dismayed. "Well," said Skye. "Well," said Solange. There was a third 'well' from Toby who, as always, was never far from wherever Skye was.

"Ulric isn't keen on leaving Contessa, Guyanne," said Skye, "and with Zia here, it would be best for the three of them to stay together." Skye

CYNTHIA D'ERRICO

was thinking of how the implacable calm that was Ulric would be just the thing to counteract Zia's anxiety. Zia had already made herself known directly to Ulric by walking up to where he was standing patiently beside the trailer, and it was Zee, not Ulric, who was answering Contessa who, still stabled, was wondering what was happening out there and who the stranger mare was.

"She's a very take-charge sort, isn't she?" said Solange, as the three watched the horse talk going on.

Skye smiled. "Yes, she is, has been ever since the very first day, the very first time . . . . I'll have that tea now," she said to Solange, as abruptly as if someone had pulled down a shade. Guyanne was a little disappointed that Ulric wouldn't be coming along. But as far as Yanne was concerned, whatever Skye Spahro thought best was best. Point final, 'that's it—that's all,' as Ollie often said.

Last Call

S OLANGE HAD KEPT cousin DeeDee abreast as much as she
could, although Dee's research and teaching schedule made it hard
to reach her a lot of the time. She never had gotten around to asking
Solange if she could intervene on her behalf with Rash nor told her
the government had finally named le Canadien a heritage breed. The
ceremony was months away and with all Solange was dealing with these
days—especially with Ollie and Guyanne away—she thought it could all
wait till life was less hectic for her cousin. Anyway she hadn't heard from
Rash since the day of the earthquake and she began to believe that the theft
of the Zia page had nothing to do with him and maybe more to do with
mindless vandalism. So, that night, when she saw a limousine pull up in
front of the dorm, she thought nothing of it. A knock on her door at that
late hour however was enough to change her mind instantly, so before the
door was fully open, Rash heard, "You've got a new limo." He'd changed
his mind about using the Senator as his goat with the Directorate—at
least as a first option; the subtler way was to approach DeeDee first and
see if she'd play ball—or at least give him more information about how
the bird-woman's Institute worked. He wasn't into intimidation at all
where women were concerned, but he thought it wouldn't hurt if she
knew that he now knew her address; that might go some way to mending
the rift between them. God knew he'd be beyond happy to be back with
her even if nothing else, like useful information, came out of seeing her
again. He could always expedite the Spahro matter through other means.
There's more than one way to skin a cat.

At about the same time of night, somewhere in the Verchères region,
two men, stark contrasts in age, nature, education and lifestyles, were
nursing a couple of Molson's. Apart from Belle, the two couldn't have

had less in common; the best that could be said was that neither minded getting down and dirty—soil and manure both generically dirt, washable and compostable. Chano hadn't questioned Ollie's offer to drive with him to Verchères even though they'd met only that one time when he'd tracked down Belle at Solange's. Initially, he'd seen this as an opportunity to get to know Belle through her father. His view of her mother was still forming; he'd never met anyone even remotely like her which made his powers of analysis useless and any style of approach questionable. Ollie, on the other hand, had warmed to him almost at once and despite having been a father in absentia, seemed to have gotten the lay of the land much faster than he had. But as they grew more acquainted, Chano realized that Olibade was the one out for information—about the daughter he'd never known and about the kind of man such a daughter cottoned to after so long alone and unaccompanied.

Olibade who was no stranger to love, especially the ill effects of separation, had decades of experience over the young man and knew that the boy needed to talk—vent, more like—and so he let him. He let him be or more to the point, he let him be himself. Discreet and self-assured, Ollie had never become one of those old codgers more intent on reminiscing about past glories than learning about new glories from the young. And as he listened, he grew to trust him—not just because he believed that his love for his daughter was genuine—but because he could sense that he was someone as full of integrity as his beloved Skye, someone who, if only he'd laugh a bit more—and he'd learn that in time—would remind him in many ways of his great friend, Lucien Deschambault. So Chano found himself more disposed to talk than he'd expected, aware that he wasn't any further ahead in his quest to learn more about Belle, but curiously enough, easy in his mind that whatever he revealed about himself to Ollie would work in his favour in future, maybe sometime soon.

It was almost last call in the Verchères bar when the two men called it a night. At the uni dorm, Rash's limo driver was having a snooze.

Home Safe

WHEN SOLANGE DROVE Skye home, she'd had no intention of staying till nearly nightfall but, just as Dee had been on her first visit, she was impressed by the pastoral peace of Holdout Bay, its oval of great trees encircling the Institute pastures like an open-air basilica. Just before they'd left Huis Clos, she had lingered for just a moment to grab the papers showing a mixed pinto named, JustinTime, as offspring of her own Contessa. Up to now, with all the intrigue over Zia, Solange had said nothing to Skye about it or to anyone else for that matter. JustinTime would be about nineteen now, she figured, and from the little Chano had told her, he was a credit to his species—in looks, personality, and intelligence. She wanted to see him for herself, and then she'd talk to Skye. As it turned out, it was Skye who spoke first.

"I have a feeling that you know Justin from somewhere," she said, looking at Solange as she watched Justin grazing among the ponies. Skye continued filling the oat bins. "Many of our rescues come from well-known stables or big farms, and what we try to do is erase their pasts. We change their names to give them new identities, although sometimes if we're sure there is no danger that the prior owner will try to take them back, we keep their original names. It's always fun when the name suits them to a 'tee,' like our Justin's."

"JustinTime suits him better; in fact, it tells the story of his birth," replied Solange with a knowing smile, and proceeded to tell Skye about Jericho, his outlaw father, and how she would dearly love to have Contessa meet her long-lost baby again. Skye was delighted at the idea and excited for Justin who'd been with her almost as long as Zia had. Toby, perched up high, watched as the women, smiling and laughing, agreed not to tell Justin or Contessa but to make it a surprise. Then a noise beyond human hearing made him as still as the branch he sat on. 'It must be that birdwatcher again,' he thought. He waited, listening, but only heard a car door slam somewhere near the cemetery. 'Still,' he thought, '. . . best to check it out,' as he vectored through the trees till he was on the cemetery side. He lit on the church steeple offering a view an eagle would envy.

The dark-haired birdwatcher looked grim, throwing black looks at the trunk of his car. Volpone was not happy. He'd been sure the blonde wouldn't make a move until daylight, and had returned just before daybreak to find the mare gone, vanished. He didn't bother to sneak onto the property or into the stable to check. It seemed that this motley pony crew lived outside most of the time—one of those 'natural horsemanship' methods—and that champagne coat which normally stood out a mile was nowhere among them. The only real horse there was that pinto—a brute mass of meat if ever he'd seen one. Toby watched as the man looked up and squinted as if whatever he was looking for was to be found heavenward. 'He can't be much of a birdwatcher,' thought Toby, 'here I am, and he hasn't even reached for his binoculars.' Toby had come across hundreds of birdwatchers in his time and although this man looked more like a hunter—a special softness of eye was altogether missing—he decided that here was no threat and flew back home as soundlessly as he'd come.

Solange had just taken her leave and was pulling out of the driveway, yelling through the window that Guyanne would be there tomorrow or "at the crack of dawn probably or maybe even tonight—I know she can't wait!" She'd shared with Skye her worries about her daughter and how happy she was that Guyanne had finally found herself, and in a calling which so closely followed the Deschambault line. "It's as if Papa himself answered my prayer and arranged everything just so," she'd said. Skye waved, then eyed her little herd; some resting in the grass, recumbent, and others, standing peaceably, enjoying the comfortable cool of the dying sun. Her mind was finally at ease about Zee. She knew Solange's was the best hideout; the Huis Clos property couldn't be seen from the narrow dirt road that ran through Pointe-de-la-Méduse making it even more hidden than the Institute was on Holdout Bay. Until this matter was dealt with—and she fully intended to phone the Sûreté tomorrow—Zia would stay with Solange. She scanned the treed perimeter for some time, satisfied herself that all was well and no-one was about, and then held the door open for Toby as they entered the house for the evening.

Road Mishaps

BELLE WAS AT a loss. She'd already arrived in Sorel when it struck her that she had no idea exactly where Chano would be carrying out his field work—if that was even what he'd been called to Sorel to do: maybe he was caught up in meetings or conferences, or in a hotel somewhere producing reports or doing net research. He could be anywhere, doing anything. It wasn't like Belle to just fly off without a plan or clear destination or even, she fretted now, without announcing herself. But Skye's sense of urgency—not to say, fervour—that her daughter follow her lover had been contagious, so somehow, almost before she knew what she was doing, she was behind the wheel on the road towards Sorel. She pulled in to a local *Tim Horton's* to look over a map and decide what to do next, but delinquent thoughts kept pulling her back to the day Skye had told her that she not only knew about Chano but that she was happy, so happy and relieved, that Belle had fallen in love, and that her daughter couldn't for a minute think of foregoing love; that love was a rare and blessed thing, and that life without it, wasn't a life at all. Belle was stunned on many counts, but mostly on that one. Skye herself had been guilty of sacrificing love, hadn't she? Giving up Olibade—and at that tender age when romantic love was the be-all and end-all; that ecstatic spiralling, that dizzy inner spin that rendered all other contenders to happiness before and to come a blank nothingness in comparison—and instead devoting herself to—Belle hesitated—to the love and protection of animals. Yet when young, she'd often heard Skye say, 'it doesn't matter who or what you love, my bell-elle; it only matters that you love,' and that staunch mantra had embroidered their life together, their life's work together. But it was that life's work, Belle recognized, that Skye was questioning on behalf of her daughter. The rescue and care of the abused was Skye's calling, but was it, and should it be, Belle's as well, and that, forever?

Belle put her coffee cup down. She couldn't imagine living differently than she had been all her life. But really she thought, to be honest, she could imagine a life with Chano. It would be different; a big adjustment, she knew. Yet if love meant looking past the flaws and reaching for the love, they were already there. They'd already seated themselves comfortably at a table for two where the bill of fare was the ebb and flow of a life together. She just didn't know if she wanted to or not—no, that wasn't it, that wasn't true: she loved Chano. What she didn't know is whether she was brave enough. It was past suppertime. She decided to spend the night at a nearby *Super 8* and try to find Chano in the morning. A good night's sleep might bring respite from her barrelling thoughts, if not a few answers. She sighed as she paid the bill. Answers, she thought, were as flighty as sparrows.

Answers were exactly what Solange had as she headed for home. She knew now for a certainty that Justin was in fact the foal—lost to her father, Lucien, so long ago—of the regal Contessa. She was sure too in her own mind that Skye was some kind of fated signpost for her daughter, Guyanne; a living, breathing sign that Lucien himself had put in Guyanne's way: as if the youngster's wheels weren't rolling as they should be, and Papa had purposely put *un bâton dans les roues* to re-set the young woman's heart. 'And God knows,' Solange thought, thinking back, 'it had needed a good jump-start.' Then her grateful smile vanished as she heard the blow-out. 'Damn.' Still, you don't spend years covering the news in less-than-developed countries without learning how to change a tire. Night had fallen so the first thing she reached for in her well-equipped trunk was the flashlight. As the headlights of a pick-up pulled up behind her, she thought herself lucky that anyone was on this road at this time of night.

"Ouais . . . c'est toujours quand il fait noir qu'on tombe en panne," Volpone said as he walked over to Solange's truck. When he set himself to changing the tire, unasked, it wasn't that Solange wasn't grateful; it was that he insisted on following her home, as if she were a teenager or, worse, a feeble-minded woman. But since he was so insistent, she let him follow her, knowing that once he used her phone—he had to phone his wife and explain his lateness, he claimed—she'd give him the bum's rush, politely but firmly.

When she turned off the main road, Volpone wasn't even sure there was a road to turn onto—it was almost impassable with low thick branches sliding off the windshield obscuring his view. He followed her into a sharp turn into what appeared to be a thick thatch of trees. Then the treeline broke abruptly and Huis Clos Stables was laid out before him. He let out a low whistle. Finally, he pulled up behind her in a long and wide driveway. The horses were up and fully about and the dogs of course were barking fiercely. Zia recognized his scent immediately. 'Damn,' she snorted as she lifted to and fro, 'he's here! The devil is here!'

When the man left—and Solange found him an unctuous blowhard despite his gallantry—she looked again at the note Guyanne had left on the table, smiling at her daughter's eagerness to be with Skye. They'd just missed each other; she must have left for Skye's only minutes before Solange pulled in. She went out onto the verandah and looked out. All seemed quiet: no swift kick swooshes, no self-pitying sounds after an unjust bite or nip, no neighing—just quiet. 'Bon,' she thought, 'Tout le monde s'est adapté l'un à l'autre . . . tant mieux pour moi.' She went back inside and opened a window so that if there were any unusual horsey exchanges during the night, she'd hear them, and since she was alone, she invited the dogs in to sleep in the warm parlour. The dogs looked at each other. They couldn't believe their luck.

As Luck Would Have it

SOMEONE ELSE WAS feeling lucky. When Volpone saw what a well-groomed estate Huis Clos was, he decided instantly that Zia couldn't possibly be there. It was much too posh a place for a nag like her, and his sense of the flat tire woman—another lucky break that got him right into her house—was that she wouldn't lower herself to take in a rescue even though she'd seemed friendly enough with the Institute owner. The mare must still be where he first saw her at the Institute or maybe holed up somewhere nearby. He was pretty sure the blonde was all alone there at the Institute. He'd watched all day and had seen only the two women, no one else. That made what he had to do easy. He decided to go have a very late leisurely supper; these things were best done after midnight anyway.

'Idiot,' Guyanne muttered, as the driver behind illegally passed her and turned in to a local diner's parking lot. But nothing, not even a Montréal driver, could dampen her enthusiasm tonight. She was going to work with Skye. Fortune had smiled on her, she knew, and in that, she saw the hand of Papa Lucien. Yet as much as she appreciated what she considered her great good fortune, she threw her head back at the thought of how much she had to learn—and that was everything, really, wasn't it? But with Justin and Zia in mind, she gripped the wheel: she meant to go on as she'd begun. As she passed the only gas station along this road, she veered to the shoulder and pulled a u-turn. It was past eleven and she was only ten minutes away from Skye's but thought she'd better fill up now rather than later.

The bed shaking woke Belle up with a start. 'I must have been dreaming,' she thought as she looked around the still hotel room. She made herself a cup of tea, picked up Delphine's diary and sat in the wingback facing the white sheers of the patio door. She'd only had time, so far, to read twenty or thirty pages or so; a sleepless night like tonight would be a perfect opportunity to read on. But as she fingered its sturdy faded cover, her mind began to race again. Here she was, having left her mother with an inexperienced young woman—which is to say essentially alone—to care for the Institute, and at a time when someone was bound to cause trouble about Zia. What was she thinking? That's just it: she hadn't thought. She wasn't even sure where Chano was, or, as she thought back, even whether he was in Sorel. Hadn't he said Verchères *then* Sorel? Maybe she wasn't even in the right city. It was no good. In less than an hour, she'd checked out and was on the road again, this time with a clear destination. She turned her brights on and headed home.

Contessa couldn't say she was sad to see Zia go. She didn't dislike her and they'd gotten along well enough, but she certainly had been bossy. When Ulric told her he'd seen the mare spook and take off, to places unknown, she'd replied that there'd be hell to pay in the morning when Solange found her missing. Ulric agreed but said he knew she was one of Skye's, and if she'd been brought here, even temporarily, there'd been a good reason for it. "It was when that dark-haired man showed up that she shied." Then, after thinking it over for a few minutes, he said, in that quiet but decided way of his, "I don't like the look of things, Tessa. Something's not right."

"Toby should be by soon for a visit. We'll tell him what we saw and then he can tell Skye," replied Contessa, always helpful and beginning to worry for Zia a little herself.

Not Another One

CHANO, WHO WAS somewhere around Rivière de l'Assomption and nowhere near Sorel, was too engrossed to notice whether lamps or furniture shook or shivered. He was doing what he often did late at night: reading reports from Environment Canada or the Ouranos group. The latest one dated Summer 1999 on the Verchères region showed how underwater clay beds were weakened by erratic sea rise and fall—altering shorelines among other things—and listed all the other familiar impactors that he'd measured and recorded on Holdout Bay.

He stared into space for a minute, revisiting the undulating ledges of the Bay's cemetery, the blue grass adorning what was an unwieldy mix of sediment and silt: a landslide risk waiting to happen. The increase in waves from passing boats and ships would cause those ledges to creep, one over the other; and, at some point, unable to bear one crumpled weight over top another, they would slide, smooth as you please, right into the St. Lawrence. Or it would be a more dramatic plunge heralded by an unusually energetic tremor, like the one he'd been present for only a little while ago. And not only the dead and buried would be displaced. The cemetery shared the same shoreline as Belle's Institute; it was only a few thousand yards away obscured by a single file of massive trees that met the water's edge and dispersed into a dense marsh. That whole sector of shore, except for the tree line, was composed of the most fragile silts and clays. And Belle's house was parallel to the topmost of the seventh level of the cemetery ledges; not even as high up as where the church sat. Although, he mused, nature swallows the sacred and profane alike; when the earth gets riled, there would be no more sanctuary there than anywhere else. As he reached for the light switch, he felt his arm sway. 'I must be tired,' he thought. He knew a cure for that. She'd be in his dreams.

A Light Homeward

POINTE-DE-LA-MÉDUSE WAS AN outcropping of land attached to Isle-Saint-Jean-Baptiste like a wart on a thumb. You'd never even know it was there with its stringy little road, overgrown and unmarked. Waterside, early mariners had had to look smart and maneuver around this cocksure little land mass thrusting itself into the great river where they least expected one. They hadn't named it after the medusa for nothing. Zia wasn't sure where she was and kept trying to find the shoreline so she could follow it back home. When she spotted a hobby farm, she kept herself well out of sight. The last thing she needed at this point was more human intervention. A last quarter moon shed a stingy light amongst the trees, but the dark held no fear for the determined mare. The only thing that did was that devil-man. She knew that he was out to get her, her herd and her Skye, and she meant to put her bulk between him and her loved ones if it's the last thing she did. Carlights shone up ahead. She trailed after their brightness until she came up finally to a paved road. As she and Skye had done only the night before, she kept just beyond the culverts and followed, the car's headlights providing just enough frontal light—and welcome light it was, too. It would lead her home to Skye.

Apart from bad dreams, there was nothing of the night that could scare Skye either. When Guyanne pulled in, she could see Skye's silhouette standing inside the door of the darkened house.

"It's only me, Skye!" she called out as gaily as one could at such a late hour. Skye held open the door as she carried in her belongings. She jumped back once, startled, as Toby whizzed by her and made for the trees. "He prefers to sleep outside," said Skye, "and now that you're here, he doesn't mind leaving me. So it's just the two of us girls now, eh Guyanne?"

Horses made of Iron

JUST BECAUSE NOBODY knows another way in to a place doesn't mean it's a secret entrance. It wasn't a secret to Belle or Skye or any of the horses, but it certainly was to Volpone. It wasn't his fault. He'd done his homework reconnoitring the Institute property, all about and around it, but as he watched the blonde emerge like a ghost from the woods on the north side, he cursed himself for not checking the ins and outs a little more carefully. It was after 2am; what was she doing out at this hour? He looked over at the little herd; you couldn't miss that tall pinto even in the dark. But she was walking towards the house, not heading for them at all. Maybe she'd already checked them out and gone in to the woods for a pee. Nah, why would she go in the woods when she was so close to the house. Funny that she was awake though, and up and about. He shrugged. Maybe she had insomnia, like him. It'd give him something to talk to her about when he did her, and he could do her in the great outdoors just as well as indoors. It didn't matter to him. He jumped down from the tree bough, hitting a ground strewn with leaves that crackled and popped noisily. He swore again.

You could draw a perfectly straight line across the grassy pastures between where Volpone had just left to where Zia was hiding across the way. She hadn't realized until Belle pulled up just north of the Institute that it was Belle's headlights she'd followed all the way from Pointe-de-la-Méduse. It had been a solid two-hour drive from Sorel and Belle was tired, but not too tired to remember that some cords of firewood had been ordered and should be at the north entrance. She'd told the man not to look for a gate—there'd be no gate or sign—and to drop the load next to the tallest fir he saw just past the culvert there—riverside of course, not landside.

His knees locked into a standing sleep, Justin raised his head when he heard some brush crackle louder than even a raccoon could make. Since Zia had left with Skye, he was the lookout, keeping watch at night, and keeping care of the little herd during the day. He heard Belle's footsteps at the same time as he caught another scent. Cam was already pacing. "Coyote" he whispered into Justin's neck.

"Coyote" echoed between Belle's ears. As she looked around to put a face to the voice, she froze on the spot as she saw a lone coyote skulk towards her from the left. Volpone, who'd moved in closer to the house, watched as the blonde came to a dead halt. He thought she'd seen him so he didn't stir. 'Where there's one, there's a pack,' thought Belle, not daring to breathe. She looked toward where the horses were. 'Oh Zia, where are you when I need you?' She didn't dare say it out loud. When a voice, different from the first and as hollow as a bell, replied, "I'm in the woods hiding. Leave this to me, Belle, and take Skye away from here," Belle's legs gave out from under just as if she'd had no legs at all.

Solange couldn't sleep. And the dogs were acting funny. As warm and toasty as their beds in the house were, they'd all asked for the door about 40 minutes ago and not come back. And the horses were quiet, so quiet. Two purebred Canadien mares—you'd think there'd be some back and forth, some nipping and lipping. Zia was—well she'd seen for herself—an uppity type, used to being boss, but Contessa was no slouch herself. Lucien had often said of Contessa that she picked her battles and those she picked, she always won. And since when did the dogs turn up their noses at a chance to sleep indoors? Solange pulled on jeans and a windbreaker and went outside. "You mangy darlings . . . I'll fix you!" Twenty minutes later, she was back in the house, searching frantically for Skye's number. 'It would be better to drive there, be on the spot,' she thought, as she grabbed the keys. 'Damn mare! Why'd everyone have to go away all at once anyway—no Belle, no dashing young man, no Ollie—especially Ollie?' Frustrated and worried, she whipped open the car door, clutching the keys and stared. She couldn't drive that distance on a spare tire, and Yanne had their other car. She turned and looked at the horses who were looking at her, ears up like posts and Contessa doing an impatient little dance. "Bombproof"—that's the other thing Dad always said about Tessa. "That pretty little girl is steel underneath, pure steel—absolutely bombproof." 'Imbecile. I don't need a car; I've got an iron horse!' If nothing else, journalists are resourceful. Solange ran to the barn and blew the dust of a decade off her even older tack. She hesitated for only a second; Tessa walked right into the bridle. After that, it all came back. All of it. Like riding a bicycle.

Skye crept into Belle's room where Guyanne was sleeping. "No!" she breathed as the girl reached for the lamp switch. "We're in trouble. No sound, no lights. Follow me." Downstairs, she pointed to Yanne's jacket as she put one on herself, grabbed a flashlight, unlocked a desk drawer and carefully pulled out a gun. "There's someone out there, probably looking for Zee. If I'm not back in fifteen minutes, call this number; Officer Grandcoeur. He'll come right away, night or day." Guyanne grabbed her sleeve roughly but Skye pulled away almost violently. "Don't worry! I've done this a dozen times. Do what I say, Yanne!"

By now so many scents competed for Justin's attention—including one he was sure was Zia's—he wasn't sure which to follow. First and foremost, he had to take on that coyote. When Belle fell to the ground, Cam and the others thought she'd fainted. Even the coyote was surprised but it didn't stop him from closing in and circling a minute later. And it didn't stop Volpone either—nor did the coyote when he finally spied him. He wasn't scared of coyotes—those chicken-legged, rapier-nosed sob's; they weren't even as big as Alsatians. "This bud's for me, pal," he said as he leaned over Belle and barely missed shearing off the coyote's back leg and tail.

It took twenty minutes by car to reach Holdout Bay from Huis Clos—fifteen if you were speeding. Solange knew the island much better than Skye who'd shadowed the main boulevard the day she showed up with Zia. There were three—no, four—shortcuts she could take—a couple through boggy marshes, but no matter. She had the right breed for tackling rough terrain. All in all, she figured she could be at Skye's in a little under forty minutes. She might even encounter the mare somewhere on the way there and could bring her back. Skye wouldn't even have to know Zia had gone missing. 'Mais non.' She frowned at herself for even thinking that. She adjusted the night light on her forehead, mounted and within minutes, as if from long ago, a cavalier astride a beautiful black disappeared into the dark of a Québec woods.

Backslider

T HE EPICENTRE OF this most recent earthquake wasn't far from Lachute but its rumblings could be felt for two days prior and as far away as St-Eustache. In what could be called the underground slipstream of a tectonic event, however, sub-events were percolating, and in the most unexpected areas. The earth seems capricious in fetching back parts of herself to herself, but truly her shenanigans are no more arbitrary than those of man, and all things being equal, she does, after all, hold all the deeds to land and water and ice and air, and flora and fauna too. Put that way, man doesn't have a leg to stand on. Hadn't he already cuckolded the planet, betrayed all that was good and vital and life-sustaining, turned brusquely away; choosing instead for millennia—in every single century, the choice of every single empire—to indulge himself in a destructive cupidity so that now, like Lot's wife, he turns timidly to look back at what he's done and is shocked that the earth is dry as dust and he is become stone? So when the ground gives way underneath—for whatever reason—one truly doesn't have a leg to stand on, or, as Skye once said to Toby, 'anywhere to stand it on if you did.' And it's in that moment when a purely rhetorical trope becomes reality that the 'unbearable' part of an unbearable lightness of being takes hold. This is a difficult concept for people like Matteo Volpone who had the still insensible Belle in a chokehold as he faced a lone pinto posturing like a stallion, both coyote and herd having fled to opposite ends of the woods. Every living creature felt the ground shake at the same time as the wolfman did, and though he couldn't dispel his own craven fear, he refused to release his hold. But the motion made him pitch forward and he went down on one knee—something Justin couldn't see but could feel in his sensitive hooves.

"Get out of there, Justin! It's a quake or something—you'll be killed!" Cam screamed from the perimeter. Justin, who by now knew that Zia was somewhere close, ignored him as if he were deaf as well as blind. Volpone thought he saw his chance when he saw the pinto take off to the other end of the pasture. 'Hah,' he thought as he pulled himself up along with the blonde's dead weight, 'big guy's scared of a little dirt milkshake.' He shook his fist. "I'll give ya something to be scared of, ya big bastard." But Justin was just warming up. He spun around and thundered back toward where Belle's scent was strongest. Volpone dropped Belle like a rock and ran to the right. He pulled out a long chain with a porcupine javelin on the end. As Justin closed in, he pitched it right at his head.

After the tremor, Guyanne just couldn't stay inside like Skye told her to. She wasn't scared; after all, Chano said these plate shifts happened all the time and rarely caused any harm. But she was worried about Skye who'd been overcome by vertigo. Yanne wasn't able to see much from the windows of a dark house looking out into a field of darkness, and she'd lost sight of the herd, even though she'd run from window to window on every floor, trying to see where they'd got to. She decided to peek through the storm cellar door before going outside. That way, she'd be sure not to interfere in whatever it was Skye was planning. But the first thing she saw when she cautiously lifted the cellar door wasn't Skye: it was Zia. Before she had time to react, another stronger tremor threw her back, off the top stair. Dazed, she sat up. 'That didn't feel like the other one,' she thought, as she rubbed the back of her head. 'That felt like something slipping or sliding, like mud.' Zia was pawing the cellar door. Yanne climbed back up and out, and Zia led her to where Skye was, crumpled in a heap against the south side of the house, the gun beside her on the ground. Yanne tried to get her on her feet but Skye was too weak to stand.

"It's okay, Skye. You stay here and rest. You can't be seen from here. I'll call for help."

"No," said Skye, clutching the girl's collar. "He's got Belle. Do you understand? He's got my daughter. I don't know what she's doing here. She's supposed to be in Sorel. Here," she reached for the gun. "Take this. They're on the west side. Go. Go with Zia. She'll help you."

"But Skye, what should I do?" said the young woman. "I know how to shoot a rifle but—but what if, what if—and that quaking, it doesn't feel like the other one. Maybe—"

"No, it's not a quake anymore, I know. It's something else. Just stay clear of the cemetery side, and just—just do exactly what I say. You only need to scare him, Yanne. These guys don't usually bring guns to steal a horse. Shoot in the air and he'll see we mean business. Zia and Justin will do the rest," replied Skye, as she laid a trembling hand on Zia's face. "Bring me back my Belle, Zee."

Zia bumped Guyanne's arm to get her on her feet, and then again, once she was up. "Okay, okay . . . I'm coming," said Guyanne, looking back, worried more about Skye than about what she was about to do. Then, resolute, she whispered, "Okay, Zee. It's high noon. Let's chase the bad guy out of town."

They'd come through the dense wood from the cemetery side. When Solange heard a man's voice, she'd jumped off Contessa and as quietly as a cat followed behind the sure-footed mare until they came to the clearing. She could just make out a body slumped against the side of the house. If that was Skye, where was Guyanne? She could hear Volpone slapping Belle awake. 'What the hell—' She knew that voice.

"C'mon wake up pretty lady. Wake up. Tell me where the expensive nag is. C'mon. I won't hurt you if you just tell me where it is." Justin's scream of pain had snapped Belle awake but she knew enough to fake it for as long as she could until she could get away from this madman. Belle wasn't a swooner despite what Cam and the others had thought, but her mind had seized up when she'd heard Zia's voice—the voice of an animal inside her head—and gone into a fugue state. A long-dormant portal had opened and somehow her conscious mind had accepted the internal change as if the ground had been laid decades ago. For the first time, Belle understood how profoundly she was, in every particular, Skye Spahro's daughter.

Solange grabbed the reins, crouched low and ran over to where Skye was. Contessa stood still as a post as she threw Skye over the saddle and the three fled back to the safety of the trees. Solange ducked to avoid a low-flying bat. But it wasn't a bat; it was Toby. Seconds later, the cry of a hawk filled the night air. Almost instantly, the trees released thousands of screaming birds whose incredible number canopied the open pastures. Terrified by the fearsome sight, covering his ears against their piercing screams, Volpone finally let go of Belle.

As Belle ran to safety, all hell broke loose, starting with the unforgiving earth giving way beneath them, beneath everything around them. As the muddied earth slouched downward, dragging Guyanne down about six feet from where she'd been a second ago, she looked up and saw Zia, still on four feet, doing a fast-stepping, sideways jig. She stuck the gun in an inside pocket and tried to climb on all fours towards her. No good. It was like being in a high-speed blender; she was being dragged further and further down towards the water's edge, bathed in layers and layers of mud. She couldn't even see the skin on her hands. The weight of it was tremendous. Only the trees seemed steadfast in the heavy moving sludge all around her. She slithered to the left and grabbed hold of a big fir. With one free hand, she wiped her eyes free of the ooze. As far as she could see, liquefied land was flowing like lava, as swift as a white-water rapid. She tried to look down but all she could see was a gaping maw of swirling mud. And she couldn't see Zia anymore—or Skye. She wiggled closer and wrapped herself around the tree trunk. Holdout Bay could hold out no longer. It was a torrential landslide and Guyanne was more alone than she'd ever been in her life.

Where Everyone Else Was

IT WAS NEARLY five in the morning. Rash had left only minutes ago, but not before promising that he'd leave the mare Zia, Skye Spahro and the Institute alone. "No harassment, no scare tactics—nothing, right? Just leave my friend alone," said DeeDee in that 'don't fool with Mother Nature' voice and the besotted rich man had apparently agreed. Dee didn't know how she did these things. It wasn't the first time she'd gotten her way without it costing her a single blessed thing. She hadn't promised anything that she wasn't willing to give. He'd asked to escort her to an upcoming charity ball and she said she'd think about it and let him know. As for the rest, she was just lucky, she guessed. She wasn't at all tired but she was hungry so she grabbed an orange and started to peel it. "Tawser . . . you can come out now, baby," she crooned. But Tawser had crawled under the sofa long before Rash had shown up and hadn't shown his face since. "I have something for you, little cat . . . something good," she said, as she shook his treat can. Nothing doing. "Oh we've had overnight company before, you silly thing, you," she said, as she turned on the TV.

"DeeDee, DeeDee . . . allume la télé," came with an urgent knocking on her door.

"Mais quoi . . . qu'est-ce qu'il y a?" Solange said as she opened the door. Her young dorm-mate picked up the remote and changed the channel to RDI, the all-news station.

"Don't you have a cousin who lives around Holdout Bay?" The half-peeled orange rolled under the sofa and came to rest right up against Tawser's nose.

Despite his best efforts, Chano had spent the night tossing and turning. Awake even earlier than usual, he paused on his way to the coffeemaker when he spotted a piece of paper sticking out from under the door. It was from Ollie. Two minutes later, a half-dressed Chano was knocking frantically on a colleague's door. He needed to borrow a car. Right now.

Ollie believed in the power of prayer but he knew even God couldn't give him wings no matter how hard he prayed. Sometimes God just says no. He tried to set the cruise control because he knew he was speeding, but in the end, gave up because it was easier on his nerves to take the risk. No matter how fast he went, he still had an hour's drive ahead of him. 'Je vous en prie . . . don't say no to this one. Keep my Skye safe. Please.'

The Fall of a Sparrow

THAT JAVELIN PROBABLY saved Justin's life. If the pain in his left leg and shoulder hadn't made him rear and whirl about like a dervish trying to dislodge its spikes from his flesh, he never would have made it to the higher ground of the north pasture—the only land the landslide hadn't claimed for itself. The javelin-thrower wasn't so fortunate. Even after the scary little birds had dispersed, he was so frozen with fear that his knees locked, making his legs stick in the ground ramrod straight, like longish golf tees. When the earth suddenly turned into an angry cream beneath him, there he was, with arms and legs akimbo, like the famous drawing of the five-pointed man. He slid face down into the brackish ooze in that same, fixed position. Whether reality had finally caught up with Matteo Volpone, special child of God, or whether he was in a state of incorrigible denial remained to be seen.

Zia wouldn't have made it at all if the house had luged straight to the bottom in the first or even second muddy churn. It had slid down about forty feet from its foundations and seemed to rest there, making agonizing twists and turns, as if unsure where to go next. Resting on the rocking house were parts of the back verandah, tipped upward, not going anywhere fast. The little jig Zia danced when she'd lost sight of Guyanne hadn't kept her upstanding for long so when the mud carried her close to the verandah banister, she'd hooked her neck and then her forelegs onto it. She scrambled just enough so that the back of the house took her weight and steadied her against the drag of the mud. When she saw two big rocks coming towards her, she leapt and landed her backlegs on them, stretching out the rest of her body like a dancing poodle. Then, springing forward, she jumped. The effort nearly killed her but she had just enough strength left in her upper body to drag the rest of her onto the solid north pasture. There, out of breath and out of sorts, she dropped like a stone.

By now, all but three—Zia, Guyanne, and the wolfman—were safe in the north wood. Justin's left shoulder was slimy with mud and blood even though Belle had staunched the bloody wound with her jacket. Though she said nothing, Contessa couldn't take her eyes off Justin; she'd recognized her son instantly. Solange was subdued, holding her head in her hands. She was praying that all those years in Girl Guides were paying off right now, and that Guyanne was safe somewhere and just didn't know where everyone was. Skye was in bad shape, struggling against the vertigo caused by the landslide. Still, when they all saw Zia collapse, Skye was the first to reach her.

She ran back almost immediately. "I need a rope. She can't get up," she panted. Skye squeezed Solange's hand. "The last time Zia saw Guyanne, she was on the west side, lower down. She's a smart girl, Solange. She'll have found a way up. And by now, I'm sure emergency crews are on their way to us."

"Mother, let me—"

"No!" said Skye, "I'll stay with her while Contessa and the rest of you pull her forward—at least until she has the strength to stand and walk by herself."

Solange unlooped the rope hooked onto Contessa's saddle and began to tie one end to the horn.

"Not like that," said Skye. She threw off all of Contessa's tack leaving only the bridle and reins. Then she tied the rope into what looked like the breastplate of a carriage harness with the long end of the rope running from her withers past her croup. Solange looked at Belle.

"Don't worry," said Belle, "she's a Canadien; she can do it." Then Belle smiled and said, "Contessa says she brought you safely through the shortcuts and the woods. How can you doubt her now?" Solange was too stunned to answer; then she embraced her old friend saying, "My God! You, too?"

Skye was almost at Zia's head. "Okay!" she yelled when the rope was securely around Zia. "PULL!"

Belle smiled at Tessa, who was already straining forward, and joined Solange who was in the rear, pulling on the rope with all her might. It was working. Zia was being dragged forward, slowly but surely.

"That's it, that's it . . . she's coming," said Skye, right by Zee's side, herself pushing as much as she was able. Then Zia's body was jerked back about half a foot. Skye could hardly see at first. "Wait a minute," she yelled. She saw an arm first and then a hand wrapped in Zia's tail. Zia cried out and tried to get to her feet. "No! No!" yelled Skye. "Leave her alone you sick bastard!" Belle ran over and began to pull Zee by her neck. "Leave it, mother! Tessa is stronger than he is!" But Skye had already scootched down to Zee's tail and was fighting to break Volpone's grip. Just before he released, Skye saw him smile. He let go the tail, grabbed Skye just above her elbow and pulled her down about five feet, leaving her to dangle just below his knee. In the woods, Justin heard Skye scream. He struggled to his feet, weak and weaving a bit from side to side. With a great effort, he steadied himself and began to make his way past the trees towards where Skye's voice had come from. But it was too late. Volpone and Skye were sliding beyond the solid ground into the morass below.

Only a botanist could say which trees—if any at all—could best withstand the irresistible force of a landslide. When the enormous fir sheltering Guyanne finally gave way, just before it reached where the shoreline had been, Guyanne hurled herself off as if she were dive-bombing into a pool. She landed on something smooth but hard that wasn't moving with the mud. The out-sized headstone appeared to be lodged or attached to something that kept it in place. She unclipped her pant belt and tied herself to the stone, leaving her limbs free like a surfer's. She didn't bother looking up or around; the boggy darkness had made her blind. She shut her useless eyes tight and prayed. 'People are on their way, I know . . . help is coming, please God, please, please, please . . . .' Minutes later, when the light from a helicopter began to pan the area, she wished she hadn't opened them again. Hanging onto the roof of the house were Volpone and Skye, scuffling: Volpone was laughing while Skye kept trying to loosen his hold on her and on the roof. 'She wants to kill him,' raced through Guyanne's mind. 'And she doesn't care if she goes with him.' Guyanne was only about forty feet across from them and could see beside and below but nothing above. When she thought about it later, she could have sworn she heard Zia scream but in truth nothing could be heard above the churning din. But she did see Zia swoop down like Pegasus onto the roof. Guyanne watched, horrified, as the mare's weight not only forced the reluctant structure downward but made it list badly. Volpone lost his grip on Skye but as she fell, she managed to grab hold of the eavestrough. The weight of her stressed the already detached pipe, dropping her further down and then she just hung there, suspended. Volpone had somehow managed to gain his footing, and precarious though it was, the relentless madman headed for Skye. Guyanne pulled out the gun in her pocket. It looked completely mud-plugged but she wouldn't know for sure unless she tried it. In that same instant when she looked over at Skye, she saw Skye look up at Zee and Zee look down at Skye. Then Skye let go.

Guyanne's eyes grew dim after that and she couldn't say what happened next. Sometime later, the helicopter pilot told a story that no one believed about this crazy horse who lunged at this poor guy fighting for his life and the two tangled up together plunged to the bottom. "It's like the horse did it on purpose, I tell ya. It was weird. And it was like the guy knew the horse was gunning for him." Some of the reports from the frogmen who went in looking for bodies had to be revised before they could be released to the press. The details were just too graphic for the public to know. Rumour had it that they'd found a man and horse down there, their limbs so entwined that the horse's foreleg was stuck down the man's throat—so far down that it pretty much disembowelled him. "This tragedy was probably caused by the combination of the horse's sheer weight and the force of the fall. The man most likely fell underneath the horse, and the natural forces of the earth—gravity and momentum—did the rest," wrote the coroner in her final report.

Epilogue

THE DAMAGE THE landslide did to Holdout Bay was incalculable—but that wasn't the worst of it. The whole area—and that was at least one-fifth of the entire island—had become an archaeological dig: a morbid sorting of the long-dead from the newly dead. The locals had been right about one thing: there were many more dead resting at Our Lady of Vigils Cemetery than had ever been officially recorded. Experts quietly celebrated discoveries of artifacts dating back 250 to 300 years with toasts of wine at intimate gatherings—the same specialists who had dismissed the regional folklore as so much nonsense.

Much later, despite all recovery efforts, when the body of Skye Spahro still hadn't been found, Belle signed papers stating that her mother was "lost at sea, deemed to be indefinitely irretrievable." All of it was just a formality to Belle—and to Toby—who all along knew that the now-quiescent earth had reclaimed Skye as part of itself and had no intention of returning to the world of man the gift he'd rejected. Out of respect for rescue protocols, Belle wouldn't call off the search before time. But there was another reason too. The rescue agencies that had toiled onsite for days had been taken aback by the number of birds and beasts who'd appear at the edges of the Bay, looking up at the rescuers now and then as if waiting for news. Some men were intimidated by the sight of so many free-roaming creatures, lounging about in such fearless proximity as if they'd never seen a hunting rifle or any other human killing device. Belle knew the animals were there to pay homage to Skye so she'd let the futile search go on.

Unscathed throughout was the diary of Delphine deBeauvilliers. When Belle finished reading the last page, there was no question in her mind that the inscription 'dD' meant 'don de Dieu,'—gift of God; something she now knew she shared with countless mothers and aunts going back generations. She gave DeeDee permission to use the copy she'd made of the diary in whatever way she thought best but like her mother before her, Belle would not give up the original. She hadn't known it then but the day she'd heard Zia and Cam, a matrilineal birthright had found its voice in her. Finally. Gift or burden, it was hers to keep.

His love lost to him, this time forever, Olibade was inconsolable. In time, he took comfort in the fact of their daughter, encouraged by her growing attachment to him, her seeking out his advice on all matters, big or small; including him in her life as if he'd always been there the way he wished he had been. Deeply in love herself, Belle understood more than ever before how much Skye had sacrificed all those years ago when she'd given up her beloved Ollie. She treasured her father more as each day passed both for Skye's sake and her own.

As for the work of the Institute, it would go on—despite the loss of Holdout Bay; Belle would see to that—somehow. Solange said nothing to no-one the day she phoned Belle and offered Huis Clos as the new location. "Skye always said it was even more private than the Bay," she said. "It's the perfect solution." And truly it was, for if Skye Spahro's dearest wish was that her daughter find love, Chano was the answer to that wish. And the two could not begin their life together, apart. Planning for her absence, Belle arranged for Ollie to oversee everything and to no-one's surprise, asked Guyanne, on the day of her twenty-first birthday, to act as rescue coordinator—"after some intensive training" Belle had said, grinning. If anyone had shown grace under fire that night, it was Guyanne. Who better than the fearless to take on a sometimes fearsome task? The young woman was beside herself, awed by the privilege of continuing Skye's good work. With her arm still in a cast, she hugged Belle as best she could, and then ran outside to share her good news with the herd. Toby beat her out; then, as he'd done all his life with his dear and special friend, Skye, he perched and waited for her.

Justin, still under vet care, was sharing a shady spot with his mother, Contessa, Ulric and the ponies. The vet confirmed that if the javelin had struck him in the head instead of the shoulder, he would have died instantly. But Justin had spotted the spiky projectile coming at him with the little bit of fuzzy sight he had in his left eye and swerved at the crucial moment. Some time later, though he was still weak, he'd recognised the scent of his mother. Ulric, Luka and Cam watched their joyful reunion; the ponies happy for their dear friend and protector, and Ulric, now herd leader, as content as he could be.

John Rash remained, as such men are, unchanged by recent events. He was sorrier to have lost his chance at the mare than at the death of Volpone whose presence on Institute property that fateful night, he'd known nothing about. He couldn't be held accountable for the actions of an employee whose zealousness had overcome his good sense, could he? He'd begun interviewing for Volpone's replacement almost the very next day.

Three months after the Holdout Bay disaster and a little more than a year after Lucien Deschambault had passed away, the province of Québec named le Canadien an official heritage animal of Québec. Leading Contessa, #3456 in Le Canadien Registry, Solange and DeeDee attended the ceremonies in Lucien's name.

Three years later, on April 23, 2002, when the Canadian breed was legally recognised as the National Horse of Canada, Lucien's granddaughter, Guyanne, was present. At the very moment official status was conferred, Guyanne looked skyward and whispered, 'une race, la nôtre, Papa . . . .'

THE END

Afterword

IMPOSSIBLE TO KNOW what horses think of us when they first encounter us, often as foals (babies). There is no reason on earth, therefore, to believe that they will know how to respect your personal space unless you teach them. Horse trainers use the term 'ground manners' to refer to a horse's behaviour when the rider is off-saddle. A horse without ground manners is considered unmanageable—even dangerous. Horses with good ground manners have learned and accepted that their rider is neither prey nor predator but different, even unique, and certainly dominant enough that they cannot bite, nip, buck, rear, step on or stampede us nor do to us a multitude of other things that could maim or kill us. Given their size, power and fear of the unfamiliar, all of these actions come naturally to a large prey animal. Some horses are excellent under saddle but have terrible ground manners. With others, the opposite is true. The horse-human relationship seems to depend on where you and the horse are relative to one another, and what your intentions towards him are. I have no doubt that his opinion of your intentions when you're with him changes by the minute.

When our intention is to render their flesh for our consumption, you might say that the relationship between man and horse has drastically changed. No longer interested in whether they have ground manners or won ribbons or great amounts of money for us, or are even athletes of the highest order—Eclipse, Seabiscuit, Northern Dancer, Ferdinand, Big Ben, Hickstead, Secretariat, and of course, Belle Bayonne, a creature of unimaginable stamina, come to mind—we are only concerned with how-much-per-pound and which horsemeat recipe is the best.

This is why the novel features the inner lives of horses who've been rescued either from abuse, as in Luka's case, or from ending up on someone's dinner plate. In today's world, it's a perilous world if you happen to be a horse. Black Beauty is *not* rescued by his old friend, Joe, but instead dies a painful miserable death over and over again, well over 100,000 times a year in Canada, after being transported thousands of miles in trailers meant for cattle—much shorter beasts. The Canadian horse slaughter industry has tripled since the US banned horse slaughter in 2007, and apart from Mexico, Canada is one of the prime destinations for US horses. One of the worst offenders in the country is the province of Quebec. The horse abattoir in Massueville, QC, has been cited repeatedly for violations—most of which have been videotaped—in both the manner in which they foul up the stunning and execution of horses, and the egregious means by which they try to disable them (a 22 rifle).

To bring the point home—in fact, right into our kitchens—the agency tasked with ensuring food safety in Canada, the CFIA (Canadian Food Inspection Agency) is unable to verify whether the horsemeat on your plate (or on dinnerware in Japan, France or Belgium) is contaminated with phenylbutazone (bute), among many other drugs commonly given only to horses yet banned in other food animals: with good reason since bute or 'horses' aspirin' is lethal to human health. Only very recently has the European Union taken note that none of the horses slaughtered in our abattoirs is routinely checked for these drugs before they're rendered into meat. Because of the European Union's new policy, Mexico has started to turn away US horse transports at their border; the drivers leaving the weakest equines to languish in misery and pain until death is their only reprieve—or rescue by devoted souls who cannot but feel that all this is wrong and this wrongness has created new wrongs which no-one had foreseen. But these developments are very new. *Ground Manners* is set at a time when even the horse advocacy groups were collating information—bits and pieces of information that have grown into an Everest of shame.

Although *Ground Manners* is fictional, it is based on facts and real events, all of which have been well-documented elsewhere: there is no exaggeration anywhere—more's the pity. Yet, in all cases, places, people and horses are composites of many, and familiar place-names and historical references have been used for no other reason than to localize the story in Quebec; the province I love. Quebec is the site of Nouvelle France, one of the birthplaces of North America, which, at the time, included what are now most of the north-eastern United States. In its relentless quest to achieve independence from Canada, Quebec's spirit—its animus—is a larger metaphor for coastline erosion, with shorelines and bodies of water shifting and shimmying dangerously away from each other—not unlike man whose surly manners towards the very ground he walks on has brought him to an impasse.

Horses are sport and companion animals in our culture, not food animals, and as the Canadian Horse Defense Coalition has stated, "they should never be in the slaughter pipeline." What we do to horses every second of the day, all over the world, fills me with dread and anger and shame. And while the geography of Quebec in *Ground Manners* may seem a bit off to some, the real terrain covered in this novel has more to do with confronting thresholds, moral and otherwise, in constant flux, than with national boundaries.

Visit *http://www.defendhorsescanada.org* to find out how you can help horses, and visit *http://www.refugerr.org* to sponsor a horse.

Acknowledgements and Sources

I AM DEEPLY grateful to Deb Harper of Abbotsford, BC, for providing the stunning photo of a Canadien for my cover, and to Jim C. Taylor of South Carolina for permission to include his incredible close-up of a bluejay; one of many great ones featured at *www.jimctaylor. com* and the one which, to my mind, best captured the character of Toby. Jim and Deb's artistic generosity to a complete stranger living miles away was heartwarming, to say the very least. I owe my first-born to Karen Burrows who came to my rescue at a crucial moment, editing the text with the penetrating insight of a word shaman. I am eternally in her debt.

Some of the horse characters in this novel are based on horses I grew up with (Zia emerged from memories of our magnificent, talented palomino, Doc), thanks to my father whose admiration of the beauty and strength of horses led him to keep a private stable for decades. Stories of abuse fictionalized here were inspired by cases of abuse (and rescue) reported on the website, in the newsletters, and at fundraisers for, *Refuge RR for Horses* in Ontario, as well as from the sites and email alerts of the *Canadian Horse Defence Coalition* (CHDC), *Animals' Angels USA, Wild Horses of Alberta Society* (WHOAS), *les écuries Diabolo, Horse Plus Humane Society* (formerly Norcal Equine Rescue) and many others.

I am particularly indebted to *Animals Angels USA's* investigative reports and the CHDC's website where details and statistics on how horses are transported to slaughter and the conditions under which they're slaughtered in Canada fuelled my anger at a morally egregious, impracticable, and inhumane practice. *Curb the Cruelty,* a report by *The World Society for the Protection of Animals* (WSPA) made for an especially grim, but thorough, indictment of animal transport in Canada. *La Terre de chez nous,* a Quebec agricultural newspaper, also provided information specific to the lot of horses slaughtered in Quebec. *La Terre* was remarkable for its balanced reporting throughout the nearly three years I've been a subscriber.

The staircase cemetery fictionalized in *Ground Manners* is based on an actual cemetery in Notre-Dame-de-l'île-Perrot, an island rich in Quebec culture and history just outside Montreal, Quebec. Cimetière-de-la-Falaise is very real and truly unique in North America, prized as one of the Seven Wonders of the Vaudreuil-Soulanges region. This eerily beautiful location belongs to the parish of Ste-Jeanne-de-Chantal which features a small chapel reconstructed with the original brickwork of the area's first church built in 1740. I am indebted to Lise Chartier, President of the *Fondation Sainte-Jeanne-de-Chantal N.D.Î.P.* for her encouragement. Mme Chartier is a well-known historian and the author of *L'Île Perrot 1672—1765* and is dedicated to preserving the entire area as a heritage site. See these sites for more information on a region that is an historical centrepiece to one of North America's birthplaces: Nouvelle France.

http://www.7mvs.com/default2.asp

http://fondationsjdc.org

http://www.ndip.org/en/index.html

Though this is a work of fiction, I am sorry to say that the suffering of horses and the manner of their transport and slaughter is as depicted—indeed, far worse than anything which appears in *Ground Manners*.

Any technical errors regarding horse husbandry or behaviour are mine and mine alone. Corrections and suggestions for improvement are always welcome on my blog *http://skipalldiscoverederrorsandcontinue.blogspot.com*. The sources below follow no particular order. Some sites may have moved or been altered since I began my research over two years ago.

http://www.refugerr.org Refuge RR for Horses

http://www.defendhorsescanada.org/ The Canadian Horse Defence Coalition (CHDC). See especially *Summary of Horse Slaughter Violations, 2005.*

See also on the CHDC blog a report by Channel 13 Indianapolis, October 2010, on *Indiana horses sent to slaughter;* one of the most thorough and balanced reports highlighting how supernumerary US horses end up in our slaughterhouse in Massueville, Quebec, and elsewhere in Canada and Mexico.

http://www.chevalcanadien.org/accueil.htm Association québécoise du cheval Canadien. A wonderful site which features personal testimonies from Quebeckers deeply committed to the preservation of le Canadien. See *Belle Bayonne* by J. Lucien Ouellet, La Pocatière, Québec. *St-Anne Marquis de Bécancour* by André Auclair, St-Paulin, Québec. *La lignée Henryville Prince. Hommage à M. Bernard Lamoureux* by Réal Sorel, St-Germain de Kamouraska, Québec.

http://www.legacycanadians.com/page/page/1098841.htm Legacy Canadians [the National Horse of Canada]. Another wonderful site. Read the history of le Canadien dating back to Louis XIV.

http://www.spvm.qc.ca/fr/sur-le-terrain/3_5_2_6_Histoire.asp The Montreal cavalry (mounted police). See also *The Montreal Gazette*, 'It's not like he's a police car.' René Bruemmer. April 1, 2009, p. A3.

http://www.montrealgazette.com

All Bets are Off. Blue Bonnets may have had its last race, but memories abound at fabled track. Paul deLean. July 13, 2008, p. A11.

Fun in rural Quebec: cutting off the heads of chickens. Don Macpherson. August 21, 2008, p. A21.

http://www.northernhorse.com/wildhorses/index.php Wild Horses of Alberta Society (WHOAS)

See *The History of the Horse in Alberta,* by Bob Henderson, and the Society's ongoing fight to save our Canadian mustangs from extinction. Bob's photos are exquisite and his blog on the day-to-day lives of each herd will move you to take action on behalf of our mustangs—as iconic as the Sable Island ponies (which are protected) and Canada's polar bears (which are threatened). Please sign their petition to save and protect our remaining mustangs.

http://www.animals-angels.com/index.php?pageID=start_us&
sessionLang=us

*Animals' Angels Investigation at Richelieu Meats Horse Slaughter Plant in
Massueville, Quebec. External Report.* 09/17/08—09/22/08.

Also see *Undercover Investigation Underscores USDA-documented Brutality.*
August 6, 2009, for information on "kill horses" abandoned to suffer and/
or die in both Canadian and Mexican slaughterhouses.

Also see *Investigation at Natural Valley Farms Horse Slaughter Plant,
Neudorf, Saskatchewan. External Report.* 26/09/07and *Investigation into the
transport of American horses to Canada for slaughter. External Report.* 6/1/07
- 6/3/07.

http://www.savingamericashorses.org/home.html

See information on the trailer to the forthcoming movie, *Saving America's
Horses,* featuring Paul Sorvino, Tippi Hedren and others.

http://www.hsicanada.ca Humane Society International/Canada

Working with the CHDC to help pass Bill C-544 to ban horse slaughter
in Canada permanently.

http://www.peta.org People for the Ethical Treatment of Animals

See factsheet, *The Horseracing Industry: Drugs, Deception and Death.*

http://www.ifaw.org/ifaw_canada_english/index.php

International Federation for Animal Welfare

http://www.gan.ca/home.en.html Global Action Network, Montreal.

http://www.wspa.ca/ World Society for the Protection of Animals

See especially their 2010 report, *Curb the Cruelty: Canada's farm animal
transport system in need of repair.*

http://www.rachelcarson.org/

http://www.cfhs.ca Canadian Federation of Humane Societies

See joint report with BC SPCA: *Report on Horse Slaughter Practices in Canada.* April 23, 2010.

http://www.equinecolor.com/color.html

http://www.ciwf.org.uk/ Compassion in World Farming

Government and related sites:

http://www.gov.pe.ca/infopei/index.php3?number=19654&lang=E

http://earthquakescanada.nrcan.gc.ca

http://earthquakescanada.nrcan.gc.ca/histor/20th-eme/1929/1929-eng. php#tphp

http://atlas.nrcan.gc.ca

http://www.ec.gc.ca/default.asp?lang=En&n=-1&

Environment Canada and the Centre St-Laurent.

http://www.ouranos.ca/en/ Ouranos

http://www.gov.pe.ca/infopei/index.php3?number=1965&lang=E

Government of Prince Edward Island (PEI)

http://laws.justice.gc.ca/en/H-3.3/index.html Federal Health of Animals Act 1990 c.21

http://www.animaquebec.com/ Anima-Quebec, organisation charged with enforcing the Animal Health Protection Act in Quebec.

See also Animal Health Protection Act (R.S.Q. c. P—42). Division IV.1.1 Safety and Welfare of Animals.

http://www.cosewic.gc.ca/eng/sct5/index_e.cfm

http://www.sararegistry.gc.ca/default_e.cfm

COSEWIC and SARA (Species at Risk Registry)

http://www.ndip.org/en/index.html City of Notre-Dame-de-l'île-Perrot, Quebec

http://faculty.marianopolis.edu/c.belanger/QuebecHistory/bios/index.htm

http://www.banq.qc.ca/accueil/index.html?bnq_langue=en

Bibliotheque et Archives nationales Québec

http://www.newadvent.org/cathen/03567a.htm

http://adaptation.nrcan.gc.ca/assess/2007/ch5/index_e.php

See *From Impacts to Adaptation: Canada in a Changing Climate 2007.*

http://www.em.gov.bc.ca/Mining/Geolsurv/Surficial/landslid/ls2.htm

For information on landslides.

http://archives.radio-canada.ca/environnement/catastrophes_naturelles/dossiers/51/

On the 1971 Saint-Jean-Vianney landslide.

http://www.cra-arc.gc.ca/charities/ Charities Directorate, Canada Revenue Agency

http://www.inspection.gc.ca/english/fssa/meavia/man/ch17/annexee.shtml

Canadian Food Inspection Agency (CFIA)

http://www.laterre.ca

La Terre de chez nous website. See issues May 2010; April 23, 2009, *Abattage au bout du champ* (exposing clandestine farmer slaughterers); and, issue June 4, 2009, *La Loi sur les abattoirs de proximité adoptée.* Also see *Les chiens sur la ferme,* May 1, 2009. Also see *Chronique. Embargo sur l'abattage de chevaux.* January 10, 2008 and *Courses de chevaux au Québec. Les Mordus ne lâchent pas.* December 2008. See also *Animaux morts. Gestion 101.* Jean-Sébastien Laflamme. *Bovins du Québec,* Winter 2010.

http://www.hebdosdusuroit.com

Horsewoman Evelyne Villers' articles in *Première Édition,* especially issue dated January 16, 2010 on horse euthanasia.

L'Étoile, Société secrète et dévots en Nouvelle-France. January 2009.

L'Étoile, Noël à travers l'histoire. Temps des Fêtes=occasion de pécher. Stéphane Fortier. December 17, 2008. Second part of a lecture on Quebec history delivered by historian Jacques Lacoursière at the municipal library of Vaudreuil-Dorion. See his account of Christmas 1759 when the citizenry held a demonstration in downtown Montreal against the Church enjoining them to eat horsemeat: "their argument was that horses are considered as friends, and one doesn't eat one's friends [my translation]."

http://www.horse-canada.com/ Horse-Canada magazine

See issue December 2009. *FEI Update on drug use in horses.*

Ibid. *The Versatile Standardbred. Life After the Track.* Mark Harling. This article appeared shortly after Montreal's Attractions Hippiques declared bankruptcy and ended harness racing in Montreal. The sad lot of many of our pacers and trotters thereafter was the slaughterhouse.

http://www.canadianhorsemagazine.ca Canadian Horse Magazine International *http://www.equinewellnessmagazine.com* Equine Wellness

http://www.horseillustrated.com Horse Illustrated

http://www.thehorse.com The Horse

http://nbcsports.msnbc.com.

From *The New York Times. Many owners, trainers are silent on drug issue. U.S. continues to have world's loosest medication policies for thoroughbreds,* April 29, 2009.

Ibid. *When horse races are over, an uncertain fate. Significant source of deaths is slaughter industry, driven by overbreeding.*

Bob Langrish & Nicola Jane Swinney. *Spirit of the Horse.* Parragon Publishing, Bath, UK. 2005.

Bernadette Faurie and Penny Swift. *The Complete Guide to Caring for your Horse.* New Holland. 2004.

R.S. Summerhays. *The Observer's Book of Horses and Ponies.* Frederick Warne & Co. Ltd., London, England. Third reprint, 1973.

The Audubon Society. *Birds of America.* Garden City Books (Doubleday), Garden City, N.Y. 1936.

Ellen Levine. *Up Close: Rachel Carson.* Puffin (Penguin Books), UK. 2007.

Rachel Carson. *Silent Spring.* Houghton Mifflin, Boston. 2002.

Peter G. Brown. *The Commonwealth of Life. Economics for a Flourishing Earth. Second Edition.* Black Rose Books, Montreal, Canada. 2008.

Serge Gaboury and Brigitte Ostiguy. *Parlure et parlotte québécoises. Illustrées.* Les Éditions du chien rouge. Québec city, Quebec. 2008.

Interview with the Author

When reading the book, it feels like there is a difference in tone between the first two parts and the last two parts. Were you aware of that when you were writing *Ground Manners?*

I WAS, YES, very much so. I felt that I had to move from lightness to dark, even though the first part especially deals with the various reasons these horses are even at a sanctuary: abuse and imminent slaughter. I wanted the reader to fully accept the literary conceit of animals who talk, feel and have opinions before anything else. You're almost sitting on the edge of a razor there because traditions of anthropomorphism in literature range from the comical or childlike, like *Dr. Doolittle* or *Charlotte's Web,* to the political satire of *Animal Farm*, so the challenge is to present it without sentimentalizing or being reductive. Jane Austen wrote that 'second-hand conjecture is pitiful,' and when we ascribe human qualities and language to animals, we're really only showing that we are unable to conceive of communication beyond our own limited parameters. That pig may be singing to the moon, or he may be doing something totally beyond our ken. Impossible to know for sure. Finally, I just had to trust that the reader would suspend disbelief and accept the conceit and read on.

Some readers were surprised by your Afterword. It's much more didactic than the storyline would lead one to expect.

The entire storyline in *Ground Manners* is backlit by the larger issue of horse slaughter and abuse. The Institute exists because abuse exists. It didn't seem necessary to me to belabour the point once I'd outlined how Luka and the others came to live at a refuge. I think Zia's nightmare of what happened to her is a glimpse of what happens to horses all over North America and elsewhere. As we went to press, I learned that the Bouvry slaughter plant in Fort MacLeod, Alberta, was just shut down due to poor sanitation policies, including contaminating the Qu'Appelle Valley with horse blood. That's good news. We'll just knock 'em down like bowling pins until Canada passes Bill C-544 banning horse slaughter forever in this country. I worked for women's rights and founded a women's centre in the seventies during the 'second wave,' and I can tell you, that's the only way real change happens—one victory at a time.

But there is an episode in Part Four where Skye goes on about how man only values his own sentience or "interiority" as Skye puts it. Isn't that proselytizing a bit?

Well, up to that point, the reader doesn't really know Skye very well as a character except that she has this inherited gift and is a tireless machine when it comes to saving horses. To some extent, I did that on purpose because we can assume that the inner workings of autistic savants or any other gifted individuals are different from the average person's—even the bluejay figures that out—but that makes it harder for the reader to sympathize with someone like Skye. It helps if the reader knows why Skye does the work she does so I gave her a belief system which, as it turns out, is the same as the moral agenda embedded in the story. So I am guilty of preaching, yes—but just a little, I think.

That brings me to the question of who the hero or heroine is in this story. It's true that we don't know Skye well enough to identify with her and—without giving away the ending—it doesn't really seem to be any of the horses, so . . . ?

That's entirely up to the reader but personally, I would vote for Guyanne. She's a character who undergoes the hero's journey from innocence to experience—she is a walking epiphany waiting to happen from the moment she appears. Her reactions to what she's learning incorporate catharsis, fear, pity and all of that, starting with the moment she connects to something or someone outside herself. In fact, the only other character who evolves in this book is Chano, and for the same reason: love.

What about Justin, the blind horse, being the hero? He takes the lead while Zia is away.

He does but he always could have been a leader or a hero. Justin has a fearless nature—something no-one identifies as an attribute of leadership or heroism in him because all they see is that he's blind. He doesn't undergo inner change the way Guyanne does; he doesn't have to. He's a natural hero but he is underestimated because of his handicap. Assumptions are made throughout the book—whether by Cam the pony or Toby the bluejay—which turn out to be patently wrong. Justin is not only brave but extremely smart—something Cam doesn't pick up on until much later because Cam's perception of Justin begins and ends with his blindness. Toby is wrong about Volpone being a harmless birdwatcher. Rash is wrong about why the Institute does what it does and Volpone is wrong about just about everything, including who the blonde-haired woman is. People live their entire lives based on assumptions that are usually wrong or misinformed or misguided or what-have-you. We can all be blinded by our own assumptions, and most of those assumptions are based on our narrow perceptions. I like to think that *Ground Manners* presents a wider field of vision as a way of challenging our limited perceptions of animals, and, to some extent, explaining where the commitment to champion them comes from. There are dramas going on every day, every second, in the world of animals which I find more compelling and certainly more poignant than our own.

You mentioned earlier that Guyanne has to connect to something outside herself in order to grow. What role does 'connection' play in the story's overall theme?

In many ways, the entire book is about connecting and disconnecting... even the collapse of the ground being a metaphor for our being disconnected from the earth or perhaps the earth's alienation from us. Quebec's conflicted relationship with Canada made a perfect backdrop for that theme—always on the brink of separation but not ever quite there—as well as all the parents separated, for one reason or another, from their children—Justin from his mother, Luka from his, Solange from Guyanne and Belle from her father. Even Skye's name implies separateness, as the sky is from the ground. In a very special way, she is not of this earth; she's not like anyone else, and her ability to connect with animals both grounds her and separates her from others at one and the same time. Sparrows don't perch anywhere for very long; they are almost constantly in flight, and in terms of the disintegration or instability of our coastlines, you have to wonder if they know something we don't. That's where love comes in. There are a number of love stories in *Ground Manners*—not just between people, but between people and animals, and animals and animals, and in a larger way, between us and the planet. Love connects—and the question becomes 'do we have any love left for our planet, for the earth beneath our feet, or don't we?' While I was writing I had in mind the image of the Mayan Venus emerging from her annual battle with the Sun, all smeared with gore and broken, but ready to fight another day: that became my vision for Skye. There is something of the fierce goddess about Skye. She stands alone. But we find continuity—connection, again—in Guyanne whose legacy and background tie her to Quebec and to its national breed, and she picks up the gauntlet. I liked that continuity on so many levels through Guyanne.

Can you talk a bit more about Quebec and its preferred breed, le Canadien?

Our heritage breed, yes. There's a scene in *Little Women* in which the Professor tells the heroine, Jo, to "write about what you know." I grew up in Quebec and I know the Montreal area intimately. Quebec fascinates me—and that's why I argue with it constantly. If I didn't care, I wouldn't argue. To me, indifference—not despair—is the worst sin, so I couldn't set the story anywhere else, and as I said earlier, there is a centuries-old "two solitudes" mentality in Quebec which made it a perfect setting for the connections and disconnections in *Ground Manners*. Partly because it was set in Quebec and partly because of how much I've learned to love le Canadien horse breed, I had to feature them in the book. My sources section will give readers a much more detailed history of this amazing breed than I can.

Is there anyone you identify with most in *Ground Manners*?

I'm in the landscape, where the water meets the sand, and I'm the last piece of ice; the one that resists melting . . . the last hold-out. I am everywhere and nowhere in the novel which is where the writer should be.

Glossary of Québec French

À bout de souffle   breathless

Ah oui . . . il y a quelque chose qui se passe là sans doute.   Ah yes . . . something's going on there without a doubt.

Ah regarde, quelqu'un s'en vient. On a de la visite.   Oh look . . . someone's coming. We have company.

allume la télé.   Turn the TV on.

Bien sûr.   Of course.

Bon qu'est-ce qui se passe?   What's happening?

Bon voilà mon trésor . . . nos biens de la saison.   Here you are, my love . . . our gains of the season.

C'est ça . . . parfait.   That's it . . . perfect

C'est comme ça.   Some things just are./That's the way it is.

C'est moi DeeDee.   It's me . . . DeeDee.

C'est toi le boss.   You're the boss.

Ça fait partie de notre patrimoine.   It's part of our heritage.

Ça m'est égal.   It's all the same to me.

Ça ne me regarde pas.   It has nothing to do with me.

Ça ne se fait pas.   It simply isn't done.

Ça se peux-tu?   Can it be possible?

Ça va?   Is that okay with you?

ci-pâtes (also six-pâtes)   a traditional Québec dish made with various meats, especially game.

Comme nous, les chevaux aiment jaser de temps en temps.   Horses like to chat every now and then, just like us.

Comment ça va? Ça va bien.   How are you? How is it going? I'm fine/all goes well.

compte rendu   to give an accounting or summary

coup de foudre   lovestruck

de chez nous   one of our own; ours

Désolé.   So sorry.

Dis-moi pas.   Don't tell me.

don de Dieu   a gift from God

Écoute madame . . . .   Listen, ma'am . . . you must come . . . it's beyond me. I have two ponies here—one of them is very nearly strangled. Bring the vet cuz it's a sure thing that these poor creatures can't be saved.

Écoute   Listen

écuries   stables

En tous cas . . . .   Anyway, it's good to see you, Hugh.

Enfant prodige   a gifted child

Est-ce que ma fille Guyanne est chez vous?   Is my daughter Guyanne at your house?

fait au Québec, produit de chez nous   made in Québec . . . a homemade product

fermette   hobby/horse farm

Gran Écurie (also Haras National)   National/Royal Stables

gros nounours   a foolish person

gros parleur, 'ti' faiseur   a person who is 'all talk and no action'

Huis clos   no exit; end of the road

Il était dans son assiette.   He felt good in his own skin.

Inquiète-toi pas   Don't worry

j'ai trouvé le bébé de Tess-ah . . . notre bébé perdu.   I've found Tessa's baby . . . our lost baby.

Je me souviens   I remember

je t'embrasse   hugs; I send you hugs.

Je vous en prie   I beg you

l'abattage au bout de la pelle   running an animal down with the shovel of a backhoe

Là c'est ça . . . là on lui demande si on peut aller avec lui . . . on y va!
There now! Now we ask if we can go along with him . . . let's go/and we're off!

La Canadienne brouillée . . . t'la veux-tu toujours? . . . Oui certain, toujours. Bon . . . ce soir après minuit. Emmène la van. Elle sac' son camp. The smoky coloured Canadien . . . you still want her? . . . Yes, certainly. Well then . . . tonight after midnight. Bring the van. She's ditching this place.

la patrie   the Québec nation; our homeland.

Le Canadien, historique   a book on the history of le Canadien horse breed.

le grand destin québécois   the destiny of Québec

les grands manitous   the big bosses; the grand poobahs

Mais ces hommes là étaient des ignorants.   Those men were ignorant.

Mais qu'est-ce que tu veux, mon bébé, mon petit don de Dieu, hein? What do you want, my baby . . . my little gift from God, eh?

Mais qu'est-ce qui te prend?   What's come over you?

Mais quoi . . . **qu'est-ce qu'il y a?**   What . . . what is it?

Merde   sh*t

Mon dieu ça l'air pesant ce computer-là.   That computer looks heavy!

mon oncle   my uncle

mon trésor   my treasure

Non pas du tout   no not at all

On ne mange pas son ami   One does not eat one's friends

Ouais . . . c'est toujours quand il fait noir qu'on tombe en panne. Isn't it always at night that we get stuck somewhere?

Ouais . . . pis? Yeah . . . so?

oublie moi pas là. don't forget me

Oui j'arrive. Yes, I'll be there shortly.

pas de méchancété no malevolence

petit cheval de fer little horse of iron

Peux-tu venir dans maison? Could you come into the house for a minute?

Point final Period! (no further argument)

pure laine old stock; descended from the first settlers in the new land.

Qu'est-ce qui se passe? What's going on?

Remarque ma fille Take note, my girl

sais-tu ya know

sans faute without fail (in this context); otherwise: without flaws

stimés, moutarde chou steamed hot dogs garnished with mustard and coleslaw

Sûreté du Québec the Québec provincial police force (the QPP)

T'as le tour You've got the knack; you've got it down pat.

T'es malade dans tête touais. You're sick in the head.

Tout le monde s'est adapté l'un à l'autre . . . tant mieux pour moi.   Everyone has adjusted to each other . . . all the better for me.

un bâton dans les roues   a wrench in the works (literally: a stick jamming the wheels)

un bovin canadien   a breed of cow called the Canadien (another Québec heritage animal)

une race, la nôtre   the breed that is ours alone; one breed, ours alone

Verglas   the 1998 Québec Ice Storm